TIME TO YOUR ELF

TIME TO YOUR ELF

REG RAWLINS, PSYCHIC INVESTIGATOR #14

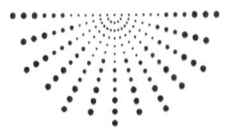

P.D. WORKMAN

PD WORKMAN

ISBN: 9781774681558 (IS Paperback)
ISBN: 9781774681565 (KDP Hardcover)
ISBN: 9781774681541 (KDP Large Print)
ISBN: 9781774685006 (KDP Paperback 2 ed)
ISBN: 9781774681527 (Kindle)
ISBN: 9781774681534 (ePub)

ALSO BY P.D. WORKMAN

FIND MORE BOOKS AT PDWORKMAN.COM

MYSTERY/SUSPENSE:

Reg Rawlins, Psychic Detective
Paranormal Mystery & Adventure
What the Cat Knew
A Psychic with Catitude
A Catastrophic Theft
Night of Nine Tails
Telepathy of Gardens
Delusions of the Past
Fairy Blade Unmade
Web of Nightmares
A Whisker's Breadth
Skunk Man Swamp
Magic Ain't A Game
Without Foresight
Careful of Thy Wishes
Time to Your Elf
Undiscovered Tomb
Missing Powers
Thrice Spared (Coming Soon)
Cloaked Campaign (Coming Soon)

AND MORE AT PDWORKMAN.COM

To those who want to move forward instead of back

CHAPTER ONE

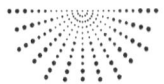

*T*he sun was down and Reg was feeling energized as she looked through the appointment book on her kitchen island. It felt good to have some business coming in again. Her bank account had almost dwindled away to nothing and she had been feeling the pinch.

But she had come back from her most recent adventure determined to get things running again, and her efforts were definitely paying off. There was at least one appointment scheduled every night for the next couple of weeks, and in some cases a couple of readings and a seance.

She had been worried that she wouldn't be able to get any work. There had been quite a reaction in the paranormal community when they discovered that her mother was a siren, and the backlash had not been pleasant. But her landlord, Sarah, had been correct when she had said that it would settle down and people would forget all about it in a few weeks when it was no longer big news. The work was coming back in, and Sarah's wards and charms kept the more militant witches away from the yard and cottage so that they didn't have to keep cleaning raw egg off Reg's front door and the remnants of spells and curses that had been left behind in the yard. All in all, things had been pretty peaceful the last couple of weeks, letting Reg get back into the swing of things.

There was a tap on the door and Sarah let herself in. The older woman was dressed for a night out. A green sequined dress clung to her curves and, despite her more mature figure and a bit of extra padding around the middle, she looked very fetching. Reg was sure that she would have a fun night with whatever group of friends she was hanging out with.

"Just thought I would check in before we go," Sarah announced, smiling. Starlight came running in from the bedroom and jumped up on the island counter, yowling at Sarah in a pleading, plaintive voice that clearly announced that Reg had been neglecting him and no one ever fed him when Sarah was not around.

"Don't believe him!" Reg warned.

"Oh, I know he exaggerates," Sarah agreed. She petted Starlight. "But I don't think it would hurt for me to give him a little treat, do you?"

"For a beast who is starving, he's getting pretty fat," Reg observed. "You'd better not give him too much. I'm going to have to start giving him that special food for overweight cats." She looked Starlight in the eyes, one of them blue and one of them green. "That low calorie, high fiber kibble."

Starlight made a cross meow and turned to look at Sarah and to rub lovingly against her hand.

"You're all ready for your readings tonight." Sarah looked Reg over and gave an approving nod.

Reg didn't know how Sarah could get up so early in the morning when she stayed out half the night with her friends. Weren't old people supposed to need more sleep than younger folks? Even if Sarah only looked to be in her sixties, Reg knew—or at least had been told —that she was actually centuries old. So she should need a lot of sleep, shouldn't she?

But Sarah was always up before Reg was and *tsked* and shook her head over the fact that Reg didn't usually manage to get dressed for the day before noon. Young people these days.

"Good to go," Reg agreed. "I'm just going to grab a bite to eat before my first appointment arrives." She looked down at the book. "Eugene Franklin."

"Eugenia," Sarah corrected. "You'd best get that right!"

"Oh." Reg looked at it again. The letters were carefully printed, but Reg had only glanced at the first few letters and assumed the rest. She was not the best reader and used a lot of shortcuts. Sometimes that worked and sometimes it didn't. "So... Eugenia. That must be a woman."

"Yes."

"Got it."

There was another tap on the door, and Reg looked over to see Letticia, the older witch who led Sarah's coven. While Letticia's lined face always looked serious and foreboding, Reg had learned not to make assumptions from her looks. Letticia had helped Reg out in the past and was not quick to prejudge her as others had. She was a lot more compassionate than she looked.

"Are we ready?"

"Just one moment. I need to get the cat something to eat."

Reg rolled her eyes.

Letticia tilted her head and looked amused. "I don't think that cat is going to starve. For someone who claims not to like the creatures, you do tend to put a lot of time into this one."

"Well, somebody should keep an eye on things."

Letticia shook her head slightly, but didn't point out that Reg was standing right there and the cat was clearly not starving to death as he claimed. She waited patiently while Sarah found some tuna and put a spoonful in Starlight's dish. Starlight jumped down from the counter and started to wolf it down.

"What are you guys doing tonight?" Reg asked.

It was probably not a coven night, since Sarah usually dressed in formal black for those. But Reg supposed some of the witches from the coven might go out together for a social activity. It wasn't all chants and spells.

"There is a new club in the city that we are going to check out."

Letticia was not dressed in a slinky, sequined dress like Sarah. Letticia didn't have Sarah's curves and probably wouldn't be comfortable in something like that. She wore black slacks and a satiny blouse that came up high on her neck. She wouldn't have looked out of place in church or a courtroom, but Reg wondered what kind of club Letticia would feel at home in. Maybe they had a seniors' night.

"Well, you girls have fun and don't stay out too late," Reg told them with a smile.

Sarah gave Starlight one final pet and nodded. "I hope your evening goes well. You really should come out with us one night and relax. Too much work will just burn you out. You need to regenerate too."

"Yeah. Maybe some night," Reg agreed, though she had no intention of going out partying with the older ladies.

"Marian is coming too," Letticia said. "It isn't all witches."

Marian was a psychic like Reg. Her competition. In the beginning, Reg hadn't gotten along with her. Marian had been adversarial toward Reg. Jealous of the work that she was picking up, maybe, or the reputation she was getting for being one of the better psychics in town. In Black Sands, there was no lack of psychics and other practitioners to compete with.

But they had reached a tentative truce. Marian had even sent a couple of referrals over to Reg recently and Reg was watching for the opportunity to send some business back Marian's way. It was better if they cooperated, or at least didn't openly compete with each other.

The two older witches were soon on their way, and Reg looked in the fridge for something that would be good for a quick bite to eat before Eugene showed up.

CHAPTER TWO

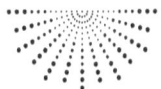

*E*ven after meeting the thin blonde, Reg kept thinking of her as Eugene, which didn't help the reading go particularly well. She tried not to be distracted by the woman's unusual name, but she kept worrying that she would slip out with "Eugene" during the reading.

Despite her distraction, Reg was able to give the woman a few tidbits that she thought were worth her money, so Eugenia went away satisfied with the session. At least, as far as Reg could tell. Maybe the woman thought she was just an idiot or a charlatan, but if she did, she didn't announce the fact or think it obviously enough for Reg to read. Hopefully, she would tell her friends that Reg was the real thing and get them to sign up. Reg had started to offer referral discounts so that if Eugenia got her friends to sign up for sessions, Eugenia could get a lower rate at her next reading. That encouraged repeat business and referrals, both of which were helpful to Reg in rebuilding her business.

Her next appointment was a seance for a group of friends, one of whom had received the session as a birthday gift. Oddly enough, seances were an increasingly popular birthday gift, at least around Black Sands. Reg was happy to take advantage of the trend. She enjoyed doing seances. The energy of the group was a boost, and in the odd event that there were not enough spirits around to provide commentary—and Reg rarely lacked for extra voices in her head—it was easy to ad lib and keep the clients happy.

"This is Sharon," one of the women pointed to a dark-haired Latino girl. "She turns *thirty* today! At midnight! And this is Rachel, Sunny, Deb, and I'm April."

Reg blinked at the quick succession of names. "You might need to remind me if I get the names wrong," she apologized in advance. It might be a good idea for her to start supplying groups with stick-on name tags so that she didn't have to remember them all. It just wasn't a good idea to call people by the wrong name in the middle of a seance. It could be brushed off as the mistake of a confused spirit or perhaps the name from a past life, but it was always best to get them right in the first place.

"We'll let you know!" April laughed. "We're always confusing people. Should we sit down here?" She gestured to the dining room table, eager to get right to it.

"Sure," Reg agreed. "Make yourselves comfortable. Does anyone want tea? Drinks?"

"Drinks!" one of the women, perhaps Deb, echoed excitedly.

"You've already had enough margaritas," Sharon told her. "If you keep it up, you won't remember anything about tonight. How about tea?"

"No, drinks," the others protested as a group.

Sharon shook her head at Reg and rolled her eyes. "I guess it's drinks," she sighed.

"Shall I make you a tea? I can…"

"No, no point in going to the extra work. I'll have the same as everyone else."

Beverages were arranged and, in a few minutes, everyone was sitting at the table, drinks in hand, giggling nervously about the upcoming seance. With them so well-lubricated, Reg didn't foresee any problems. They would all be very suggestible. The only question would be whether they *would* remember it in the morning. If they didn't remember the seance, they couldn't exactly recommend her to others.

"Okay, if you are all ready, we'll get started. Is there someone in particular that you are trying to reach? Or a question that you would like answered?"

They all looked at each other, reluctant to speak up first.

"Birthday girl?" Reg suggested, looking at Sharon.

Sharon shrugged, blushing. "I don't know. I've never done anything like this before. It's just kind of a gag."

Reg nodded, smiling, so that Sharon would know that she wasn't offended. "A lot of people come just on a whim, to see what they get out of it. That's okay. Nothing then? Nothing special?"

Sharon shrugged and shook her head. "No... just, whatever. I guess. Will you do that thing where you say there is a spirit whose name starts with G and does anyone know someone who died whose name started with the letter G?"

"No. I don't do that. I can see who a spirit is attached to, if they are attached to someone. And sometimes, it's just one of the spirits that I'm familiar with, who might have a message or insight to be passed on. It just depends on who speaks to me."

"Does someone always speak to you?"

Reg shrugged. "That's what I'm here for."

"So you're a real medium? This is real?"

Reg pointed to the placard on the table. *For entertainment purposes only.* That little disclaimer that kept her from getting charged for fraud by people who decided they didn't like what she had to say or thought that she wasn't a real medium. She preferred to keep the police out of her life, if she could.

"Oh." Sharon nodded, looking disappointed.

"Let's join hands," Reg suggested. She sat down in her seat at the end of the table and held out a hand to each of the women sitting next to her. The girls quieted immediately, and everybody put down their drinks for the moment and grasped each other's hands.

Reg rolled her eyes upward and listened to the voices, waiting for one of them to come to the forefront.

"We reach out to the spirit world," she announced, "on behalf of this group of friends. Do any of the spirits have messages to be passed on?"

There were plenty of voices. A lot of them fought and bickered with each other like old married couples, they had been with her for so long.

"Perhaps someone here has recently lost a loved one?" Reg suggested. "Or maybe someone looking for love?"

There was a ripple of laughter around the circle, which seemed to be directed at April. Reg felt a surge in the energy level, and watched a rosy aura develop around April. A seeker. Reg could find one in most groups. The one person who was most likely to believe what they saw and heard. Not a dupe, exactly, but the one who really wanted to receive a message.

"April," Reg intoned. She listened to the voices whispering around her. She closed her eyes most of the way but could still see the faux candles flickering in their jars around the room. Little twinkle lights, because it was too dangerous for her to have real candles in the house without an experienced firecaster around to make sure that Reg didn't accidentally burn the whole house down around her. That would not impress Sarah. "April has come looking for love."

I see, a voice whispered in her ear, *let me tell you what I see.*

"Do you have a message for April?" Reg asked, wanting to make sure that she didn't give a message to the wrong person. It would be just like some impatient spirit to speak up and pass along a message intended for someone else. They needed a bit of managing.

Yes. A message for April, the spirit insisted.

"What message do you have?"

A stranger he is, but soon they will meet.

Reg spoke the words in her own voice and gave herself over to the spirit to give the rest of the message.

Handsome but dangerous. The man in black. He will come soon.

Handsome but dangerous. Reg gave a little shiver at the words, thinking of Corvin. She couldn't think of who fit the description better. The warlock was one of the most attractive men Reg had ever seen. Maybe the most handsome she had ever met in person. And his magical charms made him even more desirable. And for an unsuspecting woman who didn't know that he could steal magical gifts, he was very dangerous. He was very clever at getting his own way. Reg could not recall the morning she had woken up to silence in her head without a shudder and a sense of deep loneliness and loss. He had given her powers back to her, something that was never, ever done, but the circumstances had been unusual.

Reg never wanted to feel that emptiness again.

And she never wanted anyone else to experience it either.

"Be careful," she warned April, opening her eyes and being sure to meet the other woman's gaze. "Please beware."

April nodded. But her eyes were shining with excitement. She wouldn't be careful. She would be looking for this handsome stranger wherever she went now, eager to meet him and fulfill the prophecy.

Reg opened her mouth to inquire whether there were more messages for the group or whether there were other questions that the women hoped to have answered.

But something strange was happening in the living room. Reg blinked her eyes a few times and tried to focus on the dancing lights that had suddenly materialized. They swirled around like fireflies, or like moths around a light, but Reg couldn't tell where the light originated.

The women started to ask questions. Most just wanted to know what Reg had seen, why she was so distracted. Or wondering whether it was some kind of show she was putting on. But April gasped, her eyes focused on the swirling lights.

"What is that? How are you doing that?"

"It's not me," Reg told her.

They both watched the space, mesmerized.

CHAPTER THREE

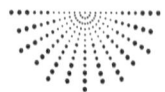

*A*s Reg and April stared, the lights multiplied, swarming around each other, with more and more of them appearing until they nearly formed a solid mass. And then they were solid. Or *he* was solid.

A man. Surely it wasn't April's handsome stranger already. The spirits' prophecies were rarely fulfilled quite so promptly.

The women were all silent, mouths hanging open. Reg gathered that even the less receptive ones could see him now. They were all wondering how she had made a man appear out of thin air.

And so was Reg.

He *was* handsome. Rugged, with long golden-brown hair, dark eyes that twinkled, and dark clothing that seemed to shift and change color as he looked around. He had a closely shaved beard that added just the right touch of masculinity to his gentle face.

But dangerous? Was this the handsome and dangerous stranger?

"Who are you?" Reg asked.

The man looked around at them all as if confused. He put on a pair of dark glasses, which couldn't have helped him to see, clothing the already dim room in complete darkness. He took them off again and looked at Reg, as if checking to see whether she were still there.

"I am Orri."

"Orri. Why are you here? Why have you appeared before us?"

"Well…" He looked around the table in consternation. "I didn't mean to appear to *all* of you."

Reg laughed. "They were prepared for a spiritual manifestation, so…"

He touched his chest. "But I am not a spiritual manifestation."

"Oh? What are you then?" Reg was not put off. Spirits frequently did not believe that they were dead until they were confronted with incontrovertible proof.

"I am physical." He blinked at her. "Aelf."

"What?"

"I am Aelf."

"I thought you said you were Orri."

"I am." He gave a nod of confirmation. "Orri. Of the Aelf folk."

"An elf?" Reg asked, trying not to let her voice rise in excitement at the possibility. It was rare for humans to see elves, and she had been visited by them once before. The odds of having a second visit from elves was astronomical.

"Yes," Orri nodded. "Elf."

Reg remembered the lights that had danced around and the sounds of bells that accompanied them on their last visit. She should have guessed that the dancing lights had something to do with elves.

"We are honored to have you here. Can I… get you anything?"

Fairies, she knew, liked milk. But elves? She had no idea what kind of a diet they ate, and whether they drank tea or alcohol or milk. Maybe they weren't even allowed to eat or drink in human houses. She knew next to nothing about their race.

"Perhaps… mead?" Orri suggested.

Reg was flummoxed. She looked at her human guests around the table, but none of them appeared to be capable of speech, let alone able to tell her what mead was. Reg knew it was sometimes served at the community parties, and that fairies were particularly partial to it, but she didn't know what it was. She was pretty sure there wasn't any in her cupboards and fridge, even with how well Sarah kept them stocked.

"Uh…"

Orri's eyes traveled over the women at the table and their cups. "Wine?"

Reg nodded with relief. "Yes. Wine. I can get you wine."

She stood up and went to the kitchen to pour him a generous glass of wine. She hoped that it wasn't too cheap. She didn't want to offend a person of another magical race by offering him an inferior beverage. Reg didn't buy the cheapest wine at the store, but it wasn't exactly premier stuff either. Nice enough to keep groups of women like April and her friends happy, but not anything a connoisseur like Corvin would compliment.

She walked over to the elf slowly, worried about scaring him off with any sudden movement. She was a bit anxious around creatures that could disappear in the blink of an eye. But Orri did not appear to be worried by her and did not disappear. He took the wine goblet from her with a polite nod. Reg bent her knees in a slight curtsy, not sure what else to do.

A curtsy? Reg had no clue what the proper protocol was. Why couldn't it have been a night where there were other practitioners present who could help her out and explain things to her? Reg never asked her clients whether they had any magical experience or not, but she could usually tell. And April and her friends gave no indication that they knew that real magic even existed.

"Is there... a reason you're here?" Reg asked tentatively, after the elf had a sip of the wine and didn't spit it back in her face. "Did you want to see one of these women?"

"You are Reg Rawlins?"

Reg nodded. She felt butterflies in her stomach over the elf knowing her name. She had a reputation among the elves? She hoped it was for something good, not something she had done wrong. He was there to see her. She assumed that if she had done something wrong, he wouldn't want to see her.

"Yes, I'm Reg."

"My message is for you."

"For me? Not for..." Reg motioned to the women seated around the table, "You're sure it isn't for one of them? They came to make contact with the spirits..."

"I am not a spirit," Orri pointed out. "I am corporeal." He patted his chest as if to demonstrate his solidity. Of course, he had already been drinking wine, which was a pretty good indicator that he had a physical body. If he didn't have a body, the wine would just dribble to the floor, wouldn't it?

"Yes, you are. I just thought that since they were looking for messages, maybe you had a message for them."

"No."

There was a little sigh of disappointment from April. She'd been hoping that the message was for her. Maybe more about the handsome stranger. Or maybe Orri *was* the handsome stranger. But he did not appear to be there for her. If she wanted to attract his attention, she would have to work pretty hard.

"Okay." Reg steeled herself. "What is your message?"

It probably wouldn't be good. In Reg's experience, unexpected messages from beyond were rarely good news. Why did omens always have to be of evil? Why couldn't they be good, at least half the time?

"This is my message," Orri announced. He held his hand up dramatically for silence. It wasn't as if there were a bunch of conversations going on around him. He took a deep breath and announced his message to Reg. "Beware fair folk bearing gifts."

CHAPTER FOUR

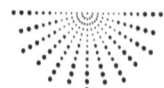

*R*eg looked at him, waiting for more. That couldn't be the whole thing. She stared at Orri, waiting for him to finish. "That's... not it, is it?"

Orri nodded. He looked disappointed that this had not gotten a better reaction out of her. He had clearly thought that it would have an impact.

Reg smiled reassuringly. It was a good warning message; it just wasn't one that would be of any help to her.

Reg had already received a gift from the fairies. Orri was right, of course, she should have been more careful and maybe even not have accepted the gift in the first place. Fairy gifts, she had since found out, rarely brought the receiver any kind of joy or good luck. Fairies tended to take away at the same time as they gave, so that a person might end up with less than they started with. And might have a lot of bad luck or magic to contend with.

"It's good advice," Reg told Orri reassuringly. "It's just that... I already accepted a gift from the fairies. And I already figured out that it wasn't such a good idea. I appreciate you coming all this way just to let me know..." Who knew how long or far he had traveled? If he was supposed to give her the warning before she had received the gift, then he was months overdue.

"You already know?" Orri repeated.

Reg nodded.

Orri slapped himself on the forehead. "You already know! It's too late! This was the wrong time!"

"It's okay," Reg assured him. "I'm really grateful that you came to tell me. That was very thoughtful of you. It's just that I already know."

"The fair folk…"

Reg nodded. "The Papillon family of the fairies. I know. You're right. I should have been more careful. But it's all been straightened out now, so…"

Of course, claiming that it was all straightened out was more than a bit of a fib. Reg had managed to deal with some of the gems, but there would be many more trips and consultations needed before she could trace all of them… it was a big job, but hopefully Reg had the time she needed to do it.

Orri didn't need to know all the details. Just that Reg already knew everything she needed to and he didn't have to worry about it.

Orri took a large swig of the wine. Reg shrugged and grimaced. "I am sorry."

He looked at the table and the women interrupted mid-seance.

"You talk to spirits?"

Reg nodded. "That's what I do. These are clients, people who want to communicate with spirits or… otherworldly folk. Maybe you could give them a message too."

Orri looked doubtful, starting to shake his head.

"Come on," Reg prompted in a whisper. "You can just tell them something vague and mysterious sounding. They won't know what it means, but they'll think it's wonderful."

Orri hesitated.

"They were already told to watch for a handsome stranger." Reg fluttered her eyelashes at him. "And… here you are."

He actually blushed. Reg couldn't contain a laugh. She tried to keep a serious expression, but it was impossible.

"Maybe…" He looked at the women, trying to come up with something.

"Maybe you could give them my warning. It's a pretty general one. No one should accept gifts from fairies without due caution, should they?"

He shook his head in agreement. He straightened, puffing out his chest slightly and looking at the women with a beatific expression. "Beware fair folk bearing gifts," he announced importantly.

There was a gasp from the women at the table. They started to whisper to each other. Reg glanced at them for a moment, and when she looked back at Orri, something was happening. The fireflies and moths were swirling around him again, bright spots of light swirling around and around, closing in on him until he was obscured from view, and then dissipating, the cloud of insects getting smaller and smaller until just a few stray lights floated around the room.

"Best birthday gift ever!" Sharon announced.

CHAPTER FIVE

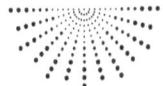

*R*eg slept restlessly after her guests were gone, wound up by all the excitement. She had pushed all thoughts of the fairy gems to the side while she'd been working on building up her business again. A person could only work on so many things at once. But the visit from Orri had reminded her that she needed to be dealing with the fairy gems, and not keep putting it off. It would take a long time to deal with all of them, so she should get started before they became a problem. Take one bite at a time. That was the way to eat an elephant. Or so she had been told.

Reg had never been very good at starting a big project. She got bogged down by the details and everything that she could see had to be done, and had problems breaking it down into smaller, manageable steps. One thing she had learned about herself was that she should just do *something*. Even if it were the wrong thing or started her off in the wrong direction, it was the easiest way to get some traction and to figure out whether she was going the right direction or not. Otherwise, she could be left fussing about a project for days, months, or years without any forward movement.

The first thing she could think of to do with the gems was to see whether she could liquidate a few of the ones that had already been cleansed. At least it would be possible to get rid of the cleansed gems, converting them into cash that she could deposit into her bank account. And the first people she thought of who might be interested in stones of power were the dwarfs. At least, the first people she could think of who would pay money for them. Plenty of others would try to steal them or to claim rightful ownership over them without giving anything in return.

She had the phone number for Gwythr, one of the dwarfs who she had talked to the last time she had visited the dwarf mountain with Corvin, Davyn, and the others. The phone rang a few times before it was picked up, and Reg wondered whether Gwythr might be out of range.

She had not expected the dwarfs to be able to get a good cell signal underground, but they had seemed to operate pretty well. She thought they might have some kind of signal booster underground. Or maybe they ran on a completely different service provider or kind of infrastructure.

Eventually, the call connected. "It is Reg Rawlins!" Gwythr announced enthusiastically.

"It is," Reg agreed, unable to suppress a smile at his excited tone. "How are you doing, Gwythr?"

"I am well! And thou?"

"I'm doing pretty good." And it was true. Reg had gone through some difficult times in the recent past, but she was in a good place with her business picking up and people talking to her again. Things would work out.

"You are calling to inquire after Nico, Warrior Cat?"

Reg hadn't been calling about Nico in particular, but she was interested in how he was faring with the dwarfs. And it was important to hear about him for other reasons.

Although Nico looked just like any other black cat, he was far from normal. Shortly after Reg's arrival in Black Sands, the Witch Doctor, an immortal going by the name Samyr Destine, had been raising a zombie-like race known as draugr to do his bidding. The draugr could shift into the form of a small black cat, a kattakyn, to enable them to get from one place to another unobtrusively. When Reg and the others had done battle with the Witch Doctor, he had sent what was left of his being out into the nine kattakyns to escape annihilation. Francesca, a charmer, had been able to bind the kattakyns in that form, so that they could not shift back into draugr again. Francesca and Reg had found new homes for the nine kittens around the world, each with a practitioner suited to their personality and abilities.

This would, Francesca promised, keep the witch doctor from being able to re-form for at least a thousand years.

But that had been on the assumption that no one would be able to undo the binding and that the kattakyns would be unable to find each other for a long time once the binding wore off.

But things had changed.

Reg took a deep breath. Nico was her favorite of the kattakyns. A mischievous, hyperactive, terror of a kitten who attacked her, broke lamps and vases, climbed the curtains, and defended her from the dwarfs when Reg had initially met them. The dwarfs, in turn, venerated the little black warrior cat and had made him custom armor. Nico had stayed to train with them when Reg and her friends had returned to Black Sands. It was the best home they could have found for him.

"Yes, of course," Reg agreed. "How is Nico?"

"He has learned much," Gwythr told her. "He is growing very strong and is getting bigger. We have had to refit his armor several times. You would hardly recognize him now."

Reg hoped with a pang that she would recognize him if she ever saw him again. And that he would recognize and remember her. He had never been her pet; she had known when she took him off Francesca's hands that it would only be for a short period of fostering before they found him a permanent home. But she still thought of him with fondness.

She understood Nico at a level that most others did not. His hyperactivity and distractibility. The way that he wouldn't or couldn't conform to the rules and type of relationship that seemed to come naturally to other cats. Reg knew what it was like to be different. She had never fit into the foster families she had lived with. She had always been an outsider, only there temporarily until her social worker could find her somewhere better. But the perfect home and family had never materialized, and when she had aged out of foster care, she was already on the street, trying to find a way to make it on her own.

But Nico had, hopefully, found his forever home.

"He's happy there?"

"Yes, very happy. He enjoys the training and the fighting. He is very skilled."

"That's good." She hoped that he had someone he could cuddle with at night too. That he was more than just a warrior cat that had to fight every day for his keep. He needed someone to take care of him too. "I'm really glad that he found such a good home with you."

"As are we," Gwythr agreed.

"I also was wondering…"

"What can the dwarfs do for the great Reg Rawlins?"

"Well, I thought that I might be able to do something for you."

"Indeed?"

"I have come across… well, I have some precious stones that I thought you might be interested in."

"Stones," Gwythr repeated.

In her mind's eye, Reg could see him nodding and stroking his long beard. When she had last seen Gwythr, he had been wearing a Cookie Monster t-shirt and jeans, with a sword on a belt. The mixture of modern and traditional dwarfwear was a little jarring.

"I could send you some pictures," she offered, "if you would like to look at them. And I have an evaluation from a jeweler, with the weight and cut and clarity and all that."

"Yes, that would be helpful," the dwarf agreed. "But why have you not sold them to this jeweler?"

"Well… that's a good question, I guess. You see… these gems have a bit of a history…"

"All gems have a history."

"Of course." Reg imagined that most of the gems that the dwarfs acquired were probably ones that they had mined themselves. Maybe they had been passed down from generation to generation over the years. Though maybe they had bought a few on Amazon or eBay. But the gems that she held had a more… storied past. "They were… uh… cursed for some time."

Gwythr cleared his throat.

"They aren't anymore. They have been cleansed. And I could sell them to a regular jeweler in the city. But some of them are more powerful, and I would rather find them a good home with someone I know. Somewhere I know they would be safe, and not be stolen again. Where their power would be used… in *positive* ways."

She did not want them to end up in the hands of a magical warlord like General Mbombo. She had seen the kind of harm that a man like he was could cause. The maimed villagers. The child soldiers. The poverty of the people who were pulling one of the world's most precious resources out of the mud.

"We appreciate that," Gwythr acknowledged. "Most humans do not understand how gems need to be properly cared for."

"Yeah. I didn't used to. But now that I know how they can be damaged by misuse and the trouble they can cause, I didn't want to sell them to just anyone. They could end up anywhere. I wouldn't have any control over it."

"You cannot control where they would go from here, either."

A heaviness settled in Reg's stomach. She had hoped that if she sold them to the dwarfs, they would be guaranteed to stay in the dwarf mountain. The dwarfs would keep them as heirlooms and not sell them anywhere else.

"No, I guess not. But I think that… someone like a dwarf who understood gems would be careful about who he sold such gems to, or how he used them."

There was a brief silence from Gwythr. She wondered whether he was thinking this over or had muted his mic and was talking to someone else in the background, going over strategies and negotiations. Eventually, there was a soft click and he spoke again.

"We will need to discuss this. Send me the pictures and specs. We might need to send someone to have a look at them firsthand."

"Okay. That sounds good. I'll send you the information." Reg let out her breath slowly, hoping the tension in her muscles would soften. "Give Nico an ear-scratch for me. He's really doing well?"

"He fares very well," Gwythr assured her.

"And… no one has come to see him?"

"Come to see him." Gwythr's voice hardened. "Who would come to see him? Has Reg Rawlins sent a delegation?"

"No. I haven't sent anyone. If anyone shows up to see him, it isn't because of me. I'm trying to make sure that no one bothers him."

"Why then? Who would bother him?"

"No one. I don't think." Reg thought of Harrison, and how to explain him to the dwarfs. Her immortal godfather? A powerful magical being with a penchant for cats and chocolate cake? Someone who didn't much care about human lives that could be lost while he and his kind amused themselves?

"Who?" Gwythr insisted.

"There is… a magical being. I don't know. I haven't told him where to find Nico, but I think he could search him out if he wanted to. He has… visited some of Nico's litter mates recently. I just want to make sure that he can't get near Nico."

"What does this being want with him?"

"I can't be sure. He likes cats. Maybe… he knew Nico in a previous incarnation. An old friend… I can't really understand it very well."

"When will he come?"

"I don't know whether he will. I hope not. But just… be aware."

"We shall," Gwythr agreed, his voice low and gravelly. "This person shall not bother our warrior cat."

CHAPTER SIX

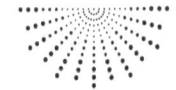

*R*eg hung up the phone after talking to Gwythr. She focused on Starlight, who was sitting directly in front of her, staring at her intently. She hadn't even been aware of him during the phone call with Gwythr. But she was sure that he had heard every word and had probably understood the situation better than either of them.

"I'm sure it will be fine," Reg told him. "Right? I'm just worrying over nothing."

He blinked at her slowly, then opened his eyes again and stared at her, blue and green eyes drilling deep into her thoughts.

"The dwarfs will take the gems. I don't have any doubt about that. The only question is whether I can negotiate a price that both of us will be happy with."

The dwarfs were good at bartering. But they would want the gems once they had seen them. They would be ready to deal.

And Reg really didn't have anything to worry about as far as Harrison was concerned. She had already told him to stay away from the rest of the kattakyns. Harrison was her protector. He would not do anything that could cause her trouble. Not after she had warned him. The world was safe from the kattakyns and the danger of the

Witch Doctor re-forming again in her lifetime. That wasn't going to happen.

The phone rang. Reg looked down at it, expecting to see a call back from Gwythr with further concerns or inquiries. But she hadn't even sent him anything about the gems yet. He wouldn't want to negotiate until he had seen what it was that he was buying.

And it wasn't Gwythr's name that she saw, but Corvin's name and incredibly handsome face. Something fluttered in Reg's stomach, and it wasn't worry and dread this time. She tried to keep her voice calm and relaxed and not give away that she was glad to hear from him. They hadn't spoken much since she had returned from her trip across the ocean to deal with the first batch of gems. He was kind of miffed by the fact that she hadn't waited for his help, hadn't even let him finish his research into how to cleanse the gems before her little excursion. Reg supposed that he had a point. She had asked him for help, and when things hadn't happened as quickly as she had hoped, she had found another way to deal with the problem. Corvin probably felt used. Unimportant.

"Corvin. Hi."

She shouldn't sound too friendly, since she was usually more reserved with him, trying to avoid being charmed by the warlock who could use his wiles to gain control over her if she weren't careful.

"Regina. We haven't... *talked* lately, and I was thinking of you..."

"Yeah, it's been a while. Everything going okay with you?"

"I am well, thank you. And you?" His voice took on a purring note. As if he really cared about her and wanted to know. That voice could get right under her skin and worm its way into her brain. Reg took a deep breath, trying to get air into her lungs. But she still sounded breathless when she answered him.

"Yeah. Things have been going a lot better for me, actually."

"Maybe divesting yourself of the cursed stones has had an effect."

"Maybe," Reg agreed. He didn't know how many gems she had started out with and how many she had been able to find new homes for. And how many gems were still sitting in a wooden box in her closet, waiting for her to take another trip. "What have you been up to lately? Working on any interesting projects?"

Not that she was really interested in any of his business. She didn't understand what he did as a warlock, when he wasn't stealing others' powers, and she found his collegiate studies to be extremely boring. But she felt she should at least inquire.

"I have applied to Davyn to reinstate me to the coven," Corvin told her.

It hit Reg like a punch in the gut. It shouldn't make any difference to her whether he were an active member of Davyn's coven or still being shunned by them. She had continued to be friends with him, despite the treacherous things he had done, so what did it matter whether he was being disciplined by his coven or not? If she, the victim in his case that had gone before the tribunal, was still on speaking terms with him, then why not the friends he'd had since before he even met her?

But that would mean that it was over. That the magical community felt that he had been fully punished for what he had done and was a full member of their order once more. He would be able to pick up more business, since he could now see and talk to the others in his coven without any restrictions.

Maybe he would stop calling her so often if there were other people he could call when he got bored with his solitary life.

It felt like a betrayal. Like the amount of damage that Reg had received from him had been measured and deemed to be compensated for. She should be over it now, since they had decided that he'd been shunned for long enough. No lasting harm.

Nothing they could see, maybe. That didn't mean that what he had done hadn't left scars that she would never get over.

"Are you still there, Regina?"

Reg considered just terminating the call. Why was she still on the phone with him anyway? Why had she even answered it to start with? Why would she even consider having anything to do with someone who had attacked her and taken something so precious from her in the past?

"Regina?"

"Yeah."

"Did you hear what I said?"

"Yes."

"You don't have anything to say?"

Reg licked her lips and swallowed. "What do you expect me to say?"

"I don't know. I expected you to go off, to be honest. Full-blown tirade about how I should never be released from my punishment after everything I have done. I expected... a lot of four-letter words, if nothing else."

"Well... however the coven wants to deal with you, that's their business." Reg cleared her throat. She felt very off balance but tried to act as if everything were normal. "I'm not the one who brought the charges against you in the first place."

"No, you didn't. I always thought that said something about you. And maybe about how you felt about me."

"Just that I didn't want anything more to do with you," Reg told him with a snap.

"Really, Reg. I think we're past that childishness, don't you? You and I have had some very enjoyable times together since then. We are far more alike than we are different."

Reg supposed he was referring to the fact that she was a siren and he was a warlock who had inherited certain abilities from his patriarchal line that allowed him—or to hear him tell it, forced him—to steal the powers and gifts from others to satisfy his unending hunger. Such things were not spoken of in the community, and that reluctance to talk about it had led to Reg being tricked by him into giving him her powers. She had never felt so empty and bereft as she had when she had woken up that morning.

In a bizarre twist of fate, Corvin had returned her powers to her, something that was previously unheard of. But he'd been trying to get them back ever since.

"We are not the same," she told Corvin coldly. "I am nothing like you are. What your coven does about you is their own business. It's got nothing to do with me."

"I'm sure Davyn will be calling you. You could, perhaps, happen to mention that you have no axe to grind. If you truly don't care whether I am readmitted to the coven or not, then tell him so."

It was a challenge for Reg to put her money where her mouth was.

"You could tell him that you are not afraid of me," Corvin prodded. "Inform him that you don't think I'm a danger to you any longer. That would go a long way to showing how much I have rehabilitated."

"You haven't rehabilitated. You haven't changed at all."

They had been psychically joined so many times that Reg couldn't ever fully separate from Corvin or keep him out of her own head. So even though he was only on the phone, she saw the smirk on his face and felt the chuckle that was too low to hear.

"Regina. I've changed so much. You know that. Look at how many times I have helped you. With the Witch Doctor and the draugar. With giving you the strength that you needed to help protect your younger self from Weston. Giving you strength to heal Calliopia and keeping you from blowing up the dwarf mountain. Can you really say that I haven't been the perfect gentleman, always willing to help you out whenever you called? Even if there was nothing in it for me?"

"No, I would not say that," Reg snapped.

"Well... I suppose everyone has a different perspective. But you can bet that I will be telling the tribunal of our many adventures together and how often you have called upon me to assist you. Whether you ended up taking my advice or not. I think if you look back at it, you will see that I have more than paid for one small mistake."

"Is that what you called me about? Just to gloat over how you are going to get reinstated into the coven? Because if that's all you're calling about, I have other things to do now."

"I'm sure you do. But I did want to give you a heads-up. It seems like the right thing to do. I wouldn't want you to get blindsided by this."

Reg breathed out slowly. Was she ever going to get to the point where she wouldn't react to Corvin's goading? Where she didn't care about what he was doing or thinking or had to say to her? It shouldn't matter to her what he did with his life. They were not a couple. They were not family. There was no tie between them, other than a psychic connection that both of them would prefer to break. Corvin was attracted to her, yes. Having once held her powers for that brief period, he didn't seem to be able to give up on the idea of talking her out of them again. But Reg knew too much now and she would never let him get the upper hand over her again. His powers had grown much stronger, but so had hers and, so far, she had been able to resist him.

And she would not give in to him again.

"You do what you have to," she said coolly. "It doesn't make any difference to me."

"I will, then," Corvin agreed smugly.

CHAPTER SEVEN

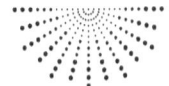

*R*eg was glad to get off the phone with Corvin. She didn't need the aggravation. He could go ahead and do whatever he wanted to. It was Davyn's problem to deal with, not Reg's. She didn't have to make any kind of decision about it. And she certainly wouldn't beg.

"What a pain in the neck," Reg told Starlight crossly.

Starlight, curled up on the couch with his nose touching his back feet, raised his head slightly to look at Reg. Who was a pain in the neck?

"Not you," Reg reassured him. "I'm talking about that warlock."

He blinked at her, then eventually closed his eyes and put his head down again, apparently satisfied that she wasn't criticizing him for something he had done.

"What would make me happy is if he just left me alone," Reg muttered to herself. She wasn't crazy. Not really. Talking to herself was just a way of sorting things out in her mind.

It wasn't as if she were talking to the voices in her head.

The voices had, unfortunately, been very loud recently. She thought it was her increased psychic activity. She was doing so many readings now that she was always open, always vulnerable to what the spirits had to say.

Or those who were not spirits but still, somehow, managed to worm their way into her head.

"That Corvin is lovely," one voice simpered, the accent and cadences as familiar to Reg as the sound of her own voice. "He is a wonderful specimen. You should get together with him. Go for a walk at the beach."

"Shut up, Norma Jean," Reg said evenly. "I can't even hear you."

"If you can't hear me, then how can you answer me?"

"You're not there," Reg pointed out. "You're all the way north in Maine or wherever you ended up. I'm just having a nervous breakdown."

"Of course you can hear the voices of your sisters."

Reg blinked, trying to process this. She petted Starlight, digging her fingers down into his thickest fur and trying to ground herself. "This is ridiculous," she told Starlight. "Even if I could hear Norma Jean, she is my mother, not my sister. Why would I think that?"

"We are all your sisters," Norma Jean's voice informed her.

"*All of you?*" Who else would Norma Jean be talking about? The other voices that Reg fought to ignore were not living beings like her mother, but those who had passed on. Reg had carried Norma Jean's voice in her head for a long time before Weston had changed the timeline, making it so that her mother had not died at the hands of Samyr Destine when Reg was four. Reg assumed that her familiarity with Norma Jean's voice after so long with her was the reason she could hear Norma Jean's voice even though it couldn't really be there. Reg had just gotten so used to it, that was the voice she had assigned to her internal voice.

At least, that was what she had been telling herself.

Everyone had an internal voice, right? She had heard writers talking about internal narrators. And that had to be what Norma Jean was now. No longer a ghost trying to communicate with her still-living daughter, but Reg's own brain, making observations about things around her. Helping her to make decisions.

But who else was Norma Jean talking about?

"No more. I'm tired. I need a break."

"You said he was yours. You claimed those waters, but you have not anointed them. You must seal your claim. Soon."

Reg shuddered. The last thing she needed to do was to take Corvin to the beach again. The last time she had nearly succeeded in pulling him into the water. Heart pounding loudly in her ears, she could almost smell the sweet scent of his blood that she had been able to sense that day. She had wanted so badly to just pull him into the water.

"Seal your claim," Norma Jean's voice insisted, losing the fake southern accent. "You must seal your claim with blood."

Norma Jean was joined by a chorus of creepy voices, most of them chanting words she could not understand, their voices starting low and hoarse and gradually rising until they were high-pitched and piercing. Reg poked her fingers into her ears, trying to drown them out.

Why couldn't she block them out? Why could she still hear Norma Jean's voice when she was miles away, and no longer a ghost, but attached to a physical body? None of it made any sense. Reg closed her eyes as tightly as she could, holding her breath, trying to force them to be silent.

CHAPTER EIGHT

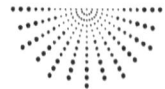

*T*here was a whoosh of air, as if something very large had walked into the room or the door had been opened. Reg's eyes flew open and she looked at the door. There was no one there. It was still shut.

Reg looked around the room, spooked. It had felt like there was someone else there with her. She was sure she wasn't still alone.

"Norma Jean?"

"Do you want me to be Norma Jean?"

Reg turned all the way around to look into the corner of the living room, where Harrison was crouched down, looking at the TV and pressing buttons to try to make it do something.

"Harrison?"

"Regina?"

"What are you doing here? You startled me."

"Yes."

"What are you doing?"

Harrison pushed on the front of the TV. Not one of the buttons, just the TV screen itself as if it were a touch screen.

"I am experimenting."

"With the TV?"

"Yes."

"What are you trying to do?"

"Trying to play yesterday. There was a story I wanted to show you."

"You can't play yesterday. Unless you recorded it. And since you were not here yesterday, I am assuming you did not."

"Recorded it?" Harrison echoed.

"Yes. Onto the hard drive. If you didn't record it onto the drive, you can't play it back."

"I can be here yesterday."

Reg shut her eyes and pressed her temples with her index fingers. "Don't mess up my timeline any more."

"Mess it up? I would not do that."

"Whatever you call it. I don't want you changing my timeline at all. Got it?"

"How about me?" Weston suggested.

Reg whirled back around and saw the immortal bending down to look at Starlight and to scratch his chin.

"What are *you* doing here? When did you get here?"

"Yesterday?" Weston suggested, his tone tentative. He looked at Harrison questioningly, and Harrison nodded obligingly.

"You guys are not funny! Quit the comedy routine!"

The sad thing was, they didn't even know how ridiculous they were being. They could probably go back to yesterday, tape whatever show Harrison wanted to show to Reg, and then return to play it for her. If he had any understanding of technology. He would probably have more luck if he took her back in time and just showed her the movie himself. Or maybe it was a TV show or a documentary. Or even just a commercial. He might want to show her a commercial for underwear to ask her opinion of it.

As usual, Weston was the more conservatively dressed of the two; Harrison was the flamboyant dresser and could never quite get the styles that he wore *right*. Something was always missing, out of place, or worn the wrong way. He had on a Hawaiian shirt that she had seen him wear before, or one quite like it, and a sailor's cap like she had seen on an old TV show. And he wore long tan shorts. Going on a safari? Harrison put on a pair of dark sunglasses to complete the ensemble and looked at Reg for her response.

"It's... very nice," Reg told him. "You look great. And so does..." She looked at Weston. She didn't even know what to call him. The immortal might be her father—and Reg was still not convinced of that fact—but he had never been a father figure to her. The immortals were extremely quirky. Self-centered, impulsive, and impossible to get any information from. If they were all-knowing, they hid it very well.

"So... why don't you tell me about the TV show?" she told Harrison.

"The TV show."

"You said you wanted to show it to me."

"But alas..."

"You can't. So why don't you just tell me about it? What was it about?"

Harrison made a gesture to wave it away. "Maybe we will go back there."

"No. Don't mess up my timeline. Listen, while you're here, I want to talk to you about—"

"Coffee?" Harrison suggested, walking into the kitchen toward the coffee machine. Reg turned toward it.

"I'll make the coffee. It's about Destine." She used the name that she had heard Harrison use for his old friend or enemy in the past. She still wasn't sure what the relationship between them was. If they had been rivals, then why was Harrison so interested in the kattakyns? Francesca was sure Harrison was going to try to free them to allow the Witch Doctor to re-form.

Harrison watched Reg put coffee grounds into the hopper. "The coffee?"

"The coffee what?"

"You said it is about Destine."

"No, I want to talk to you about Destine."

"Ah." He watched the coffee machine intently as Reg pressed the buttons and started the coffee brewing. "I thought it was about the woman."

"What woman?"

Harrison looked at Reg, and then over at Weston. Without his saying anything, Reg understood that "the woman" was Norma Jean. She put the discussion about the Witch Doctor on hold and thought about that. If Weston was in the mood to talk about Norma Jean, and could do it clearly, then it would go a long way to finding out why Norma Jean was in her head again. Maybe Weston had changed the past again, so that her mother was dead as she had been in the past Reg could remember. That would at least explain why she was talking to Reg again.

"You wanted to talk to me about Norma Jean?" she asked Weston.

"No."

"Why can I hear her again?" Reg asked, ignoring his answer. He obviously knew something. She couldn't give up the opportunity to find out what she could.

"You can hear sirens," Weston contributed. He looked around boredly.

"Sit down," Reg invited. She walked over to the living room to sit down, hoping to keep him there. She couldn't very well have a conversation if he disappeared into thin air again. Harrison stayed in the kitchen watching the coffee maker. "I know I can hear sirens. But why can I hear Norma Jean when she isn't even here?"

Weston followed her over to the living room, but didn't sit down. Reg wondered whether he had just followed Harrison there and wasn't really interested in visiting with Reg. Maybe the two of them were buddy-buddy now. They had been together when she'd seen them on her trip to the Everglades, but she hadn't seen Weston since then.

"Sirens can hear each other."

"So can humans. Why is that anything special?" Reg reconsidered her answer. Humans could hear each other when they spoke to each other aloud. They couldn't usually hear each other's thoughts, or she wouldn't be able to make any money as a psychic. But Norma Jean's voice was not actually audible. Maybe sirens, like gnomes, usually spoke to each other telepathically. "Do you mean that all sirens can speak with each other in their heads?"

Weston rolled his eyes to the ceiling. "Clearly."

"There's no need to be rude about it. I don't know anything about sirens and how they usually communicate."

Reg remembered Harrison saying more than once that "humans don't know anything." It was too true, in Reg's case in particular. Not having been raised in a community where paranormal powers and races other than humans mixed with them socially, Reg felt herself at a distinct disadvantage. Many things that might have been clear to the people who grew up in the community were completely unknown to Reg.

She looked at Harrison, who at least was more likely to talk to her and explain things than Weston. "Is that how sirens normally communicate? Telepathically?"

He shrugged. "Perhaps. I never paid any attention."

"How far can you communicate telepathically?"

"Me?" Harrison touched the side of the coffee pot, then jerked his finger back. "Distance is not a barrier."

"But you always come to see me in person. You don't just talk to me in my head."

He considered this for a moment. "When you were smaller, and there were many other voices, I had to visit you."

Reg nodded. There were still many competing voices and, as she had just demonstrated, she couldn't tell the difference between Norma Jean's spirit voice and her siren voice. If Harrison had just started speaking to her in her head, would she have known he was any different from the ghosts?

When she was little, she hadn't even been able to tell the difference between living playmates and ghostly ones. Or she hadn't known how to treat them any differently. Hadn't understood that playing with spirits would only make her a target to bullies and to grown-ups who thought she was too old for imaginary friends or thought she was psychotic.

"I like that you visit me," she told Harrison. "I like being able to see you physically."

"I like being able to see you too," he said generously.

"You are not as beautiful as the woman," Weston said bluntly. He clearly preferred his lover over his child. Reg had been surprised that an immortal could be charmed by a siren. Norma Jean was not a full-blooded siren, and her body and looks had been ruined by drug addiction and life on the street. But Weston had still been entranced with her, treating her like a beautiful princess.

If the immortals were all-seeing and all-knowing... but Corvin had corrected her more than once on this note. They did not have the attributes of the Christian God. They were very powerful and long-lived, but they didn't know everything and were quite naive in human matters.

"Have you seen Norma Jean lately?" Reg asked Weston, choosing to ignore the sting of his telling her she wasn't as beautiful as a drug addict living in squalor. Norma Jean didn't look like that anymore. In this timeline, she had recovered. Her skin was clear and her hair was thick and luxurious. Her rotting teeth had been replaced. She was a beautiful woman again, and her siren wiles meant that she was capable of ensorcelling pretty much any red-blooded male in her vicinity, including an immortal.

"I have seen her," Weston acknowledged.

"Recently?" Reg wanted to make sure that Norma Jean wasn't back in Florida. Just the thought of her mother being in the vicinity again set her heart beating faster and the anger and anxiety flooded through her whole body.

"All times are recently," Harrison reminded Reg.

To a being who lived forever, or at least for hundreds or thousands of years and who could travel back and forth in time as easily as walking into the next room, how could there be any long ago or recently? Reg knew from experience that trying to pin Harrison or Weston down to a human measurement of time would be impossible.

"Where is she right now?"

Harrison looked at Weston, passing the question back to him. Did that mean that Harrison didn't know? Or just that he wasn't interested?

Weston looked out the window, his hands loosely in his pockets, uninterested in Reg's question. Reg didn't know why he was there, why he had bothered to join Harrison. If he didn't want to talk to her, then why be there?

"Weston? Do you know where Norma Jean is right now?"

He looked at her, but his eyes were not focused properly on her face. Maybe he was remote viewing Norma Jean, checking in on her to answer Reg's question.

"She is… in her body. Where she always is."

"Yes, of course she's in her body. And where is her body?"

Weston made a vague gesture to the north.

Back in Maine, or a block away? Or outside the cottage?

Reg looked out the window Weston had just been looking out, fearing she was going to see Norma Jean lurking outside. That would, at least, explain why her voice had been so strong in Reg's head.

"Is she in Florida?" Reg asked, turning back to Weston.

But he was gone. And so was Harrison. Reg was alone in the cottage once more. Just she and her cat. And a coffee maker that was dribbling onto the counter, the coffee pot mysteriously absent.

CHAPTER NINE

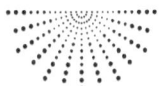

*R*eg tried to get the coffee maker to stop, but it was determined to keep dribbling fresh, hot coffee all over the counter and onto the floor. Reg shoved a coffee cup under the spout to catch the remaining liquid and tore a length of paper towels from the roll on the counter. She started mopping up, the hot coffee soaking its way through the paper towels and hurting her hands. Reg swore under her breath. Why would Harrison have disappeared with the coffee pot? He didn't even drink coffee. Chocolate, he liked, but he wasn't interested in coffee. He was just fascinated with the machine. He could have vanished the whole thing, so why hadn't he done that instead of just taking away the pot?

She muttered angrily to herself as she mopped up what she could, then ran cool water over her hands, which were turning a bright red.

Reg started to see bright spots in front of her eyes, and for a minute she thought that she was going to pass out. But they were not the bright sparklers that she saw when she was about to faint. They were sparking, glowing bugs—fireflies and moths and little things that Reg didn't have a word for. She turned away from the sink to look behind her, and saw a room filled with the brightly glowing insects, which gradually gathered and coalesced into a form that she had seen before.

Orri.

The day just couldn't get any better. A call from Corvin, Norma Jean's voice in her head, an appearance from Harrison and Weston that left her with a counter and floor covered with pools of coffee. And now the weird elf was back.

"Hi," Reg greeted.

Wasn't there any way to keep magical beings from appearing inside her house? With all the wards and charms Sarah had set, wasn't there anything that would keep the immortals and elves from coming and going as they pleased? It wasn't just malevolent humans and pixies that Reg wanted to keep out of the house.

Orri took off his sunglasses and looked around. "You are Reg Rawlins?"

"Yes... and you are Orri, the elf. I remember."

He cocked his head slightly, considering that. Did he really think that humans were so forgetful? That she could have a visit by an elf one day and have forgotten about it a day or two later?

His eyes moved from her face to the sink, where Reg was still holding her hand under a thin stream of cold water to relieve the minor scalding from trying to mop up hot coffee. The elf took a step toward her, looking concerned.

"It's fine," Reg said, pulling her hand away from the water and showing it to him. "Just a little bit of a burn. Nothing serious."

"I have a message for you."

"Don't take gifts from fairies?" Reg inquired.

He frowned.

"Sorry, go ahead." Reg told him. "Tell me your message." Even if he had already delivered his message once before, it was rather rude to upstage him. How many times had she gotten in trouble from foster parents for being a smart aleck? Even if she knew the answer, she knew better than to mouth off about it.

"I have a message for you," Orri repeated. He straightened, lifting his chin higher. "Waters be thy friend and foe."

"Oh." Reg nodded politely. She supposed that was why he had been concerned about her holding her hand in the water. Maybe he came prepared with a warning about water and seeing her standing there with her hand under the tap had confused him. "I see."

He waited, as if expecting some kind of reaction from her. Or maybe a tip. Did one tip elves who delivered warnings? Where did the warnings come from? Had someone paid him to deliver them? Or was it a compulsion?

"So... is this your job? Delivering messages to people?"

"No."

"Then... you're just doing it... for fun? As a hobby? What?"

"Waters be thy friend and foe."

"I know." Reg nodded. "Friend because it gives me strength, but foe because I can't control myself when I'm close to or in the water. I love the water; I always have. But with this whole siren instinct thing, I have to stay away from it to protect the people around me."

"Yes."

Reg nodded. "Well... thank you. Is that it, then, or was there something else?"

He frowned and looked around as if trying to figure out why he was there. "Have I been here before?"

"Yes. You showed up during a seance. Gave all my ladies quite a thrill. That time it was a warning about gifts from fairies."

He rubbed his forehead, frowning. "I'm not very good at this."

"You've done fine," Reg assured him. "Really. You found me, you gave me the message, what more could you do?"

He shook his head, clearly irritated with himself.

Did he have some kind of elf dementia? She hadn't even heard of an elf delivering warning messages before. If it wasn't his job, then why was he doing it? And it wasn't like the messages were wrong. They were apt, just... she'd already learned the lessons he was trying to warn her about. He was a bit late, that was all.

Orri strode up and down the room, scowling and looking around. He muttered something under his breath in elf-tongue. Finally, he shook his head at her, and the fireflies began flying around him again, and eventually, his shape dispersed.

CHAPTER TEN

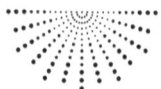

*S*he thought that was the end of it. There were no more strange messages or messengers for the rest of the day, nor for the next day, nor the next. She started to relax again, not expecting to run into her mother or Harrison or the strange new elf at every turn. It was just a coincidence that she had heard from them all in a day. They didn't seem to have anything to do with each other and did not show up again to warn Reg of things that were to come.

Just a strange day. Nothing she needed to worry about more.

Reg sat in the garden behind the cottage with a cup of coffee. She had replaced her missing coffee pot within a day; there was no way she could get through life without coffee when she got up in the morning. It was a drowsy, warm, pleasant day, the garden buzzing with bees, birds cheeping away in the trees, and a mild wind blowing the branches and leaves.

"Hail, Reg Rawlins!"

Reg realized that she had shut her eyes to listen to the wind and the birds. She opened them and saw a little man in front of her, with a red cap and brown and green clothing. She thought in the first instant that it was Forst, the gardener, but in a split-second, she realized that it was his twin, Fir, who Reg had once done a favor for, delivering him from the clutches of human law-enforcement. Reg's experience with the police had come in handy and she'd been able to spring him from jail without much trouble.

Fir, how are you? Reg greeted, speaking to him in her head. The gnomes preferred to converse in their "inside words," and were awkward and terse when forced to resort to verbal communication with humans. That gave Reg an advantage over anyone who was not telepathic.

We are well, Fir advised, nodding pleasantly.

Reg took a more careful look around. He had said "we," so that must mean that Forst was there too. The gnomes were often difficult to spot in the garden despite their red caps. Reg had her own suspicions about how they managed to hide themselves so well.

She didn't find Forst, but Zinnia standing nearby, off to the side looking at Reg shyly. Reg smiled back at her. *And Zinnia. It's so good to see you. How is newlywed life?*

It was the first marriage for Fir and the second for Zinnia. They were an older couple, past the point where they would be bringing up children together. Forst, Fir's twin, had grandchildren. Six of them, because his daughter had twins and his daughter-in-law two sets of twins, very fertile for a gnome.

We are happy, Zinnia told Reg, her cheeks growing redder. *I am very glad your canna brought us such good luck.*

Reg doubted that they could credit the plant that she had grown from a seed planted during the spring equinox with their happiness. And even if the plant had been the cause, the magic that had made it grow and flower so quickly had not been Reg's own, but was, she thought, because of the equinox and the large magical population that had visited Black Sands during the Spring Games. There had been a lot of magic in the air.

Could I give you a gift? Reg asked, thinking about the gemstones that had been cleansed so far. She had enough that she could spare one for a newly married couple. They could keep it as a treasure, use its power, or sell it and decorate their house and garden together. *I have something for you.*

No, no, Fir interjected, shaking his head vigorously. *You came to our wedding. Brought the canna into the garden. That is what gnomen do. We do not give gifts like humans.*

You're sure? Not even something little? I would like to do something for you.

Reg Rawlins has already been most gracious, Zinnia asserted. *To do more would be an embarrassment.*

The gnomes were very retiring and did not seem to like to have attention brought to them. So Reg shrugged and smiled and turned her hands palms-up to indicate that she would give them nothing else. Zinnia smiled at this and nodded approvingly.

Do you know anything about the forest people and their wedding traditions? Reg asked them, thinking about the Bigfoot Etienne and his fiancée Ilka who had come all the way from Russia to meet him face to face and marry after being pen pals for some time. Empress Ilka was far above the station of humble Etienne, living by himself in the Everglades. Reg was sure there wasn't anything that Ilka would need that she couldn't buy for herself, but maybe there was something she would like for the house. Or some convenience that she would never ask for.

Zinnia and Fir looked at each other and shook their heads.

The forest people are very private, Fir said. *Do not share their nuptials with others.*

Not at all? No wedding? Even with their family members?

Very private. Maybe family. Mother, father, brother, sister. He shook his head. *No others.*

Wow. I guess I should probably be flattered that I met Ilka at all, then.

Fir nodded. He pulled a curvy pipe out of his pocket. It was just like the one that Forst used. Fir filled the bowl with tobacco. *Forest people are very large. Many humankind look for them and they be hard to hide.* He lit his pipe and smoked a few puffs. *They cannot gather.*

That's very sad... I'm sure they would like to have a lot of family members around them...

Zinnia nodded. She looked around the garden, maybe remembering their wedding and how many of their family members and friends had been able to come to watch and wish them well.

The breeze blew through the trees, and Reg watched the dappled sunlight shifting with the movement of the leaves and branches. A burst of white butterflies flew into the air all at once. There was something there, something coming out of the shadows.

Fir's eyes grew wide and round and he nearly dropped his pipe. *Elven folk!*

Reg groaned. *Not again!*

Zinnia gasped and covered her mouth, looking at Reg in shock.

I mean—elves are great. I love having them around the garden, but this one is starting to get on my nerves!

Zinnia giggled.

Elves helped to cure Starlight when he was sick and cursed, Reg went on. *They really helped him to start feeling better. Forst probably told you. But... Orri...*

The fluttering butterflies eventually resolved into the familiar shape. Reg shook her head.

"Orri."

He looked at her and took off his glasses. "Reg Rawlins."

"Another message? How many of these meetings are there going to be?"

He looked perplexed. "I do not know."

"Well... why do you keep coming to me?"

"To warn you."

"Why?"

"Reg Rawlins is a friend to the Aelfen folk."

"I'm a friend? Why?"

He raised his brows and looked at her. Reg squirmed under his gaze. She should be used to looks by now. The hungry looks that Corvin gave her. The looks that she had received as a child when she had done something particularly bizarre or since she had moved to Black Sands and people expected her to know about the magical world when she didn't have a clue. She should be used to people not understanding or believing her by now.

"You are a friend," Orri said.

There was another flurry of sunshine and butterflies, and another shape started to resolve near her. Regina figured it would be another elf, come to get Orri and maybe to take him back to whatever institution he had escaped from. But as she looked, she saw Orri forming again. She looked back at the one who was already there. There were minor differences in his dress, but otherwise he looked the same. A twin? A clone? Maybe, like gnomes, elves always had babies in pairs. They looked identical.

"Who are you?" Reg demanded.

Zinnia giggled again behind her hand. Reg supposed people didn't usually talk to elves that way. Elves were one of the races that were rarely seen, easily frightened away, so people probably didn't speak to them in a way that might be taken as harsh or rude. But Reg wasn't going to tiptoe around. This elf was taking over her life. He didn't just come and bring her a message once, so that she could learn from it and go on with her life. He kept showing up at inopportune times, warning her about things she already knew of. And he didn't seem to have a clue what he was doing or why.

The new elf said nothing. He looked at the first Orri, took off his glasses, put them back on, and looked around. Butterflies started to swirl around him, and Reg assumed that he was going to disappear as he had before. But rather than dissolving into the sparkling lights, something else was forming. Another elf. Another Orri. Triplets?

Reg bit her tongue and didn't announce "Another one?" She just looked at Zinnia, who giggled and shrugged as if she didn't understand what was going on either. At least that made Reg feel a little better. Elves must not typically come in identical triplets, or Zinnia would not have been surprised.

The elf started to speak as soon as he was solid. "Fall not to—"

The second Orri cleared his throat. The third turned to look at him, and startled. He looked at Reg.

"Reg Rawlins? I have a warning for you."

"Apparently it's going around."

He looked at her and then back at the second Orri, not understanding Reg's comment. The first Orri raised his voice. "*I* have a message for Reg Rawlins," he said firmly.

The other two looked at him. Reg looked from one elf to the other.

"I assume you all have a message for me."

They nodded more or less in unison.

CHAPTER ELEVEN

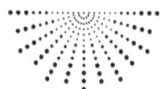

*T*here was a buzz like a swarm of bees. Reg looked around, her skin crawling. She didn't like buzzing insects. Especially ones that stung. A fly buzzing against the window was irritating, but a bee or a wasp sent her anxiety into overdrive. Maybe she had listened to too many tragic stories of bee stings when she was younger. Not just about how much getting stung hurt, but about people being killed by an allergic reaction before anyone knew what was happening. Tragedies that came with a warning to stay away from bees and wasps and not to do anything to anger them.

Reg looked around and saw a swarm of bees drifting into the garden. She got to her feet. She'd heard of how entire colonies of bees would go out looking for a new home or queen. There were people who specialized in taking care of them. She wasn't one of them. In fact, she wasn't getting anywhere near a swarm of bees. She backed toward the house, trying to avoid attracting the attention of the swarm as she made her way back inside, where it was safe.

They started to coalesce into a dark shape. Another one? Maybe this elf had been sent for the Orri triplets. It was all just a misunderstanding. For some reason, three elves had been dispatched with her message instead of just one. There was a logical explanation for it. Bound to be.

But, as she feared, the fourth figure was Orri-shaped as well. Reg looked from one elf to the other, shaking her head in disbelief.

Do elves only come in one model? Reg asked Zinnia. She hadn't noticed when the elves had come into her house before. But she had been so worried about Starlight that she really hadn't paid much attention. She knew there had been men, women, and children, but she couldn't remember what any of them looked like and just how diverse they had been.

Zinnia shook her head. *No. Not like this,* she projected into Reg's thoughts. *Very strange.*

Well… I don't know what I'm supposed to do about this. Isn't there any way to make them stop? A way to chase them away? Pretty soon, this yard will be so full of elves that there won't be any room for the rest of us.

Fir and I go, Zinnia offered, *make more room for more elves.*

Reg chuckled. *No. No, I'll try to make them give their warnings, and then they will go. Right?*

Zinnia's eyes were wide and round. *I know not.*

"What are your messages?" Reg demanded of the four Orris. "Can you just give them to me and go back?"

They all looked at each other.

"Waters be thy friend and foe," the second offered.

Reg pointed at him. "Got that one already. You can go."

"This is not—"

"I got it. I know that. You can go back where you came from."

Lights began to swarm around him, and eventually the elf was gone. Reg looked at the others.

"Next!"

"Beware fair folk—"

"Bearing gifts," Reg finished. "That one too."

The first Orri looked offended. "I warn you…"

"I got it. Fairies with gifts. Don't accept them. Figured that out before you ever showed up. So you can go."

He turned into a swarm of lights that dissipated into the garden with a clash of discordant bells. Zinnia looked at Reg, eyebrows raised, worried about the trouble she was causing. Reg looked at the two remaining Orri's.

"That was mine too," the bee-swarm Orri said, putting his hand partway up like he was in a classroom. The bees started to swarm and his shape moved back out of the garden again. Reg was glad to see that one go. She hadn't wanted to deal with that annoying buzzing any longer than she had to. Her shoulders dipped a little as she relaxed. She looked at the final remaining Orri. The second who had appeared, she thought.

"Do you have a different message?"

He nodded. "I have a warning for Reg Rawlins."

"A different one."

Another nod.

"Okay. Go for it."

"Fall not to strange keys."

Keys. Reg had already learned the lesson of the keys as well. She had learned a lot more than she had realized since moving to Black Sands. Maybe the purpose of Orri's warnings was just to remind her of that fact. That she had learned a lot since she had gotten there, both about magic and about herself.

"Thank you," she told him politely.

Orri nodded in satisfaction. He dissolved into fluttering moths and dots of light and then was gone. Reg looked at Zinnia and Fir.

One does have to take care with strange keys, Fir advised.

I know. Keys can unlock things that you don't want unlocked. Like immortals that have been hidden away under the stairs for decades.

Well, Fir frowned, *I don't know about that.*

Trust me. They can. And you don't want to give someone else your own keys, because that gives them the ability to enter your house. Even if you have wards set against them.

Zinnia and Fir both nodded about this. It was probably basic stuff for them. But it had been an important lesson for Reg to learn. One that had almost come too late. It would have been nice to have been warned before the event. The same was true of the other warnings too. If they had come at the right point in her life, she would have appreciated them much more. Not hearing the warnings until after she had failed to protect herself or make the right decision was a real pain.

Learning from experience was only one way of learning life's lessons, but unfortunately it seemed to be the only one that worked for Reg. Try as she might to learn from other people's experiences, positive or negative, she just didn't seem to learn until she had been through something herself. A character trait that had made foster mothers despair.

We will... leave you to your thought and drink, Fir told Reg, motioning to her coffee cup, almost forgotten in all the drama. He tamped out his pipe and put it carefully back into his pocket. *Fare thee well. Pay heed to the warnings of elves.*

Reg nodded. *Okay. Will do,* she agreed.

Fir and Zinnia joined hands and pushed their way into the vegetation, and in a moment were gone from Reg's sight.

She had a sip of her coffee and rubbed the center of her forehead, which was pulsing with pain.

CHAPTER TWELVE

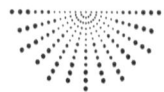

*R*eg was excited to be starting a new level of training with Davyn, a warlock who was the head of Corvin's coven and a firecaster. Being an experienced firecaster, he was helping Reg to develop her own gift, which had been neglected and repressed for many years as she had tried to keep out of trouble in foster care.

Lighting fires was not a way to endear oneself to foster families. Even though Reg had thought that it was always the other children who had lit fires in homes she had been in, she had realized that Davyn was probably correct in his assessment that she had been the one to light them without realizing it, knowing that such a thing was not allowed but unable to completely suppress her gift.

So other foster children had been blamed for the accidents and Reg's involvement in the fires had been overlooked.

And now, after several months of training with Davyn, Reg had improved her control enough that Davyn had taken her out of Black Sands to practice some new skills and techniques. Before, she'd had to stay in the house, in an enclosed area where Davyn could quickly put out any fires that got away from Reg.

"How are you doing today?" Davyn asked. "Feeling calm and focused?"

Reg nodded eagerly. "Sure." She examined their surroundings. A farmhouse far from any prying eyes. The sweet-smelling citrus trees around them were green and well-watered, as most of Florida was. They didn't have to deal with the same risk of forest fires as California or other more arid locations.

"I want you to take the time to think about it," Davyn cautioned. "Really look inside and examine your feelings and motivations. You will need to be able to stay in control. This is not an amusement park."

Reg closed her eyes. More to feign concentration than to look inside herself. Of course she was ready. She'd been ready for weeks, but Davyn had been holding her back, insisting that she keep running through his preschool-level firecasting exercises until she could do them blindfolded and with her hands tied behind her back. So to speak.

She was ready to move on to more complicated exercises. Eager to build on the skills she had developed so far. She knew that her inner fire was very strong; she had proven that to herself and everyone else in the dwarf mountain.

"I'm ready," she told Davyn in a calm, even voice that he couldn't fail to recognize as being focused and teachable.

"Okay. Let's start with some of the exercises that you are familiar with, just to get warmed up and to make sure that you are able to keep your focus in this new environment."

Reg rubbed her palms together briskly, warming them up, and then drew them apart, slightly cupped, as if she were holding a basketball between them. She conjured a ball of fire, small and well-behaved, suspended between them. Davyn had her make it bigger and smaller, hotter and cooler, and Reg performed perfectly. There was no way he could find fault with any of her actions.

"Let's try a campfire," Davyn suggested. "You've done that before."

Reg nodded. She had done that plenty of times without his help, even before she had known that she was a firecaster. At camps in her childhood, she had always been the one who could build a fire and get it going the quickest, even if the fuel were wet. She had thought then that she was just really good at knowing how the fire would behave, what it needed and how to feed it the combination of fuel and oxygen that it needed. One match, and the whole thing would burn happily. Now she knew she didn't even need that one match. She'd lit a campfire when they went on their quest to the dwarf mountain and when she had been across the ocean to find the owners of the first bag of gems. Without any supervision by Davyn.

She made a space for a campfire in a flat, rocky area where there were not many green plants, just a few weeds that had pushed their way through the gravel and rocks. She surrounded it with a ring of larger rocks, although she knew that neither of them really needed any kind of firebreak. They would be able to keep the fire contained in the area they wanted to. Then she gathered firewood, bits of old lumber and building materials from outbuildings that had long since collapsed. Dry old wood that would light in an instant.

The hardest part was waiting until she had everything ready for the campfire. A couple of times, wood started smoldering in her hands before she even got it to the ring of stones, and she had to snuff it out.

Eventually, she had a small pile of tinder, kindling, and large pieces of wood ready to be lit. She looked at Davyn.

The way that he smiled at her, Reg knew that he was aware of the struggle she'd had in not lighting the fire prematurely. He nodded.

"Go ahead."

Reg didn't go through the exercise of holding a ball of fire between her hands to start with and then using it to light the campfire. She didn't point at the wood or bend down to touch it and ignite the pile. She just released the fire she had been holding inside and the wood was ablaze in an instant.

"Keep it contained," Davyn cautioned.

Reg monitored the size of the fire, the edges, and the embers that floated off into the air, tracking and mapping them all in her mind. The fire was an extension of herself, like a dream she controlled.

"Good," Davyn approved.

"I've done this before," Reg pointed out. "This isn't hard."

"I know that. We need to start with what you are comfortable with. Start with the skills that you already have."

Red rolled her eyes. But she stayed focused on the fire. She knew Davyn would test her, try to distract her or get her emotional, to see whether he could get her to lose her focus.

"So things have been good lately?" he asked. "You have been doing more business lately."

"Yes," Reg agreed. "More readings and seances. I had a dry spell for a while there, but I'm doing better now."

"People were worried about you being a siren."

Reg gritted her teeth. She didn't like the way that he put it. Reg wasn't a siren. Her mother was a siren. Or part-siren. Reg wasn't a siren, because she hadn't acted as a siren. She had kept her siren instincts suppressed and had not followed through on the impulses that the water brought out in her. So she *wasn't* a siren. She just happened to have a mother who was a siren.

"Yeah," she agreed. "That's what people were worried about. But they're starting to calm down now. And I've been able to find other clients. Non-practitioners who don't know anything about *that.*"

"That's good. I'm glad you've found your place. Been out to the water lately?"

The campfire flared. The heat warmed Reg's face. She breathed in and out slowly and brought the size back down again.

"I'm mostly staying away from the water right now," she admitted.

Water be thy friend and foe.

She had been out on a boat with Corvin when she was trying to understand what to do about the gems. Corvin was one of the few people who had experienced the power of her siren instincts, but he wasn't afraid of her. He had his own power, and he had known when to back off and to put space between them so that Reg could not overcome his defenses. It had been a relief to go out on the water, to feel the waves rolling beneath her feet, but it had also been frustrating to be so close to fulfilling her siren desires and to have to back off, to leave the underwater world she could feel beneath her and go back to the land.

The thirst had been very strong. Stronger than she wanted to admit to anyone.

"Reg," Davyn prompted.

Reg focused back on her fire. She had expected to find it burning higher, out of her control because she'd let herself get emotional again, but instead she found that it was dying out. Just a few flames licking over the wood. Reg frowned.

"What...?"

She focused on building it up again. It took only a minute to get the campfire blazing merrily again. When it was the appropriate size and heat, Reg looked sideways at Davyn.

"Did you do that?"

"Me? No. Why would I do that?"

"To challenge me. You're always doing things to see how I respond."

"I did not quench your fire. Think about where your focus was. What were you thinking about? Where did your mind wander to?"

Reg sighed. "To the ocean. Water."

"You have a very strong affinity to two elements. An affinity for water is very rare in a firecaster. Just as I imagine it is very rare for a siren to have an affinity for fire. I believe that you can use both abilities to temper each other."

"I can control my fire by thinking about water."

Maybe that was how she had scalded herself on the coffee too. As a firecaster, it was pretty hard for her to burn herself. But maybe it was different with hot water.

Davyn shrugged. "That would appear to be the case. If so... it may be easier for you to quench your fire, even when you are angry, than it would be for the average firecaster."

It was funny to hear Davyn talking about the average firecaster, when she knew how rare firecasters were. Davyn was the only other one she had ever met, as far as she knew. Certainly the only one who had ever declared himself to her.

"Okay."

Davyn nodded. "I was talking to Julian the other day."

CHAPTER THIRTEEN

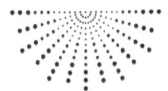

*R*eg's gut clenched and the fire leaped before she could suppress her reaction. Davyn had introduced the topic without any warning. If he had worked his way up to it, she might have been able to handle it better. Reg controlled the fire, keeping her focus on it.

"Yeah? What were you talking to Julian about?"

Davyn smiled. Maybe because he was pleased to see how Reg was able to keep her control now. Or maybe just because he was happy thinking about Julian and their conversation.

Reg didn't know what he saw in Julian. The magical investigator was still as much of a self-important bully as he had been when he had been Reg's foster brother many years before. He had physically abused her. Tormented her with his magic. And nearly gotten himself killed in the process. Coming back into her life to investigate what had happened in the Everglades, he had done everything he could to prod her into action, wanting to add another notch to his belt and prove to the Endangered Species Division what a good investigator he was. He had even drawn his wand on her, which really hadn't been a good idea.

But Davyn was attracted to Julian despite his dark side. Maybe because of it. Some people were just attracted to bad boys. He said that he saw something else in Julian. But Reg didn't know what. She knew that Julian was damaged. Whatever he had gone through in his early life before going into foster care had scarred him deeply, just as Reg's experiences had shaped her. Neither of them would ever be normal and whole on the inside. They would always be apart from everyone else.

"He mentioned you," Davyn said. "Asked how you were doing."

"That was nice of him."

"We might do something over the summer. A vacation of some kind. Get away from things."

"He's coming here?" Reg tried not to engage with the news, but to keep her emotions flat and the fire controlled.

"We haven't decided yet. Maybe we'll meet here and go to the Everglades. Maybe somewhere else."

"You should go somewhere else. He's already seen Black Sands and the Everglades. Go somewhere neither of you have been."

And keep Julian Sabat far away from her.

"We'll have to see," Davyn said pleasantly. "We haven't made a decision yet."

"Uh-huh."

Reg looked for some way to change the topic. She knew that Davyn was just trying to get an emotional reaction out of her, but she had herself under control now. He would not be able to push her into action.

"Have you heard from Corvin recently?" Davyn asked.

Reg swallowed. Davyn certainly was not making it easy for her. She focused on keeping the size of the fire down, but she let it grow hotter, hoping the intensity would relieve some of the stress.

"Yeah, I heard from him," Reg agreed. "He said he was going to give you a call. Or something. I don't know, maybe a formal letter. Did he send something by crow?"

"He talked to me directly."

"Great. So you're all over this application of his for reinstatement."

"It's on my task list," Davyn acknowledged. "I'm not about to rush it through, though."

Reg breathed steadily in and out, watching the flames, feeling the white-hot heat at the heart of it. "What's the process, then?"

"We will add the matter to the coven's agenda. Get feedback from what other members think. Talk to the parties involved." Davyn looked significantly at Reg. "And then the tribunal will be called to consider his application. As you know, this is not the first time he has applied to be reinstated."

The previous time had been mere weeks after Corvin had been kicked out of the coven. He figured that his fight with the Witch Doctor had proven his goodwill toward the community and he should be allowed back in immediately.

But they had turned down his application. Maybe they would again.

Reg wasn't counting on it. She remembered how she had been told before the hearing that removing Corvin from the coven had a negative effect on everyone in the magical community, not just him. He was a powerful warlock, and that meant that his powers would not be available for their use. They would have to do without him. And it had been long enough now that they probably really wanted him back. It wouldn't be as easy to turn him down a second time. There would be witches and warlocks who believed he had been disciplined enough for a minor failing.

"You think you'll approve it this time?"

"I've been keeping a close eye on him. I'm not sure that he has reformed as much as he would like us to believe."

"He hasn't reformed at all. He's no different than he was."

"And reformation is our goal. Of course… we can't change his nature. His condition is not his fault. We have to remember that what he is will never change."

Reg nodded. Corvin too had another set of instincts. She didn't know how much he could control and how much his predatory instincts took over his decision-making ability.

"How do you feel about it?" Davyn asked.

"I don't know. I haven't really thought that much about it."

"You and Corvin remain... friends."

"Not friends, exactly." Reg tried to explain it. "He's not someone I would pick out to be friends with... but we're connected. Like people in the same family. You don't get to choose whether you want to be family or not, and you're not responsible for what the other person does. But you're still... connected."

"He's like a brother to you?" Davyn asked, his tone dripping with sarcasm.

"No!" Reg's face grew hot, and it wasn't because the fire was getting out of her control. She would never have feelings like that for a brother. But she couldn't control the feelings he inspired in her. His magical charms and the pheromones he exuded had a physical effect on Reg that was difficult to overcome. That wasn't a moral weakness. It was just the power that his kind had over others.

Especially women.

And especially Reg.

"I'm just saying that we're connected. I can't help that. And since he's been shunned by the coven, there aren't many people that he can talk to."

"So you think that our punishment has had a negative effect on you? That it would have been better if he'd been able to remain in the coven, so that his attentions were not... directed elsewhere so much?"

"I don't know. I would have been really ticked if you hadn't punished him at all. And what else are you going to do? Give him a fine? A slap on the wrist? I know you were talking about binding him, but that would be harder, right?"

Davyn nodded. "It would take power away from the community. Binding a warlock of Corvin's power... I don't know if we could even have done it. Not for any length of time. And the negative implications on the rest of the community..." He shook his head. "You don't want to hear all this, I'm sure. You just wanted him to be punished. And maybe we didn't make the best choice for you."

"I don't know what would have been better," Reg conceded, shaking her head. "I guess you did the best you could. And now..."

She pressed her lips together, trying not to show any emotion over the discussion. "Well, you do what you do, right? Whether you reinstate him or not doesn't really have any effect on me. He's still connected to me. He'll still keep coming back whether he's part of the coven or not."

CHAPTER FOURTEEN

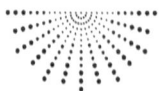

*D*avyn dropped Reg off in front of the big house that Sarah lived in.

"Make sure that you get plenty to drink," he advised. "You're going to be dehydrated after all the work you did."

"Yeah, I will."

"That's water, not alcohol. Alcohol will just make you more dehydrated."

Reg rolled her eyes. "I think I know that."

"I don't know what you know. Just stay away from the alcohol tonight. Or you'll be miserable in the morning."

Reg nodded. "Yes, *Dad*. I'm going in now."

Davyn snorted. He shifted the car into drive, gave a little wave, and pulled out into the street.

Reg walked along the pathway that went around the side of the house and into the backyard and the guest cottage. She was tired, but she was awake enough to keep an eye out for Corvin. He had ambushed her as she was going back to her house more than once, and it would not happen again. She might be superstitious, but she didn't want him showing up for a chat because she had been thinking about him.

All was quiet, and no one stepped out of the bushes or confronted her before she could get to the gate that marked the boundary of the wards and protective charms that Sarah had set. Reg stepped through the gate with a sigh of relief. She had left the evening clear, Davyn having warned her that she would probably be tired after their session. So instead of preparing for more client readings, seances, or other work, she could just relax with Starlight and not think about Corvin or Julian or anyone else she didn't want to think about.

Reg unlocked her door and went into the cottage. "Did you miss me?" she called out.

She heard Starlight jump down from wherever he was perched, and he came strolling out to see her, stretching first his front and then his back legs and giving a big yawn. He sat down and started to wash.

"Did you have a nice nap?" Reg asked him.

He stopped and stared at her for a moment before going on with his grooming routine.

"I figured we'll have an early supper, get into jammies, and then veg out the rest of the night. Just you and me. How does that sound?"

He gave another wide yawn that ended in a squeak.

"Great. Glad you approve. Now, what's in here?" Reg approached the fridge. She knew that she should eat something that was good for her body, before whatever Sarah had left in there went bad, but she wasn't a big fan of healthy eating. Truth be told, Sarah wasn't either, which was probably why so many of her dishes ended up in Reg's fridge. Reg browsed through the covered bowls and fast-food leftovers for anything that looked appealing, but wasn't inspired by anything she saw. It was time to clean out the fridge. She didn't even know how long half of the food had been sitting in there.

Reg pulled out a garbage bag and started tossing out all the fast-food cartons and bags. She even went so far as to pull out the larger bowls of Sarah's and to dump the contents into her garbage, then placed the bowls in the sink to rinse them out, hoping that way it wouldn't be so obvious that she had just dumped them instead of eating them. She looked back in the fridge.

Much better.

She could eat a few of the remaining items over the next few days.

When she felt like making a sandwich or warming up some pasta. And that meant that she could order in something good.

* * *

With her belly nearly bursting with the excellent Chinese food from Tasty Lotus, Reg lounged in front of the TV, checking through the streaming media channels for something that she could watch for a few hours without getting bored. Starlight was curled up on her lap, purring away in his sleep, eyes closed tight.

There was little Reg found more comforting than a purring cat in her lap. She was sorry that she had missed out on it earlier in life, having never been able to have a pet before. But now she had Starlight, a cat that had chosen her more than she had chosen him, and all was well with the world.

* * *

Reg stirred.

A voice called to her.

She was so tired. Reg rubbed her eyes, trying to remember what she was supposed to be doing. Had she missed a client appointment? She didn't think she had meant to fall asleep where she was.

"Reg Rawlins."

Reg blinked, trying to bring the room into focus. She was pretty sure she hadn't had anything to drink. Davyn had told her not to, hadn't he? She wouldn't have gone ahead and had drinks anyway.

Not without a really good reason.

"Mmm." She tried to let the voice know that she wasn't dead, and give herself the time to wake up completely.

Had she gone out? Or was she still home?

Reg felt for Starlight and found him cuddled up against her. So he was there and she must be home because she wouldn't have taken him out anywhere.

Then who was in her cottage?

Reg forced her eyes open, alarmed. *Who was in her house?*

"Who's there? Who are you?"

She managed to pry her eyes open, and sitting up and squinting around, found a figure sitting in the chair across from her. Reg was stretched out on the uncomfortable wicker couch with Starlight, and he was sitting in one of the chairs.

An elf with twinkling eyes.

Aelf.

Orri.

"My name is Orri," he told her, leaning forward to talk to her in an intimate voice.

Reg shook her head, trying to get some perspective and to remember everything that had happened during the day. Had something happened since she saw Davyn? She was pretty sure that she had just been watching TV and vegging out.

Starlight stirred beside her, but he didn't seem alarmed. He stood up and arched his back and stretched luxuriously. She loved watching him stretch and always thought it looked so utterly satisfying. She would like to be a cat just once to know whether it felt as good as it looked. Starlight sat and started to wash.

At least if he weren't bothered by Orri, that probably meant that the elf was okay. He was not a danger to Reg, or Starlight wouldn't have been calm around him. He'd be hissing and spitting and nipping the elf's ankles.

"I know who you are," Reg said tiredly. "We have met."

"We have?"

"This morning, there were *four* of you. Are you identical quadruplets? Clones? Robots?"

"Four of me," Orri repeated thoughtfully.

"Yes. Four of you."

"I'm really not very good at this."

"Good at what? You seemed to have no problem appearing to me out of a swarm of bugs."

"This kind of travel can be very difficult."

"I would think so. I wouldn't want to travel in a swarm of bugs. How do you even steer them?"

She knew she was being mouthy, but she didn't really care. If Orri were going to keep appearing to her at random intervals with his useless warnings, then he would have to put up with a bit of sass.

"I am not in the bugs," Orri said with a frown. He looked as if he were going to try to explain his method of travel to Reg. She held up her hand to stop him.

"No. I really don't want to know. Just... give me your stupid warning and swarm out of here. And don't come back. I really don't want you to come back again."

"I can't help coming back. It's already happened."

Reg stared at him, blinking and trying to make sense of this statement.

"Just go home, okay? I don't need your warnings. Go warn someone else next time. Please. And don't wake me up. It's really rude to wake someone up out of a sound sleep."

He scratched his head and then fiddled with one of the rings on his fingers. "I have already come to you in the future. So, I can't... not."

"Oh, good grief." Reg ran her fingers through her braids as if it would help her to get her thoughts in order. She gathered up all the braids in one bunch and pulled them back behind her shoulders. Maybe it was time for a change. Maybe she should twist them into a knot or consider a different style. "How could you have already come to me in the future?"

He raised a finger and opened his mouth to explain.

Reg shook her head. "No! No, I'm not asking. I don't want you to explain it to me. I just want you to stop. So... whatever you are planning for the future, stop it now. Hasn't anyone ever told you that humans don't like people messing around with their temporal timelines?"

He rubbed his whiskered chin. "No."

"Well, we don't. So stop doing it. No more, you understand?"

"I have to do what has already been done."

"Argh!" Reg pulled on a handful of her hair, forcing herself to focus on the jolt of pain instead of trying to understand the convoluted story he was going to give her. She didn't want to hear anything about paradoxes or the unpredictable effects of time travel. She'd seen Star Trek, but had discovered for herself that things just didn't work out like they did on TV. TV had all the answers about time travel paradoxes, but they were all wrong. "Just stop!"

Orri looked down, nodding. "Yes, Reg Rawlins."

"I need some sleep. I need you to go, okay? So go home, and we're done. No more of this."

"I have a warning," Orri said apologetically.

"Of course you do. But you've already given them to me. Multiple times. I don't understand why you have to keep coming back and giving them to me."

"I want to help."

"If you want to help, then leave me alone. Driving me crazy won't help anyone."

Orri stood up and moved around restlessly.

"Well?" Reg prompted. She made a shooing motion with her hands. "Swarm away."

"I... can't."

"Why not?"

"I have a message for you."

"You can't leave because of the message?"

He nodded, looking chagrined.

Reg breathed out in exasperation. "Which one is it this time? Beware of fairies bearing gifts?"

"No..." Orri hesitated, looking at Reg's face, uncertain whether he should proceed with his message or make her keep guessing.

"Just tell me."

Orri straightened, preparing for his moment. Reg rubbed her eyes with the heels of her hands, trying to rub all the grit away.

"Be not ensorcelled by fair face," Orri announced.

It was a new message, at least. Reg was glad not to have to hear one of the old ones over again. She considered it as she waited for Orri to disappear. But Orri remained there, looking at her expectantly. What did he want? A tip? Gratitude? That moment where it all came together and she understood why he had kept coming to see her?

Well, she wasn't going to tip him. Help him to the door, maybe, but no tip.

"Okay, thanks."

He played with his rings again, not meeting her eyes.

"You've given me the warning, so you can go now, can't you?"

"Be not ensorcelled by fair face," Orri repeated.

"Yeah. I heard you. I'll be sure to take that into account when a handsome elf keeps transporting himself into my house." Reg gave a laugh.

Orri looked horrified. "No, not *me!*"

"I think I've learned my lesson about good-looking men. Since my experience with Corvin…"

Orri's face fell. "What? You and the warlock have already… met."

"Yeah, you're way late if you were trying to prevent that. That was when I first got here."

"But I thought I went back far enough."

Reg shook her head. "No. Sorry. But… don't try again. You can just stop now. You don't need to keep trying."

"But I *must* warn you. I *must* repay you…"

Reg didn't know what he thought he had to repay. She shook her head. "No, you and me are good. No need to keep warning me. I've had enough insights into the future. Okay? So you can go home now."

Orri stared at her, his face a picture of disappointment. Lights started to flash and dart around him, and eventually the swarm of fireflies swallowed him up and winked out, and Reg was alone with Starlight once more.

CHAPTER FIFTEEN

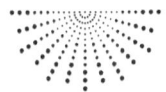

*R*eg looked out the window. It was late, the small hours of the morning. She was often still up at that time, so it was disconcerting to have been so soundly asleep before Orri's appearance. She still felt a little disoriented by his waking her up and then trying to give her his warning, as unnecessary as it was. Why did he feel the need to keep coming back to tell her to avoid things that she had already dealt with?

A light went on in the kitchen in the big house at the front of the lot. Sarah was up, back from whatever date or social event she had been out at, getting herself a cup of tea before retiring to bed. If she even slept. Reg wondered sometimes. Sarah certainly didn't seem to need as much sleep as Reg. How she found the time, Reg wasn't sure.

She pulled her housecoat on over the worn t-shirt and shorts that functioned as her pajamas and walked across the yard to the kitchen door.

"Come in, Reg," Sarah called out.

Reg opened the door and entered. Sarah smiled, her face pink as she bustled around the kitchen.

"How was your evening, Reg? Did you have a good rest?"

Sarah knew her schedule, of course.

"Yes. It was nice to have an evening to myself. I guess I need to remember to recharge now and then."

"Especially after a workout with your firecaster."

"Yeah. I like the firecasting lessons... so I don't really realize while I'm doing it just how tiring it is. How much it takes out of me."

"You need to make sure you stay hydrated." Sarah motioned to the tea kettle. "Can I get you something?"

"Sure." Reg looked at the packets of tea in the basket on the table and selected one of the commercial ones. Peppermint. While there were several bags of loose-leaf tea that Sarah had put together herself, Reg didn't have the palate for the herbs that Sarah used. They always tasted like cough medicine. Or worse. Reg had a sweet tooth, and that meant she used a lot of sugar or honey in her tea, which always made Sarah shake her head.

In a few minutes, Sarah was sitting across the table from Reg, watching as she spooned sugar into her tea. "I'm sure you need the extra energy for your firecasting," Sarah said pleasantly. "But as you get older, you may find that refined sugar is not the best thing for your body. Maybe some fruit? A banana?"

Reg glanced around Sarah's kitchen. Despite her words, Sarah indulged a little too much in restaurant food and delicacies imported from around the world. Reg did not see a bowl of fruit in evidence. Which was fine, since she wasn't big on fruit. She just shrugged.

"What can you tell me about elves?"

"Elves?" Sarah pursed her lips and stared off somewhere over Reg's shoulder. "Well, they are pretty shy. Humans don't see a lot of them. While we have some commerce and socialization with fairies, elves are different. Not haughty like the fairies... they just keep to themselves."

"So you don't see very much of them?"

"Goodness, no. Sometimes I see evidence they have been around. See lights or hear bells in the night as they are moving from one home to another, but no, the only time I have seen them face-to-face, in human form, is that day when they helped with Starlight."

"Hmm." Reg nodded.

"Why do you ask? Have you heard them again? Usually, they only move around winter solstice. Maybe summer if there were a reason for it, but it's still pretty early in the year."

"Well, no. I haven't seen more than one of them."

"More than one?" Sarah frowned.

"Yes..."

"So you have seen one."

Reg nodded.

"You are very lucky. It must be your psychic vision that has allowed you to catch glimpses of it. Him? Her?"

"Him."

"Was he very young? Maybe a child who hasn't learned how to avoid humans properly? Did he get separated from his folk?" Sarah looked concerned as she suggested this.

Reg shook her head quickly. "No. Nothing like that. Not a child. And not... trying to avoid me."

"He must be sick or injured, then. Something must be keeping him from being able to stay out of your sight."

Reg thought about that. She hadn't seen any sign that he was hurt. He didn't have any visible wounds or move like he was in pain. And he hadn't looked sick, but she couldn't discount the possibility. He had been quite nervous at times and had seemed unable to disappear when he wanted to.

"I don't know. I don't think he was hurt. Maybe he was sick. Some kind of... mental thing? Do elves get mental illness?"

Maybe he was suffering from some sort of elf dementia and that was why he kept appearing to her, talking his nonsense. Just because he said he was a time traveler, that didn't make it true. Though there were, of course, the other Orris. The ones who had appeared to her in the garden. Four identical Orris at once there to deliver their warnings to her.

If she went by what she had seen on TV, then the world should have imploded when the four of them had all appeared together in one time and place, but apparently things didn't work the same way in real life as they did on the sci-fi channels.

"I'm afraid I don't know very much about that," Sarah confessed. "I have never heard of any race other than humans having mental illness. But they might… call it something different or have remedies for it. Healing spells or herbs that don't work on humans."

Reg had seen signs of mental illness in other races. Calliopia the fairy, as one example. Ruan said she fought her demons. Reg didn't know how real the shadows Calliopia saw were. And how many of them were just in her mind, traumatized as it was by her kidnapping and the things that had happened to her as her pixie family had tried to prevent her from completing her transformation into a fairy.

"Hmm. I don't know. I don't think that mental illness is just a human weakness," Reg offered.

"Maybe not. Most of the races tend to keep to themselves and don't talk about their troubles to the meddling humans. While we are at peace with the creatures around here, it wouldn't do to reveal your weaknesses to a potential enemy. Susceptibility to any particular illness could be used against them." She took a sip of her tea. "Like the early inhabitants of this continent who were wiped out by the sicknesses the white explorers and traders brought with them."

Reg shuddered at the thought. She's always thought the settlement of the Americas was a pretty gruesome tale. The millions of innocent people who had been wiped out by men greedy for land, gold, and trade routes.

"But that's getting rather off-topic," Sarah observed. "Tell me about your elf. Where did you spot him?"

"Well… it wasn't as if I just happened to catch a glimpse of him in the garden. Though I did see him there, too."

"Too?"

"The first time was in the cottage, during a seance."

Sarah leaned forward. "Was it an elf spirit? Did he communicate with you?"

"He communicated with me… everybody there could see him; he wasn't just a spirit. He's solid enough." Reg tried to remember the word that Orri had used when referring to his physical body but couldn't recall it. "He drank wine, talked with us, he wasn't just an apparition."

"Oh, my!" Sarah's eyes were wide and round. "What I wouldn't have given to see that! As I say, the only time I have seen elves was at

Yule at your house. And that was so brief, and we didn't get much of a chance to converse and to learn about them. To see and talk to one face to face like that…"

Reg nodded. "A little more than I would like, actually."

"What do you mean? You saw him in the garden, too? You're sure it was the same elf?"

"Oh yeah. Unless all elves are identical and go by the same name."

"Well, no. I haven't ever heard anything like that. And the ones that we saw in the cottage, they did not all look the same. They were all just as individual as humans."

"So, I saw them outside," Reg ticked off the appearances on her fingers, "inside during the seance. And tonight. And when Harrison stole the coffee pot and I was trying to clean up. And four in the garden."

Sarah blinked. "I've never heard of such a thing. Are you sure he isn't injured? Something that is preventing him from hiding?"

"I can't be sure. What part is it that makes them disappear? I don't have x-ray vision. I couldn't see any injuries, but that doesn't mean he didn't… hurt his chronometer or something."

"His chronometer?"

Reg's cheeks grew warm. "I know… I shouldn't steal ideas from sci-fi and think that they apply in real life. But a chronometer, that's something that measures or controls time, isn't it? So maybe the reason he keeps showing up is that whatever is inside of elves that helps them to stay in the right timeline is broken or damaged, so he keeps hopping all over…"

"What does time have to do with it?"

"He said he is coming back in time. He's trying to come back to a certain point in my life so that he can warn me. But he keeps getting it all wrong."

"He is traveling back in time?"

Reg nodded slowly. "Isn't that something elves do?"

Sarah frowned and rubbed at her temples. "I may have heard something about this before. I don't think it is something that they do regularly. Just some of them, under special circumstances."

"Like what?"

"I have no idea. I wish I could tell you."

"When they appeared in the garden—"

"They? Did you see more than one of them?"

"Well, I saw more than one of *him*..." Reg considered. Was it appropriate to say "they" when she was only talking about one person? There had been more than one of Orri, so it seemed like the right thing to say.

"More than one... of the same elf?"

"Yeah. He kept appearing, until there were four of him. I guess they were all from the future, or from some other time. Trying to appear to me to give me a message..."

"Oh!" Sarah thumped her hand down on the table. "A harbinger!"

CHAPTER SIXTEEN

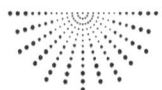

*R*eg shook her head. "What is a harbinger?"

Sarah took a long sip of her tea and put down her cup. "A harbinger is someone or something that brings you a warning of a danger that is down the road. A long time ago it literally meant someone who prepared the way ahead, booking you lodging and that kind of thing. But it changed to mean an omen or the bringer of a warning."

Reg nodded. "Okay. So that's what he is, I guess."

"I heard a story a long time ago about elves who were harbingers." Sarah closed her eyes, concentrating and trying to bring the details back to mind. "It has been so long. I believe that they are assigned or tasked with bringing an omen or warning. I don't know whether it is because of something they have done, or a gift they have, or a profession." She shook her head. "I don't know enough about elf culture to tell you."

"It sounded like it was some kind of assignment," Reg agreed. "He couldn't even go back until he had given me the warning, even though I told him I didn't want it."

Sarah's forehead creased. "Why would you not want the warning?"

"He keeps coming back. He gives me warnings about things that have already happened, or gives me the same one over again, and it's driving me crazy. I can't get away from him."

"What did he warn you about?"

Reg sighed, lounging back as much as the hard kitchen chair would allow. "About not accepting gifts from fairies. And... about water being a problem. Not using strange keys. And not being ensorcelled by Corvin."

Sarah raised her brows. "All good warnings."

"Yes, but a little too late, don't you think? I mean, I already learned not to do any of those things. I already had to deal with the consequences. So what's the point in him coming back again and again?"

"I suppose. But what about when he comes to you with a warning that isn't too late?"

"Do I have to keep putting up with him until he gets it right? What if he never does?"

"I don't know."

They sat in silence for a while.

"Maybe it's his first assignment," Sarah said. "He's just learning."

"Maybe. He said he's not very good at it. And he's right."

"We've all had missteps along the way. None of us can do our jobs the first time without making mistakes."

"Well then, maybe he should have a mentor or a supervisor. Someone to make sure that he learns how to do it the right way and doesn't keep screwing up."

"An apprenticeship would make sense. But maybe elves don't do that. Maybe it is all 'sink or swim.' Figure it out for yourself. Just because humans have supervisors and mentors, that doesn't mean that all cultures do."

"Next time he comes, I'm going to suggest it."

Sarah chuckled. "I don't see how it could hurt anything. You've already told him to go away."

"And not to come back, but he says he already has, so he can't not." Reg rolled her eyes. "I don't get how all this time travel stuff works."

"No one does, dear."

"Apparently, not even the ones who are doing the traveling."

"That would be awkward. They don't have any kind of map? No way to navigate through the tides of time?"

"I guess not. Or if he does, he doesn't know how to read it. Maybe he needs to stop and ask for directions."

* * *

Reg had eventually gone back to the cottage and managed to get back to sleep. She still felt groggy when she eventually got up around noon, but Starlight apparently decided that she'd been in bed quite long enough and would not leave her alone to sleep.

She groaned and pulled off her covers to climb out of bed, wobbling on legs that felt as if they belonged to someone else. She again felt hungover, when all she'd had was tea. She forced herself to have a glass of water before making her coffee, hoping that would do the trick, but it just sloshed around in her stomach making her feel seasick.

Starlight yowled.

"Yes, yes, I'm getting you something to eat," Reg assured him. "You just have to give me some time. I'm not a cat, you know, I don't always wake up all perky and ready to pounce on the day."

Starlight circled his dish. He had dry kibble, but Reg knew he wouldn't eat the dry food unless there were no chance of his getting anything else. And while Reg was there, there was still hope that she'd find him something better.

"Okay, let's see what's in here." Reg opened the fridge and browsed through the contents. Had Sarah been back to the cottage to fill it back up when Reg hadn't been around? Or while she had been sleeping? She thought she had cleared out most of what had been sitting in it, but it seemed like there was more than ever. Reg opened a few containers and found a tuna casserole.

Maybe the dairy and crunchy topping bits and spices were not the best for cats, but it was mostly tuna, so she knew Starlight would eat it.

"Here, have some of this." Reg took a large spoonful out and plopped it into Starlight's dish.

He complained once more, just to let her know she had taken too long, and then settled into eating it. Reg rubbed her temples and thought about the day ahead.

She didn't have any readings until the evening, by which time she would be feeling back to her usual self. But she should make the most of the afternoon before that. Maybe pick up some food from the grocery store. Put up some more advertisements on bulletin boards. And she had told Gwythr that she would get him the information on the gems that she was interested in liquidating.

The gems were at least something she could sit down and do from home without showering and dressing. And maybe after doing that, her stomach and head would have settled down enough for her to eat something.

Reg went to the closet in her bedroom and pulled out the small wooden chest full of gems. The plastic bag that contained the gems that were not cursed was at the top. Reg picked it up and examined them through the plastic for a moment. She didn't expect them to be cursed again, but she had to check just to be sure. She touched them through the plastic, closing her eyes and feeling, using all her senses to be sure that everything was in order and the gems would let her sell them.

She took them out to the living room and put them down on the coffee table to take pictures and send the details to Gwythr.

CHAPTER SEVENTEEN

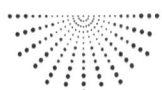

*I*t took Reg longer than she had expected to take pictures that turned out well and to compile the information she had from the various appraisers, matching each assessment up with the applicable gem, and then to send the information to Gwythr. What she had expected to be a five-minute job had ended up taking a couple of hours. Reg put the phone down and rubbed her eyes. Now time to have a bite to eat, shower, dress, and take a trip to the store. It would be evening before she knew it and she needed to be ready for her appointments.

The phone started to chime. Reg brushed moisture from the corners of her eyes and blinked to bring the screen into focus.

Gwythr.

That was quick. Reg hesitated, unsure whether to answer the call or not. Was he calling to say they would buy the stones? Or did he have more questions? She didn't really want to spend the whole afternoon in negotiations.

But he knew she had been at her phone or computer only moments ago, so it would be rude to ignore the call.

Reg sighed and picked up her phone. She swiped the call.

"Gwythr?"

"It be Brimir," another voice announced.

Reg frowned to herself. Brimir was the king's son and, as far as she could tell, he and Gwythr were not on friendly terms. So why was he calling from Gwythr's phone?

"Brimir. Uh… is everything okay? I thought this was Gwythr's number."

"Yes. He is attending to other matters."

"Oh. Okay. And did you need me, or did you just want to tell me that… he isn't available?"

"You sent him information on gems."

"Yes." Reg shifted uneasily. "Is that okay? I was asking him about whether the dwarfs would be interested in buying them. He said to send him the information. I don't think… that isn't going against some kind of protocol, is it? I didn't mean to disobey any rule."

"Whence came these stones?"

"They were held by the fairies. I can… give you more details if you want, the mines they came from initially. Gwythr didn't say he would need to know that."

Reg didn't want to get Gwythr in trouble if he'd been trying to do an end-run around the kingdom's laws, but she didn't want to end up under the bus either. If there were some other procedures she should have followed or person she should have talked to, then Gwythr should have told her that.

"They are good stones. The assessments are very promising."

"Yes. And I was hoping that they would find a good home in the dwarf mountain. I didn't want to sell them to someone who didn't know how to care for stones properly. Their history… they have been through enough without being mishandled further."

"This is true. Dwarfs would never abuse them."

"That's what I thought."

"You want to sell them to Gwythr, or you want to sell them to the king?"

"Uh… I don't really know. I don't want to disrespect either one of you. I am open to selling to both of you. I didn't mean to withhold something from you."

"We will talk. You will send me the same information you gave to Gwythr."

"Sure. What's your email address?"

Brimir gave it to her. Reg carefully tapped it into her phone for later use. "Okay, great. I look forward to doing business with you. If you're interested."

"Very good."

There was the sound of shouting in the background. Loud, angry voices. Reg held the phone more tightly.

"Is everything okay?"

"We are preparing for battle."

"Oh! I didn't know!" Reg was going to apologize for calling in the midst of their preparations, and then remembered that he was the one who had called her. "I'm sorry; you probably want to go deal with your duties."

"When do you expect the attack?"

Reg waited for the soldier that Brimir was addressing to answer the question and for Brimir to return to the phone call or to break the connection.

"Reg Rawlins," Brimir snapped.

"Yes?"

"The attack. When do you expect it?"

"The attack...? I don't know... what you are talking about."

"We are preparing for the attack on Nico. The warrior cat. When should we expect it?"

"Oh. Oh, boy. I don't... I don't think there will be an attack on him, just that someone *might* come to visit him. And if he does, that wouldn't be a good thing, but I don't think you want to start a war over it..."

"A powerful magical being coming to take our warrior cat. That is reason enough for war."

"I don't know that he's actually going to. I could be overreacting. I know he's gone to see some of the other—some of Nico's litter mates. That's all. He hasn't done any harm, but... I'm just a little worried..." Reg floundered, trying to express her concern without saying something that would push the dwarfs over the edge. If Harrison did go to see Nico, the results could be catastrophic.

Cat-astrophic.

Reg tried not to be distracted by the unintentional pun. She needed to carry on a serious conversation with the dwarf prince, not to start giggling at her own thoughts. It was a serious situation, but was preparing to do battle against an immortal the right response? Was there really anything that the dwarfs would be able to do if Harrison did show up and try to free Nico from the charms that held him bound?

"We are preparing," Brimir said sharply. "You do not know when he is coming?"

"No, I'm sorry. Maybe he won't even come, but… I don't trust that he won't. Francesca is very worried about it." She pressed her lips together, forcing herself to stop talking. She didn't want to voice Francesca's views or to explain to the dwarfs all about the Witch Doctor and the draugr and the kattakyns and the spell that held them bound.

She should probably have told the dwarfs about where Nico had come from when she realized that they wanted him to stay with them. They hadn't told any of the practitioners whom they had given the kattakyns to of their origins. They thought that it would be hundreds of years before the kattakyns could escape Francesca's spell, so what would be the point in telling their new owners what they really were?

The dwarfs, though, had recognized that Nico was something more than an ordinary cat. They didn't know what he was or where he had come from.

Or what danger there was in his breaking free from the spell that Francesca had woven around him.

"If you do not know, you do not know," Brimir growled. "At least you were able to give us a warning. You will tell us if you find out more?"

"About Har—about the being coming to see Nico? Yes, I'll let you know if I find something out. Right now, it is only a fear. I don't know for sure that he will. Maybe he'll get distracted and forget about him."

"Forget about a warrior cat? I do not think that will happen."

"Well, you don't know him… it is possible."

"You let us know when he is on the way. Or if you hear something else."

"Yes, Your Majesty. I will."

Reg didn't know if "Your Majesty" was the proper way to address a dwarf prince, but she thought it couldn't hurt. Even if it were an honorific that he didn't deserve, he would still be pleased that she had shown him that respect.

She hung up the phone and shut off the screen. Then she sat there looking at the blank screen, thinking it through. How did she manage to get in the middle of these things?

CHAPTER EIGHTEEN

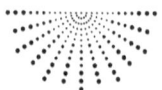

*T*he rest of the day and the evening passed uneventfully. But Reg still hadn't managed to get to the grocery store, and she knew that she had to at least get more kitty litter, even if she didn't get anything else to stock her cupboards and fridge. And she definitely needed food to stock her cupboard and fridge. It had been too long since she had bought anything herself and, while she had plenty of contributions by Sarah, Reg didn't have very much around that actually appealed to her.

She managed to get out of bed before noon and patted herself on the back as she watched the coffee drip into the new coffee pot at eleven o'clock. A *full hour* before noon. And she was barely even tired.

Hopefully, she would be able to keep that energized feeling for longer than an hour or two. She didn't want to conk out for a nap in the middle of the afternoon. Or worse yet, during a meeting with a client. Although, she could always say that it was a trance. A trance and sleeping could look a lot alike to the layman.

The coffee would help. Plenty of coffee.

She gave Starlight more of the tuna casserole, which didn't seem to have caused him any stomach problems the day before. Starlight happily chowed down and Reg checked her email, waiting for the coffee.

Nothing from the dwarfs regarding the gemstones. But she supposed she shouldn't expect anything if they were in the midst of preparing for battle.

How long would the preparations go on without an actual battle to fight? Would dwarfs get tired of playing dress-up after a few hours? A few days? Would they still be running scenarios and playing war games in a few weeks?

Or would Harrison show up before then?

Reg pushed the thought to the side. She didn't want to think of what might happen in that case. She remembered the Witch Doctor striking Damon down. Threatening to destroy them all. Bringing his power to bear against Corvin, who was well-matched due to the strength he had absorbed from the many magical artifacts that the Witch Doctor had been storing in the warehouse the showdown took place in. It had been terrifying.

The dwarf mountain was populated with not just dwarf warriors, but women and children as well. And Nico, the warrior cat. Reg didn't want any of them getting hurt. If Harrison showed up and the dwarfs attacked him, or if he tried to take Nico away or to unbind him…

Harrison might forget about the draugr kittens for a while. He was easily distracted. He might forget for a hundred years or more, and then the dwarfs would not be waiting for him and no one would know what harm he could do.

"Oh, Starlight. What am I going to do? You know him. Is there any way to stop him? What if I just ask him? He considers me his goddaughter. He would do whatever I asked, wouldn't he?"

Starlight looked up from his dish and studied her. Reg did not get reassuring feelings from him. She really wanted to feel him agree with her. She couldn't fight Harrison. None of them was strong enough to fight Harrison. He could only be matched by another immortal, and the only other immortal Reg knew, Weston, was his friend. Weston wouldn't oppose him in anything.

Immortals were unpredictable and dangerous. But Reg and Francesca could be completely wrong in their assessment of Harrison's behavior.

He might have no intention at all of doing anything to free the kattakyns and Samyr Destine.

* * *

It was afternoon when Reg got to the store, but she thought she was still making pretty good time. She pushed her cart up and down the aisles, looking for anything she might need. It was nice to have a little money in the bank account again so that she didn't have to worry about going without.

The lean years had left their mark on her. She often worried about not having enough food even when her cupboards and fridge were full. Things could change so quickly, and it really wasn't a big step from making enough money to provide for her needs to being out on the street with nothing.

That wasn't going to happen again. She had her business running again and, even if things went bottoms-up, she was sure Sarah would still let her stay at the cottage rent-free for a little while, until she figured out how to get back on her feet again.

Reg added a package of crackers and a box of cookies to her cart. Good, shelf-stable food that would keep for a long time. Just in case.

She turned down the next aisle. She needed more ice cream. And cat food and kitty litter in the pet aisle. Maybe she would get Starlight a toy, too. She didn't want him getting bored and fat because all he did was lie around all day cuddling with her or looking out the window. Indoor cats needed to stay active.

Reg picked up a bottle of olive oil.

It wasn't like she cooked. She just had the idea that if she had some things, like oil, that she needed for cooking, she might actually cook something. Maybe. Not that she knew what she would make with olive oil. French fries?

"Hail, Reg Rawlins!"

Reg jumped and looked up. Orri stood a few feet away from her.

She hadn't seen lights or heard bells; he was just there. Maybe he had already been to the grocery store ahead of her or had materialized in another aisle before finding her.

There was a smash of breaking glass. Looking down, Reg saw a pool of oil spreading at her feet. Her hand was empty, the bottle shattered on the floor. Reg stepped carefully around it, looking around to see whether anyone had seen the accident.

She looked at Orri as she walked by him, trying to distance herself from the broken bottle of oil.

"Maybe you have a warning about dropping glass bottles this time?"

He raised his brows and looked at her.

"No, I suppose not," Reg sighed. She pushed her cart to the end and rounded the corner to enter the next aisle. Orri walked along beside her. "Well, what is it this time, then?"

"I have a warning for you."

"Yeah, I figured. What is it?"

He looked disappointed that she was not taking his appearance more seriously. Here he was, a time traveling elf, showing up to give her a special, personalized message, and she acted as though it were something that happened every day.

Which lately, it had.

Reg just waited, scanning the shelves for anything she might need. Who was she kidding? She wasn't going to cook anything. At best, she would warm something in the microwave. She even turned down food that required oven cooking. She didn't like the big, shiny oven and the blast of hot air that puffed up in her face when she opened the door. A person could burn herself trying to take out a pan of fries. She could forget that she'd left something in the oven and burn the house down.

Reg thought about that for a moment. How much of what was in her head were words that she'd absorbed from her foster homes? How would she burn herself? She was a firecaster! She wasn't going to be hurt by a little heat or fire. She should have a natural aptitude for cooking, given her powers.

Orri stopped Reg, holding his hand up to make her pay attention to his portentous announcement. A couple of other shoppers walking by gave him curious looks.

"Beware Janus and the cat with nine lives."

CHAPTER NINETEEN

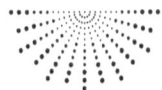

*R*eg looked at Orri. A new warning this time. One that she hadn't heard before. Janice?

Who was Janice? She didn't know anyone by that name.

And the cat with nine lives? Starlight, maybe? She knew that he had lived other lives before he had chosen Reg. He'd been powerful and important in the past. Maybe even one of the immortals. Harrison had told her that he was Bastet, an Egyptian god.

Reg found it hard to believe. He was her fuzzy, cuddly companion, who liked having his ears and chin scratched and got irritated if she didn't clean his kitty litter often enough. If he had been an Egyptian god, then what was he doing now, living with her, rubbing against the fridge door to beg for tuna casserole?

"Who is Janice?"

Orri gave a little bow, then fireflies began to blink in and out around him, swarming together, until she blinked her eyes and he was gone.

Reg looked around to see whether there were any more Orris hanging around. She saw only a couple of other shoppers, ordinary people, walking past the aisle.

* * *

Reg started putting the groceries away when she got home. Starlight jumped down from his spot in Reg's bedroom window and walked into the kitchen, arching his back to stretch, and then stretching each of his back feet out behind him in a way Reg always found charming. He'd obviously been sleeping the entire time she had been gone.

"I got you kitty food and litter," Reg told him. "Yeah. And do you really have nine lives, by the way? And is this your ninth, or do you still have a few left?"

Starlight ignored her, poking his head into the bags to see what else she had bought. Reg started putting items slowly into the cupboard and fridge. She threw out a few of the things that she thought Sarah had put there, foods that Reg wasn't ever going to eat, so she might as well reclaim her cupboard space for things that she would eat.

When there was a knock and the door opened, Reg startled guiltily and closed the garbage bin to hide the evidence. Sarah walked in, smiling and nodding at Reg pleasantly.

"Hello, Reg. Did you have a successful trip?"

Reg nodded. "Sure. Picked up a few things that I needed. I don't want you to think that you have to keep my cupboards stocked all the time. I can afford to feed myself."

"Oh, I know you can. I just end up with too much in my kitchen and figure maybe it is something that you would like." Sarah shrugged.

Or something Reg would throw out for her.

Reg put a few more cans in the cupboard. "I saw him again."

"You saw who, dear?" Sarah looked at her, then got it. "Oh, the elf? What did you say his name is?"

"Orri. Yeah. He showed up in the middle of the grocery store."

"Out in public? I've never heard of an elf appearing in public. Did anyone else see him?"

Reg wondered fleetingly whether Sarah believed her or thought that Reg was losing her marbles and hallucinating in the store.

Reg couldn't help wondering herself. Corvin had told her that the invisible friends she had when she was a child had probably been ghosts. He had told her how powerful she was. Others in Black Sands had agreed, and Reg had seemed to discover new powers and to have new adventures all the time. But what if it was all just in her mind? What if nothing was real and she was in an institution somewhere, experiencing everything in her head? Creating a new fantastical world in her own head.

What about that? What if none of it was real and she was just deluding herself?

"There were others around," she said vaguely, unable to remember specifically who might have seen Orri. Any of the clerks? The butcher at his counter in the back of the store? Friends or clients who had been there to get groceries at the same time? Black Sands was a small place. There were bound to have been people that she knew there.

"That's very surprising." Sarah picked a couple of items out of Reg's bags and put them in the fridge. "So what happened this time?"

"He scared the heck out of me. I didn't even see him materialize this time; he was just standing there."

"I imagine so. It would have scared me too. They really should be more careful. You can't just go around appearing to people and think that they won't have a heart attack or stroke."

"Or even just faint."

"Did you faint?"

"No. Thank goodness." Reg couldn't imagine what would have happened if she had fainted right in the middle of the grocery store. Would they slap her cheeks? Splash water on her? Call the police? Would she end up in an ambulance or the hospital wondering what had happened? "I didn't faint. Nothing happened."

If anyone had seen Reg drop the olive oil bottle, Sarah would probably hear about it sooner or later. The grapevine was alive and well in Black Sands.

"Did he have another warning? Or one of the same ones as before?"

"A different one this time. Janice and the cat with nine lives?"

"Janice?"

"Yeah. I don't even know a Janice. And the cat with nine lives? Is that Starlight? Francesca's Nicole? Some cat that is going to cross my path and I'm supposed to know about it ahead of time?"

"Maybe a black cat," Sarah suggested. "One that you don't want to cross in front of you, because of bad luck."

"Is it really bad luck for a black cat to cross your path?" Reg asked curiously.

"It is if you hit it. Especially for the cat."

Reg tried to stifle a laugh at the remark, snorting as she looked for a place for another box of cookies. Starlight yowled and looked at her reproachfully.

"I'm sorry," Reg told him. "But it is true. That's one of the reasons you are not allowed to go outside."

He meowed something again crossly and stalked out of the room instead of waiting to see whether she would feed him. Sarah watched Starlight's retreat.

"Well, if he's going to be so sensitive…"

Reg nodded. "He's fine. Don't worry about it."

"The cat with nine lives," Sarah mused.

"Don't all cats have nine lives? I mean, that's what they say, isn't it? It is really true?"

"Cats just have some close calls," Sarah said. "They get into mischief, and if they are lucky, they escape by the skin of their teeth. They don't *really* have nine lives."

"But they have more than one, right? Because I know Starlight has had others."

"Reincarnation, you mean? Yes, I suppose so. None of us knows how that might work, of course, or if it means that we all have an unlimited number of incarnations. There are many other traditions. Most religions believe in some kind of life to follow this one, whether it is as another person, or on another plane."

"Heaven?"

"That's one of them. There are many other names. And many other places our souls are said to go for their eternal reward."

Reg didn't want to think of those other places. She didn't believe in eternal punishment. She couldn't, not with the way she lived. She couldn't be a con and believe that people would be punished for every time they had lied and cheated.

"So do you think I already know the cat with nine lives?"

"You said that all the other warnings he has given you have already been fulfilled, so it would follow that this one has too. And the cat with nine lives might not even be a cat. It could be a person. A man who has been through several incarnations. Or who has been lucky to escape death in the past."

"Corvin? Do you think it's him?"

"Corvin." Sarah considered this. "No, I can't see that one. That doesn't mean he isn't, but I can't think of any reason that would point to him."

Corvin didn't even like cats. Reg thought about other people in her life. People that she had already known who had been threats to her. Because as Sarah had said, all the other warnings had been too late. Why would this on be any different?

"Oh!" It hit her with a flash of insight. "I know who it is!"

CHAPTER TWENTY

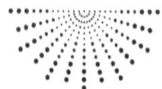

Sarah's eyes widened. "You know?"

"Of course. It's so simple. It's Jacky Lane. Maybe Janice was her real name, back in the beginning. It even starts with a J. Or maybe it's one of the aliases she took at some point."

"You think she was the cat with nine lives?"

"She had eight ghosts attached to her, right? That's eight lives. Plus her own. Nine. And she's a woman, so Janice could be her name."

"Well… yes. It's possible."

"And she was poisoning me. So of course Orri would warn me to stay away from her. It all makes perfect sense."

"You could be right," Sarah admitted. But she still sounded doubtful.

"I am. That's it."

"Then why would he say Janice *and* the cat with nine lives?"

"Because it is a riddle. That just makes it harder to solve. It doesn't mean anything."

Sarah pursed her lips. She shrugged. "Maybe. I don't know."

"Well, it's my warning, so I guess I'm the one who knows whether that's what it means or not."

Reg made herself sound confident because she didn't want Sarah to argue about it and to fill her mind with doubts. It was Orri giving her another warning about something that had already happened, just as he had done every time before. She hadn't told him this time that what he'd warned her about had already happened so, hopefully, he had gone home satisfied and would not be back. Without him reappearing in her life every single day, she could stop worrying and just go on with her life. She could work with her clients, relax with her cat and her friends, and afford to eat out or go to the grocery store when she needed to. That was a good life.

Sarah helped her to put the last few things away. She looked into the fridge for a moment. "It seems like you have an awful lot in here. We should probably clear some of it out."

Having cleared it out twice already, Reg didn't think there could be that much left. Certainly not enough for Sarah to complain about. She opened the fridge door and looked in. With the food that she had left behind, in addition to the things she had left in the fridge the last time, it was pretty full. Plus whatever else Sarah had added to it when Reg had been out. She supposed it was just a ploy to make sure that she looked through all the bowls and ate whatever Sarah had just added.

"Okay, I'll take a look later," she agreed.

Sarah nodded. "We wouldn't want anything to go bad."

Reg was tempted to wink at her and agree, but she didn't. She just nodded as if she didn't know what Sarah was up to.

"I'm glad you've worked out the warning by the elf." Sarah turned toward the door. Then she paused and looked back. "But if he warned you again about something that has already happened, then won't he come back again?"

"Not if I don't tell him."

"And you aren't worried that you still haven't been given the message that he was tasked with giving you?"

"He's given me all kinds of warnings. So, no. I'm not worried."

"You don't want to ignore a harbinger."

"I'm not. I've listened to everything he has to say."

"But you haven't received the *real* warning."

Reg rolled her eyes. "They were all real warnings. The timing was just off."

"To be a true harbinger, he has to tell you of something in the future."

Reg tried to ignore the knot in her stomach. "Then he's not a real harbinger. He just thinks he is."

Sarah tilted her head to the side and gave it a little shake. "You can think what you like, but I don't know. An omen is a sign of something to come. You don't eliminate the thing that is going to come or the omen by ignoring it."

Reg just pressed her lips together, waiting for Sarah to leave. There wasn't any point in arguing it anymore. Sarah knew her position. And Reg was sure that she was right.

Pretty sure.

* * *

Even though she had gone out for food, Reg wasn't in the mood to stay in and eat. She wanted to celebrate. Celebrate the fact that she had her business back and money in the bank. Celebrate the fact that she'd had her last visit from Orri. Life was good. Everything was good.

So she went over to The Crystal Bowl.

The last time she had tried to eat there, she had been turned away. Reg's siren parentage had only just been discovered, and the management had decided that they weren't going to serve "her kind" there.

But that was in the past now. People were forgetting about the revelation. Nothing had happened. Reg hadn't gone on a rampage. She hadn't dragged anyone to the icy depths of the ocean. She hadn't done anything exciting, but had stayed below the radar.

So she was confident that this time, they would allow her in. They had forgotten all about her history and would be happy for her patronage. She'd eaten there regularly ever since she had arrived in Black Sands, and she had missed it.

She went when she knew it would be busy. The more that was

going on, the better the chances were that the staff would completely forget that they weren't supposed to be serving sirens.

Reg had to wait in the doorway for a few minutes while the hostess found tables for people. But it never filled up all the way so, in a few minutes, people were distributed to their various tables and the hostess turned to Reg. Her smile faltered slightly.

Reg gave her a determined, reassuring smile, and waited to be helped. She could go and find a table herself. She'd done it before enough times. Sometimes the staff were busy and the regulars didn't wait as the sign instructed. Reg looked around. She would just head to her regular table and the woman wouldn't stop her.

The tables in the corner she usually sat in were already occupied. It was the supper hour. Reg looked at the adjoining tables to see what was free. That was when she saw Corvin. He looked up and met her eyes across the restaurant. Reg wanted to turn away and leave but, if she did that, she might never have the confidence to go back there again. She couldn't run away.

Corvin stood. He nodded to the seat across the table from him. When the hostess turned around to see who Reg was looking at, Corvin gestured to the seat.

"Oh, there he is," Reg said hurriedly. "He's already been seated."

The hostess looked at Corvin, not sure what to do. She wanted to tell Reg that she wasn't welcome there, but Corvin tended to have an influence over the people around him. The same charms that made him so attractive to Reg also made it possible for him to get people to do things that they would not have done otherwise.

"I'll just go join him," Reg said casually, and slipped past the woman.

But the hostess followed, not willing to leave it at that. She stood beside the table as Corvin held Regina's chair out for her and then seated himself again.

"I'm sure Miss Rawlins would like a drink," Corvin told her, his voice oozing with charm.

The hostess drew out an order pad, though Reg knew that she didn't usually wait tables. "Of course," she agreed, in a faraway voice.

Reg placed her drink order. Just one glass. Alcohol and Corvin's charms together were a dangerously potent mix. The hostess brought Reg her drink and with reluctance drew away from the table again, leaving Corvin alone with Reg. Alone, but in a busy restaurant. He wouldn't be able to do too much with so many people around. As long as she could resist his taking her away from there, she should be fine.

"Well, I haven't seen you here for a while," Corvin observed.

"No. They haven't been that welcoming," Reg reminded him.

"Ah. I told you they would get over it. Once you've been here again a time or two, they'll forget all about that silliness."

"They should," Reg agreed. "They allow *you* in here, after all, and you're a lot more of a danger to the patrons here than I am."

He smiled. A silky-smooth smile that crept under her skin and made her break out in goosebumps. He knew what he was, despite his pretenses, and it did amuse him that he could charm the hostess and probably anyone else in the restaurant into giving him whatever he wanted. He was the one who could take all their powers away, but they were afraid of Reg.

She took a sip of her drink and let it burn all the way down. It felt good. She welcomed the alcohol taking the edge off her anxiety so that she could calm down and enjoy the evening. She didn't have to worry about omens and harbingers and whatever the time traveling elf had been trying to tell her. She could just enjoy a pleasant evening with a handsome man who always made her feel special.

CHAPTER TWENTY-ONE

"*S*o how have you been faring?" Corvin asked after they had placed their orders with the waitress who approached the table and made moon eyes at him.

"I'm just fine," Reg said firmly. "No complaints."

"No? Well, that's good. You've had some interesting challenges lately. I'm glad to hear that they have been overcome."

"That's right," Reg agreed. "Smooth sailing now."

Corvin leaned forward slightly. "Maybe you would like to go sailing again sometime," he suggested.

"Yeah? You think I don't remember how you ran away last time? Seems to me that you were not so keen to get close to me then."

"Well…" Corvin shifted uncomfortably. Reg watched him try to come up with a manly explanation for why he'd had to separate himself from her. If he was so strong and had such an influence over her, then why had he found it necessary to retreat? "We *were* on the water," he admitted finally.

And they both knew what that meant. He knew that when her siren instincts kicked in and she touched him, he did not have the ability to resist her. So he had put distance between them while he still could.

Reg smiled. Score one for the "weaker" sex. "So maybe you don't want to go sailing with me?"

"Only under… carefully controlled conditions."

"Yeah. That's what I thought."

She enjoyed knowing that she could get the upper hand over him, even though she never intended to be ruled by her siren desires. It was just nice to know that she *could*.

"Have you talked with Davyn?" Corvin asked, turning his head away from her slightly and changing the subject.

"About you?" Reg shrugged. "Not much to say. He knows that I know about your application."

"And you told him that you don't care if I am readmitted to the coven?"

"Not in so many words."

Corvin's face tightened. Reg felt a definite cooling in his ardor.

"What did you tell him?"

"Nothing. They have a whole process. I'm not going to oppose anything, but I know that nothing has changed. You haven't changed."

"Everything has changed," Corvin countered. "You are not the same person you were when you first came here. You are not so… vulnerable. And me? I have acquired other powers, other abilities. I am not the same person I was either."

"You're more powerful. That doesn't exactly recommend you, does it?"

The waitress brought over their meals. She smiled and batted her eyelashes at Corvin, and coolly ignored Reg, doing nothing more than slapping the plate down in front of her.

If the waitress wanted Corvin, she could have him. Reg was not her rival.

They dug into their meals.

"What else is new?" Corvin asked after a while. "Your business is going well, you said?"

"Yeah. I'm really happy about that. Money in the bank is a *good* thing."

"Yes, it is," he agreed. "In days gone by, it was easier to live without cold hard cash. People could live off the land, barter for goods, trade, find a way to work things out. But now? Cash is king. No money means you're out of luck."

"Yeah, and believe me, you don't want to be there."

Corvin didn't ask her about what she knew of being down on her luck. But she had turned away his inquiries before, so he knew better than to ask.

"What do you know about elves?" Reg asked him. "Especially harbingers."

"Harbingers." He raised an eyebrow. "That's getting into some pretty esoteric stuff. Where did you hear about harbingers?"

"From Sarah. But she didn't know a lot about them. And with all your studies, I thought maybe you might have some information that you could share."

"Not much, unfortunately. The fables are very sparse on details about harbingers. The elves are a very secret people to begin with. They don't have much to do with humans or anyone else. To even have seen their lights or heard their bells in the garden... not many people have even experienced that. Having seen them face to face like you have is very rare."

"Well, I've experienced a little more than that."

"More?" Corvin popped a bite of steak into his mouth and chewed. "Do you mean that you've seen them again? Since Yule?"

Reg nodded.

He chewed slowly, intrigued. "And this wasn't just a fleeting glimpse or the lights and bells, was it? You mean a real... personal encounter."

"Yes."

"If you're asking about harbingers, then one of them must have given you a warning."

"Yes. Several of them."

"More than one elf gave you a warning?"

"No. One elf gave me several warnings."

"Several of them." Corvin poked his food around with his fork for a minute, then pushed his plate away an inch. "Did you... not listen the first time? I don't understand."

"Of course I listened," Reg protested. "I wouldn't just ignore him. But… he kept giving me warnings about things that had already happened."

Corvin snorted. "A fine harbinger he is to tell you the past."

Reg smiled and nodded. "Yeah. It's been kind of frustrating. What am I supposed to do? Just nod and say, 'oh yes, thank you for the warning'? Pretend that I haven't already dealt with it?"

"I don't know. What is he expecting?"

"He wants to give me a warning for something that hasn't happened yet. It seems like it is his mission. I think with the last warning, he was satisfied that he had told me something that hadn't happened yet. But thinking it over later… I think that it did happen. I just didn't know what he was talking when he gave it. Because he sort of talks in code, you know."

"Yes, omens are usually expected to be somewhat cryptic."

"I always thought that the reason fortune tellers talk that way is so that people can read whatever they want to into the reading. Like if I say you'll meet a handsome stranger, it's pretty much guaranteed that you will at some point. And then you'll know that I actually told your fortune. I thought that was just part of the con."

"And maybe it is in many cases. There are not a lot of prognosticators around who are on the up-and-up. Most of it probably is cold reading and guesswork. But a harbinger elf… well… I don't think there are a lot of elven cons around."

"There could be; you wouldn't really know, would you? They don't look that much different from humans. Maybe they like their greens and browns, but they could dress in modern style and colors and would you be able to tell them from humans?"

"Well, the fact that you rarely see an elf might be a tip-off."

"Maybe you do. Maybe they are just good at blending in with humans."

Corvin stared at Reg for a few minutes. Finally he shrugged. "Yes. I suppose if they were not afraid of people and were around them enough, they could learn to blend in. But sighting an elf is so rare, I highly doubt that would ever happen."

But if they were really good at blending in, he wouldn't know. They could be among the humans already.

"They are very shy and reluctant to communicate with humans," Corvin reiterated. "So I think that the odds that they would choose to do such a thing are pretty low."

"Maybe. But not impossible."

"Your harbinger, is he good at blending in?" Corvin asked, bringing the subject back around.

"Uh… no, not really. He keeps materializing out of nowhere, and he's got the whole 'twinkly' thing going on. I mean, he did appear in the grocery store and nobody screamed and fainted. He startled the heck out of me, but I don't think anyone else noticed." Reg took a few bites of her dinner. "The first time he appeared was in the middle of a seance."

"You're kidding. How did that go over?"

"Well, everybody figured they got their money's worth that night! I had him repeat his warning for them, so they had a real 'ghostly' warning from beyond the grave. When they tell their friends about it —you can't buy publicity like that."

Corvin chuckled and leaned closer to Reg. "You are a girl after my own heart, Reg Rawlins."

Reg felt warm and tingly all over. It was difficult to pull back from him and to put a psychic shield up around herself. She wanted to be there, close to him, warm and comfortable. The urge to touch his hand or arm to strengthen the connection between them was almost overwhelming.

"No," she said softly. "We can't go there."

She couldn't let him charm her. And she couldn't touch him and unintentionally bring him under her thrall. Why did things have to be so complicated? If he had been a man without any paranormal powers, and she had been just a regular woman, with no psychic stuff or siren stuff to worry about… it would have been different. But she wasn't sure whether there would even have been an attraction between them if not for their gifts. Corvin was handsome, granted, but did she see him as gorgeous because of his face or his charms?

CHAPTER TWENTY-TWO

*A*fter a moment, Corvin eased back from Reg as well, giving her space to breathe and allowing them both to get their equilibrium back. He toyed with his food for a moment, then started eating again.

"So what kind of warnings are you getting from your harbinger? Does he have a name, by the way?"

"Orri."

"Orri the oracle?" Corvin asked with a chuckle.

"What?"

"Seems like an apt name for someone who gives you warnings about the future, that's all."

"Is that someone well-known? Orri the oracle?"

"No, it was a joke. I'm sure he's not called Orri the oracle."

"Oh, okay." Reg shook her head. She was never quite sure when she had missed something that was from a fairy tale or was well-known in the magical community. It seemed like there were so many things she had missed by not only growing up in foster care, where her education was spotty and inconsistent, but also by not growing up in a community like Black Sands or at least a family with some knowledge of how the paranormal world worked.

"So what has he been warning you about?"

"Well... about you, for one thing."

Corvin looked up from his meal. He smiled. "Really."

"Be not ensorcelled by fair face. Sound like anyone you know?"

Corvin rubbed his whiskered chin. "Well... that could be anyone."

"Anyone good-looking, you mean."

"I wouldn't want to presume."

"You don't need to pretend that you don't know you're handsome. It's one of the ways that you charm women. There's no point in pretending to be modest about it. You're like a peacock."

"And a peacock knows that he's handsome?"

"Why would he spread his tail out like that if he didn't?"

Corvin chuckled. "I can't fault your logic."

"And it wasn't a warning about *anyone* handsome. It was a warning about someone who is handsome and can ensorcel me." She gave him a look. "And that would be you."

He had another drink of his scotch. "I don't know if I've ever been the subject of a warning by a harbinger before."

"I wouldn't be too surprised. Everybody who knows about you should be warning any unsuspecting women about what you do."

"Only those with powers."

That made Reg curious. "Do you only pursue women who have powers? Romantically, I mean."

It seemed like that would get tiring after a while. Like only eating sugary foods. Didn't he want to have a relationship with a woman who didn't have powers? To give him a break from just women whose powers he was interested in? To cleanse his palate and have a relationship with someone just because of who she was?

Corvin considered the question for a long moment. "I can... influence people whether they have powers or not and whether I am interested in them or not. Being able to persuade them to do what I want is part of my... condition. I've never had to live without that. So women without powers are interested in me."

"Yeah, but that's not really what I asked. I wondered whether you are interested in them."

He cocked his head slightly, blinking. "No..." he said eventually,

"I don't think I am. Women without powers are just... uninteresting. Weak. They don't hold much attraction for me."

"Even if they're really gorgeous?"

"Despite what the media tells you, appearance is not the only thing that interests a man. There are a lot of things that enter into the equation. And for me, the woman's gifts are a very big part of that equation."

"So if a really gorgeous woman was coming on to you, but she didn't have any gifts, you wouldn't even be interested?"

Corvin's eyebrows went up. "No."

And did that apply to a woman whose gifts he had already taken? Reg thought about the way that he had behaved toward her after stealing her powers, back when she had first moved to Black Sands. He had been aloof. Gloating. Completely undisturbed by her distress over discovering that the voices in her head had been suddenly silenced and she was as hollow and empty as an eggshell.

Until Hawthorne-Rose had started to torture her. That had changed things. That was when Corvin had decided to return her powers to her, so that they could overcome him and escape to somewhere safe.

So maybe somewhere, deep down, he did have feelings for her that were separate from her powers. Only he'd never had the opportunity to explore his feelings, constantly hungering, always needing to find his next prey.

Corvin was watching Reg, his eyes calculating. Reg pushed the topic of discussion away. She didn't want to know how he felt about other women. She didn't need to know what it was about her that he found attractive, only that he would steal her gifts if given the opportunity.

"So Orri's latest warning, the one in the grocery store."

Corvin's eyes focused on her. "Yes? What was the latest warning?"

"Beware of Janice and the cat with nine lives."

Corvin's brows went up, and he shook his head. "And you think that refers to...?"

"It's pretty obvious, isn't it? Jacky Lane."

"No... I don't follow. How does that have anything to do with Jacky Lane?"

"Janice was probably her original name. She just changed it so that it wouldn't be easy to track her movements. An alias. She had a lot of different aliases. And she had eight ghosts attached to her. So... nine lives, get it? It makes perfect sense."

"Except she is not a cat."

"Yeah, but harbinger warnings are like that. Tricky. You have to be able to interpret them."

"Hmm." Corvin did not appear to be convinced. "He said Janice *and* the cat, didn't he? He didn't say 'Janice, the cat with nine lives.'"

"Well, no. But that's just... being tricky. Making it harder to figure it out."

"It is not the harbinger's intention to be unclear, though. If he's trying to warn you, he wants you to understand what the warning is about."

"Well... maybe. I don't understand his motivations. I think he just wants to give me the warning and disappear back to his own time. He can't go back until the job is finished."

"And his job is to warn you about something that has already happened?"

"As long as he thinks it hasn't already happened. How would he know? If he thinks he's done what he needed to, he can go home and be with his wife and kids and forget all about being a harbinger. Unless it's his job, and I really hope it isn't."

"And he thinks that he gave you a warning about something that hasn't yet happened."

"I didn't realize it was about Jacky at the time, so I thought that yeah, it was about something in the future. So as far as he's concerned, it was a warning about the future, not the past."

"If he can jump through time, then won't he know whether his warning had any effect or not? When he returns to his own time, won't he be able to tell whether you have acted based on his warning? If something has changed in his own time?"

"You don't know how time travel works," Reg said, waving her hand at him. "It isn't like in all those sci-fi movies and books."

"I *did* go with you on your little journey to the past. I know as much about actual time travel as you do."

He didn't say *and more* but Reg heard it in his voice.

"Well, all that stuff about paradoxes and not being able to see yourself if you go back in time and all that is just made up. It doesn't really work that way."

"But if he comes here and warns you, and you change something based on that warning, then won't he be able to tell that in the future?"

"Maybe. Maybe not. Maybe he'll just ask the me in the future, and I'll tell him that it did. Because I'll know that I want to stop the guy from going back in time and giving me another warning."

Corvin shrugged. He ate the last few bites of his meal and pushed it to the side.

"You really don't think it was about Jacky Lane?" Reg asked.

"No, I don't. It is a good fit, but not quite. Like forcing the wrong puzzle piece into a picture. It almost fits… but it doesn't."

CHAPTER TWENTY-THREE

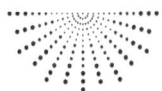

*R*eg opened the door to Francesca and let her in. Francesca had her black cat, Nicole with her. NEE-cole in Francesca's Creole accent. She released Nicole to go play with Starlight. Reg laughed as they watched the two cats greet each other enthusiastically, sniffing, licking, and play fighting. Until the two decided that they wanted some privacy and took off to the bedroom.

Nicole was not one of the kattakyns, though she was a pure black cat like they were. Reg couldn't tell Nicole and all the kattakyns apart physically, but when she thought about their personalities and felt their auras, they were quite easy to differentiate.

But the kattakyns had all been rehomed and now it was just Nicole. Nicole with Francesca and Starlight with Reg. Back to the cats they'd had initially, prior to the fight with the Witch Doctor.

"How has it been?" Francesca inquired politely. She was a white Haitian, blond with long spiraling curls. She attained a level of beauty that Reg would never achieve in a million years with thousands of dollars' worth of product.

Reg had made some tea, and she put the tray down on the coffee table where they both sat down, so they could pour their own drinks.

"Things are going well. Work has picked up. Lots of appointments for readings and seances."

"Very good. That must be a relief for you."

"It is. I feel much better. It's a lot easier to relax when you don't have to worry about where your next meal is coming from."

"It was not that bad, surely."

"It has been before. I didn't want to get back there. It doesn't take long, if you're not making enough money, for things to get really bad really fast."

"This is true," Francesca agreed. She sipped the tea she had prepared for herself. Reg spooned more sugar into hers.

"The real excitement that we've been having around here the last little while was an elf who kept appearing to me."

"An elf." Francesca looked impressed. Like the others, she knew that elves did not commonly appear to humans.

"Yeah. A harbinger, Sarah calls him. The kind that comes with a warning."

"Very rare. In Haiti—"

"Here too," Reg agreed, not really wanting to hear about elves in Haiti. Were there even elves in Haiti? "Did you ever see one?"

Francesca looked as though she would say something, then shook her head. "No. Not myself. But there are old stories. And my grandmother—"

"She saw a harbinger?"

"She told me stories."

"Did she know why they do it?"

"What do you mean?"

"I just mean… why do they appear to people to give them warnings? Why do they care what happens to humans at all? Do they give warnings to other magical races?"

"I do not know. Maybe it is penance for a wrong? Or a sense of justice that needs to be served?"

Reg nodded. She didn't get the feeling that was why Orri kept appearing to her. She felt like he was required to do it, but not as a punishment for anything he had done wrong. She would ask him if he appeared again. But hopefully he would not. It had been a couple of days since she had seen him last, and she hoped that meant that he had completed his task, or believed that he had, and he would not be back.

She couldn't help feeling a little guilty about that. Everyone else would be so excited to see an elf just one time, and she had seen him multiple times and didn't want him around.

But it wasn't like he was an entertaining guest. He didn't sit and watch TV with her or have a drink or share interesting stories. He didn't even gossip about his friends. All he did was appear, tell her that she was in danger from something or other that she really wasn't in danger from any longer, and then disappear again.

And to be honest, she didn't like the bugs either.

She was sure that elves were very clean. It wasn't like they were crawling with lice or shed cockroaches everywhere. But Reg didn't like the moths and other bugs flying around her face or in her house. They gave her the willies.

At least they weren't spiders. She really hated spiders.

"This harbinger of yours, what does he say?" Francesca asked.

"Lots of different warnings," Reg advised. She told some of the ones that she knew Francesca would find interesting. She didn't mention the one about Jacky Lane right away, because Francesca hadn't really known Jacky. She wouldn't understand the thing about the eight ghosts' lives plus her own life. Nine lives, just like Orri had said.

But Francesca showed interest in all the warnings and kept asking about more. Maybe she was more interested in Reg's experience than Reg had initially thought.

Reg told her the last couple of warnings. Francesca stared at her.

Reg squirmed in her seat and took a drink of her tea, pretending not to notice Francesca's intense stare.

"Did he say Janice or Janus?" Francesca asked, pronouncing the latter JAY-nus.

"Uh… I don't know. Janice, I think. Why does it matter?"

"Janus, he was a Roman god. An immortal."

"I've never heard of him before."

"The two-faced god. The beginning. The father."

"The father? I thought that was… Cronos. Or Jupiter."

Francesca shook her head. "Janus."

"Well, why should I beware of *him*?" Reg didn't like Francesca upending her theory that the omen referred to Jacky Lane. *Janice* might be Jacky, but *Janus* was not.

Francesca put her cup of tea down and squeezed her hands together. "You know the immortals. They are unpredictable. They have great power. They cannot be trusted."

"That's just the Witch Doctor. He's the one who fought us. He's the one who had bad feelings against the human race."

"He is not the only one. The other immortals do not have regard for humans either. We are nothing to them. They don't consider us to be... individuals with feelings and souls. We are just... animals."

"No." Reg frowned and shook her head. "That's not true."

"It is."

"Weston was in love with my mother. He still is. He doesn't consider her an animal!"

"You romanticize them," Francesca said. "Just like the ancient peoples did. But they are not special because they are long-lived. Or because they have powers beyond what we can wield. They are *not* gods."

"You're the one who said he is."

"No, I was just explaining the name. Not saying that Janus really is... a god."

Reg rolled her eyes. "Okay. So beware the immortals. And I have already met the immortals. I've already learned that lesson too. It's just another warning that he is too late on."

"Janus and *what*? What did he say?"

"And the cat with nine lives. I thought that was Jacky, because..." Reg trailed off. If Janus was one of the immortals, then the cat with nine lives didn't mean Jacky. She hadn't had anything to do with the immortals.

Francesca didn't look happy about this. "The cat with nine lives. That could mean Samyr Destine. The nine kattakyns."

Reg remembered Weston picking up one of the kattakyns, laughing uproariously. *Destine, Destine, what have you done?*

He had been able to recognize the kattakyns as pieces of the

Witch Doctor. Each of the kattakyns held a piece of him. And if all nine were put together and were no longer bound, then Samyr Destine could be whole once more. Like Weston when he was released, he could choose to go where and when he pleased, whether it was good for the human race or not.

"The Witch Doctor," Reg said finally, voicing what they were both thinking. "The cat with nine lives is the Witch Doctor."

"Samyr."

Reg's stomach knotted. "It could be." She kept her voice carefully even. "That would mean that Orri still has the wrong place in the timeline. Because he's talking about the Witch Doctor and the kattakyns being a danger. He was a danger to me back then, but he isn't anymore. Not now that he's bound by your spell. I'll be long dead by the time he can re-form."

Francesca did not look reassured.

Reg knew it was about the past. Everything that Orri had brought her had been about the past, not the future. It was all about lessons she'd already learned or battles she had already fought. Not anything new.

"Samyr Destine..." Francesca mused. "If he is the cat with nine lives, then he is not Janus."

Reg thought back to battling the immortal. He was the same being as had tortured and killed her mother when Reg was four years old. The Witch Doctor had recognized Reg when she approached, had gloated over the power that he had over her. If Reg were a harbinger, she would certainly have warned herself about that evil being and the fact that he was going to pop up in her life again. Seeing and recognizing him and the horrible feeling of dread that he brought with him had been terrifying.

"I don't know anything about Janus other than what you have told me. Are you sure the Witch Doctor isn't Janus? He can't be both Janus and the cat with nine lives?"

Francesca considered, rubbing the back of her neck. She was probably getting a headache. Reg was getting one herself. A great big one that wasn't going to go away very easily.

"He did not look like any of the images I have seen of Janus," Francesca said slowly.

Starlight didn't look anything like Bastet, either. The immortals could change their forms however they wanted to. If the form of the Witch Doctor was not one that would serve him, Destine could choose to appear as an animal, the doctor down the street, even Francesca herself. He could take whatever form he preferred, so saying that he did not look like Janus was useless.

"Janus is always shown with two faces," Francesca explained. "One looking forward, and one looking back."

"But that doesn't mean he actually has to have two faces."

"No. Of course not," Francesca agreed. "I am just thinking out loud. Trying to get it straight in my head."

"Right."

"Samyr Destine was very hungry for power. Very… angry. He did not want to wait. Violent. Raising draugar is not something that most people, even an immortal, would do. It violates the rules. Steals from death."

"So… he's probably not the god of death."

"No. Although… the god of death *could* raise an army of the dead."

"But Samyr Destine only raised one draugr at a time."

"True." Francesca nodded. "Death would, I think, have raised more of them and faster."

"So what is Janus like? Those Greek gods always had personalities. They weren't perfect like the gods in some other religions."

"No, the Greeks and Romans preferred gods that were imperfect, with vices like themselves," Francesca agreed. "Janus was not one of the ones who was always partying or chasing the women. He was the god of beginnings. He looked both forward and backward at the same time."

"The two faces."

"Right. Sacrifices were made in his temple. Not animal sacrifices, but offering up sweet cakes of spelt and honey and milk."

"Sweet cakes?" Reg repeated, her stomach beginning to do back flips.

"Yes. He was honored at the beginning of many ceremonies—"

"Like the Spring Games?"

"Well, there weren't any Spring Games yet. They came later..."
Francesca leaned toward Reg, frowning. "What is it?"

"Harrison. You don't think that it's Harrison, do you?"

"Your Harrison." Francesca rubbed the frown lines between her eyes, the psychic third-eye position. "You said that he would not do anything to harm you. That he always protected you."

"Yes. He always has. I mean, he's a little flighty sometimes. Gets distracted by other things. I wouldn't trust him to keep a goldfish alive. But... yeah. He's always been my protector."

"And what if you were warned that you had to beware of him?"

Reg's headache was getting worse the more they talked about it. She wanted to go to her room and lie down in pitch-black silence. Maybe then her headache would recede again. It felt like she was going to have an aneurysm. Harrison? She didn't have to worry about Harrison.

If she were in danger from Harrison... she wouldn't believe it. Not if just anyone told her. It would take something big to make her believe it.

Something like a harbinger.

CHAPTER TWENTY-FOUR

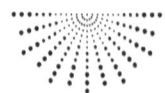

"You don't think that Orri was warning me about Harrison," Reg protested. "Harrison would never do anything to harm me."

"He does seem to like you... but that has not stopped the immortals from doing irreparable harm in the past. If something they do harms one human... or one million humans... what does that matter to them? How many of them killed their own lovers, parents, or children?"

"They have rules about not being allowed to harm their own kind."

"Perhaps. But they have not always obeyed those rules. And you are not their own kind."

"Harrison..."

He had always been so good to her. She couldn't believe that he would do anything to endanger her.

But when she had asked him to help her to fight the Witch Doctor he had refused.

He had told her that they could fight the Witch Doctor if they used all their assets, and that had proven to be true, so it wasn't as if he'd had to intervene. He hadn't had to break the rule against harming another immortal.

"And if Harrison is Janus…?" Francesca said delicately, and left the sentence hanging.

If Harrison is Janus?

The elf had told her to beware of Janus. So she would have to be careful. She would have to guard herself, even if she didn't think she was in any danger from him.

"The full warning," Francesca prompted.

"*Beware Janus and the cat with nine lives.*" Reg swallowed. "You said that Harrison had visited a couple of the kattakyns."

"And you thought it was nothing," Francesca said accusingly. "But it is not nothing. You cannot trust that he will not find and unbind each one of them. He has the power. Far greater than mine. My charms will not hold if he attempts to undo them."

"Then… what do we do?"

"What *can* we do?"

"How can we hide the kattakyns from him? There must be a way. You said that the immortals are not all-knowing. So we can keep things from him."

"You may be able to keep your thoughts from him. But to hide the kittens from him? I fear it is not possible."

Reg felt guilty, even though she had done nothing wrong. Could she keep her thoughts from Harrison? She had not done such a great job of that in the past. He appeared when she thought of him or called out to him in her mind. It was actually surprising that he had not shown up as they were discussing him.

CHAPTER TWENTY-FIVE

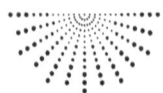

*T*here was a strange yowl from the bedroom. Reg had never heard Starlight make that kind of noise before. She was on her feet in an instant, tiptoeing toward the door to check on Starlight and Nicole. She didn't want to bother them if they were just playing together, or having a discussion, or if things were getting friendly.

Francesca was right behind Reg. They moved quickly to the bedroom, and Reg could see before she drew up even to the door that there was someone else there.

A tall, skinny shadow on the wall.

Reg looked at him. A tall, skinny man, not that much different from the shadow.

The mustached man turned his head to look at Reg, smiling pleasantly. He held a black cat in his arms.

Francesca gasped.

Reg looked at her, and then back at Harrison. There wasn't anything to be shocked about, as far as she could see. Other than his terrible fashion sense in combining a Scottish kilt that fell way above his knees with some kind of middle eastern robe. With a hood, because Harrison rarely went anywhere without some kind of hat.

Nothing horrible had happened. Harrison had a cat—one of the kattakyns, Reg assumed—but it appeared to be okay, just as when she had seen the kattakyns last.

"It's okay," Reg assured Francesca. "Everything is fine. Right, Uncle Harrison? There's nothing to worry about?"

"Why would I be worried?" he asked blandly.

Reg looked around the room. Everything was fine. Starlight and Nicole were on the bed, watching. They were both okay. Reg reached out her senses to the kattakyn. It was not Nico, but she had known that at a glance. Nico would not have been sitting comfortably in Harrison's arms. He'd be climbing up him, clawing to get away, or jumping from his arms to the curtains. She had reached out to the kattakyns before, helping to evaluate their strengths and gifts in order to match them with the most appropriate companions. They wanted the kattakyns to be happy, not to run away and look for the others. Not for their owners to decide that they had received the wrong familiar and to rehome them or send them back to Florida.

They had done everything they could to make sure that the kittens would all be happy in their new homes and not have any reason to leave. And Harrison had interfered. But all was not lost. The cat was in one piece, and they could take it back to its home or have Harrison do so. He just didn't understand why it was so dangerous. What the Witch Doctor could do if he were free again. He had nearly destroyed all of them; Reg didn't want to see what would happen if he were given a second chance.

The kattakyn was sleepy and relaxed, calm even though he had been plucked from his home by someone he didn't know. Maybe the Witch Doctor part of him knew Harrison, just as Harrison and Weston had been able to recognize the Witch Doctor in each of the kattakyns.

"Horace," Reg said to Francesca. The cat who had been sent to Egypt.

Francesca nodded her agreement. She was not psychic, but she had cared for the kattakyns in her home until they had found homes for each of them, so it was easier for her to recognize each of them by their physical attributes, even if at first glance they appeared to be nine identical black cats.

"Uncle Harrison, why did you take Horace from his home? He really should be back in Egypt where he belongs."

"I thought he should come here," Harrison countered, looking down at the cat in his arms. "This is much better."

"Why? It doesn't make any difference to you where he is, does it?"

"It makes a difference to him." A nod from Harrison indicated the cat.

Reg's stomach roiled. Did *Destine* have a preference? Was there enough of his consciousness in just one of the nine cats to tell Harrison what he wanted? Reg had thought that with Francesca's binding spell and the Witch Doctor's consciousness spread across nine different entities, Destine's self would be too diluted to be able to communicate with anyone. He was supposed to be bound for a thousand years, unable to communicate with anyone.

"To the cat? The cat likes to be with the people who feed him. With the people that he has grown to trust. He doesn't want to be here, in a home he's never known before."

"Maybe he wants to be with his mother." Harrison looked at Nicole.

"But she's not actually his mother, you know. She helped to take care of them, but she isn't really their mother. His mother."

Harrison looked at Reg. "You had other mothers."

"Yes, I did," Reg conceded.

"And a cat cannot have more than one mother?"

"He can. Of course. I'm just saying, he wouldn't really consider her his mother. He'd rather live in his home in Egypt. Where he's gotten used to the people and the way things run."

"He likes it here," Harrison said simply.

Reg looked at Francesca. She wasn't sure what to say.

"You cannot bring him here," Francesca said firmly. "And you cannot unbind them. They must remain bound for the humans to be safe."

Harrison turned his head to look at Francesca, as if he'd been unaware that she was there before. "You are the one who bound them?"

Francesca nodded. "Samyr wanted to kill Reg. You wouldn't have wanted him to kill Reg, would you?"

"He will not."

"Not if he remains bound. For at least as long as Reg lives. You can't unbind him."

"We cannot harm our own kind. It is against the rules."

"I'm not asking you to harm him. Just to leave things alone. To keep Reg safe. And the other humans."

"You should not have done this to him."

"It was the only way to make sure he could not do any harm."

"The immortals are not to be bound. They are powerful. They are to have free movement throughout the universe."

"Weston was bound, wasn't he?" Reg suggested. "And that was okay. Because it was to keep him safe. And me. You wanted to keep me safe, didn't you?"

"I did not bind him. He hid himself."

"But he couldn't get out until I released him with the key, right? So he was bound. He chose to be bound."

Harrison considered this.

"It was just for a little while," Reg continued. "He didn't mind being bound for a few years to make sure that he couldn't be punished for what he had done and I could grow up in safety."

"Weston hid himself," Harrison said slowly.

"Yes. Exactly. And we're hiding the Witch Doctor so that he can't do any harm. After a while, he'll be free again. Just like Weston. I'm sure he won't mind being bound for a few years."

"He did not choose this."

"He chose it by his actions," Francesca said, an edge to her voice that said she was not to be trifled with. "He is the one who created the draugar, a thing which is against nature. He is the one who sent his essence into the nine kattakyns, diluting his strength, when Corvin took so much of his power. He wanted to hide and escape. He wanted to be among all these cats so that he could rest."

"Where is the warlock?" Harrison asked, distracted by Francesca's words. He looked around. In a moment, there was a voice calling from the front of the cottage.

"Regina? Are you here?"

Corvin. Harrison had again transported Corvin, bringing him to Reg's cottage this time, a place Reg had done her best to keep him out of. But the immortal's powers were much stronger than hers and she couldn't prevent him from transporting himself or others right into the middle of her life.

"In here," Reg called.

Corvin appeared in the doorway of the bedroom. He looked around at the cats and people standing around. "I have dreamed about being in your room again," he told Reg in a husky voice, "but this isn't quite how I pictured it."

Reg snorted and shook her head. She looked at Harrison. "You can't just transport people into other people's houses without asking. I don't want Corvin here."

Harrison rubbed his chin. "Can I bring him?"

"You need to ask *before*, not after. Sooner or later, I would think you would get it! You understand the difference between before and after, don't you?"

He cocked his head slightly. "I don't think humans understand the sameness of before and after," he countered.

Reg didn't even want to think that one through. Her head hurt. "I don't want Corvin here. Put him back wherever he was before. *Before* you brought him here."

Corvin held up his hand to stop them. "Really, I can be on my way on my own. Don't bother."

Maybe he was right not to trust himself to the caprices of an immortal. He might end up in the middle of Siberia instead of back in his own home or wherever he had been when Harrison had snatched him up.

"This one tried to consume an immortal," Harrison said, glaring at Corvin.

"You knew about that already. In fact, you were the one who said that we needed to use all our assets if we were going to defeat the Witch Doctor. You knew what Corvin was and what he would do."

"Destine's power lies dormant. The warlock does not know how to use it."

Reg glanced over at Corvin. She didn't really want him figuring out how to access any more of the power he had stolen from the Witch Doctor. He was powerful enough without it. If he figured out how to access all that power, would he become an immortal? Had the immortals once been human, or could a human be transformed into an immortal? She knew that there were stories of half-humans becoming immortal in the Greek myths. Maybe some of the other pantheons too.

Or in reality, did a human always remain a human no matter what powers he managed to wield?

"Leave things as they are," she advised Harrison. "No good will come from stirring them up. They are… in a state of balance right now."

It was a stretch.

And saying that they were in balance was a risk, because what if Harrison didn't like things being in balance? Balance was boring. He like to stir things up. To change them. To see what would happen if he changed something in the past or interfered in some relationship. He always seemed to be playing around with something new, seeing just how far he could go in changing something.

"The warlock is no danger," Harrison decided, and Corvin was gone again.

Reg hoped that he had been returned to his house and not to Siberia. But Corvin was resourceful. Even if he found himself in the middle of Siberia, he would find a friend. He would ensorcel some woman and get whatever he needed from her to get home. A friendly smile and a shot of those pheromones, and pretty much any woman would give him what he wanted.

"Where did you send him?" Reg asked.

Harrison shrugged. Reg walked to the bedroom door and poked her head out to see whether he was just back in the living room, but it appeared he was not. Reg shook her head.

"I hope you sent him back home."

Harrison stroked Horace's head and whispered in his ear. Reg had often wondered if each of the kittens had gotten a different part of the Witch Doctor's personality. They were all very different from each other, and she thought that rather than being equal portions of the Witch Doctor, they were all different amounts of him and different aspects of his being.

Horace was probably the most innocuous of them. Quiet and content, which were not aspects of the Witch Doctor's personality that Reg had ever seen. A very small portion of the Witch Doctor with a very insignificant part of his personality. Maybe the safest of the kattakyns to awaken.

"He wants to go home," Reg tried, looking at the cat's face and speaking to Harrison. "He was probably right in the middle of a nap. You should put him back where he was. And just leave the kattakyns alone. It isn't really any of your business."

"You lie to me," Harrison accused. And for the first time, Reg saw anger in his expression. "I have always been a friend, and you lie to me."

CHAPTER TWENTY-SIX

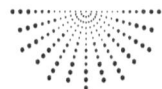

*R*eg's anxiety went through the roof.

Her heart was racing unbelievably fast, feeling like it would ram its way right out of her chest.

Harrison could squash her like a bug. She had thought that it was bad when they had gone up against the Witch Doctor? The Witch Doctor hadn't known her or understood her. He remembered her from when she was little, but back then his anger had been aimed against Weston, not Reg. Reg had only been a means of getting to him. Possibly.

He hadn't felt betrayed by her.

"I'm not lying to you," Reg said quickly. She looked for a way to convince him that he was overreacting and that everything was good between them, like it had always been. "What do you mean?"

"He does not want to be there. You sent him to the desert. To live with a warlock so old that he is turning into dust. Why would any part of an immortal want to stay with him?"

"We matched all the kattakyns up with their new owners very carefully. We matched their personalities, figured out who would work best with which cat. If Horace isn't happy there, we'll find a new home for him." Reg looked at Francesca. "Right? We can find him a new home. Our goal was to make all the kattakyns happy."

Francesca nodded. She took a hesitant step forward. "I am so glad that you brought him back here. If he was unhappy there, we will find him a new home. We want all the kittens to be happy with their new homes."

She reached out her hands as if to take the cat from him. Harrison pulled away.

"He is not yours."

"He's not yours either," Francesca pointed out logically. "One immortal cannot own part of another." She gave a tinkling laugh. "How could they?"

"You will not take him." Harrison turned away from Francesca slightly, and then she was gone too.

"Where did you send her?" Reg demanded, alarmed. It wasn't the same as it was with Corvin. Francesca was very strong-willed, but she did not have the power that Corvin did. And if Harrison were angry with her for having bound the pieces of Samyr Destine into the cats, then he might have done anything to her. He might have destroyed her. Or sent her back in time to choose differently this time and not bind the Witch Doctor as she had. He could have simply returned her to her house, where he had been once before, but considering his anger, Reg wasn't willing to bet on it. "What did you do to her? Is she okay?"

Harrison looked at Reg, his eyes icy instead of warm as they usually were. "You should not be friendly with her."

"I didn't mean to do anything wrong. We used the resources we had to beat and bind the Witch Doctor. We didn't do it to be disrespectful. He was raising draugrs. He was making zombies and making them do his bidding. People were being killed. I was almost killed by one of the draugrs. I would have been, if Starlight hadn't defended me."

"Humans are so obsessed with death." Harrison shook his head.

"Well… yes. Considering it is the end for us. Maybe it doesn't bother you because you expect to live forever, or close to it, but for us… our time here on earth is very short, and we want to get stuff done. We want to live our full lives and do all the things that we planned."

Harrison waved his hand as if brushing it all aside. "It is not the end."

"Well... maybe not." Reg had to admit that she had talked to spirits after death, which therefore meant that death was not the end of their existence. There was still something left behind, whether it was memory or an actual ghost or whether they went on to live whole new lives as reincarnated beings. "But it is a barrier that we can't see past. And we can't control what happens to us after that."

Harrison was looking at the two cats on the bed. Nicole was looking around as if confused by the various appearances and disappearances of the humans.

"Uncle Harrison," Reg wheedled. "You wouldn't want anything to happen to me, would you? You wouldn't want me to die?"

"The *little* Reg is already gone," Harrison pointed out.

"But she isn't dead, she has just grown up. Now she's me. I'm her. If you loved little Reg, then you still love me, right? You've always protected me. You've always tried to do the best thing for me."

"She wanted a kitty." Harrison looked at Starlight, and then at the animal in his arms. "And now she has one."

"Do you want... do you want to give me Horace too? Is that why you're here?" Reg smiled warmly at Harrison, trying to make him feel good toward her. "He's such a nice boy. I'm sure he would be very happy here."

She didn't want another cat. While she loved Starlight and loved having another creature around the house so that she wasn't all alone, and she loved Starlight's cuddles and the help that he gave her with her psychic readings, he also drove her crazy. Wanting to play when she wanted to sleep. Insisting that she feed him on his schedule whenever he asked her to. Getting underfoot. Even escaping or biting guests at various times in the past. He'd settled down since those early days, but he could still be annoying, and she didn't want another litter box to clean.

All of that was beside the fact that she didn't want a piece of the Witch Doctor in her house, no matter how small. She'd been happy to send the kattakyns away, all around the world. It had been tough to leave Nico with the dwarfs yet, at the same time, he had been a wild, rambunctious kitten who would sooner tear her cottage apart than to sit down and have a nap and a cuddle with Reg.

And Reg didn't want to be reminded about the destructive power of the Witch Doctor.

"You don't want him," Harrison countered, maybe sensing Reg's reluctance.

"I'd love to have him here." Reg put as much enthusiasm in her voice as she could. "Why don't you leave him here and we'll see how we get along together? I already have the food and everything else he'll need."

Harrison looked down at the languid black cat in his arms. Reg thought of him as being something like a young child who insisted that he wanted a pet, and then didn't want to take care of it. Harrison wanted the fun stuff, not any responsibility. Feeding someone and keeping them safe was not easy for someone who was so scattered and thinking of so many other things.

"He'll be fine," Reg coaxed. "You want him to have a nice time, don't you? If he doesn't want to stay in Egypt, then we need to find out what he does like. Maybe he wants to be with Starlight and Nicole. They can help us to figure out what's best for him."

Harrison looked at Nicole.

"You have the other one here as well? He can be with his mother?"

"She's not here all the time. She lives with Francesca, who you…" Reg made a motion to where Francesca had been standing until Harrison had decided to dispatch her somewhere else. Maybe Siberia. "Francesca takes care of Nicole. But she comes over here to visit with Starlight too. They like to see each other."

"They won't compete?" Harrison checked. "Eat each other?"

Reg tried to suppress a shudder. "No, they won't eat each other. And if they start to fight, we'll just separate them. But I don't think they will. They all know each other."

Harrison opened his arms and dropped Horace onto the bed, where he landed on his feet and looked up at Harrison for a moment as if he were offended that Harrison wasn't going to carry him around any more.

"He'll really like it here," Reg assured Harrison. "Horace, do you want to say 'hi' to Starlight and Nicole? This is nice, right?"

Horace eventually turned his attention to the other cats, and the three sniffed each other. Nicole tried to grab Horace by the scruff of the neck to move him somewhere else, but he was bigger than she was now. She couldn't move him around like she could when he had looked like a half-grown kitten. Reg was surprised by how big he was. Had Nico grown that much too? It was hard to think of him as being an adult cat instead of the wild kitten he had been.

Reg turned her head to make a comment to Harrison, but found that he had disappeared.

CHAPTER TWENTY-SEVEN

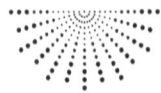

*A*fter checking again to make sure that Horace and the other cats were getting along and would take care of themselves for a while, Reg pulled out her phone and tried Francesca's number. Francesca picked it up right away.

"Reg?"

"Hi! Are you okay, Francesca? Where are you?"

"I'm back at home. He sent me back to the basement!" Francesca sounded outraged by this. Sending her back to her house was one thing, but back to the dark, damp, musty basement where Weston had been hidden was quite another. Reg wouldn't have wanted to be sent back there either.

"Good. I was afraid that he might send you somewhere else. Around the world. Or into nothingness. I had no idea what he might have done with you."

"Yes, I am fine," Francesca agreed grudgingly.

"Good," Reg repeated.

"Is Nicole still there with you? What about the immortal? Is he still there?"

"He's gone. Nicole is still here. And he left Horace too. Do you want to come get them?"

"I will come get Nicole," Francesca said slowly. "In a little while. I want to see whether I can figure out what we can do about your Harrison. We shall have to figure something out."

"Is there really anything we can do? I'm not so sure." She didn't add, "And he's not *my* Harrison." She'd told Francesca that enough times already.

And she hadn't failed to notice that Francesca had not offered to take Horace.

Francesca had been the one who had bound the kittens. She was the one who had fostered them until they had found a home for each of them, other than Nico. She was the one who was responsible for them, not Reg.

"So when are you coming? Do you know what you're going to do?"

"No. I need to figure out what to do. It is not so easy."

"No. I get that. I don't know how to handle this either. Now that we've got Horace back, we can make sure that Harrison didn't do anything to free the Witch Doctor? Find a way to prevent him from messing things up?"

"I do not know. I have to get into some books of mine and do some research. It is not as easy as you might think it is."

"I don't think it's easy. I couldn't do it on my own. I'm just hoping… that it's simple."

Something could be uncomplicated without being easy.

* * *

After ending the call with Francesca, Reg was still left with unanswered questions about Corvin. Reg could pretend that she didn't care. But she still wanted to know what had happened to him.

She tapped on his picture on the phone, but there was no answer.

Reg pondered this as she let the phone ring. Was he out of the service area? Usually if that was the case, Reg would have gotten a recorded message saying that he was out of the area.

"Come on, Corvin," Reg growled, concentrating on him and hoping that he would feel her query and make himself available for her. Psychically or on the phone, she didn't really care which one. What had Harrison done with him? *Had* he sent him to Siberia?

Reg hung up and tried again. Not only was the call not being answered, but it wasn't going to voicemail either. It just rang and rang. Maybe she had the wrong number or had reversed digits.

Again, it just rang and rang without going anywhere. Reg set the phone down, sighing. She didn't know what she would do. It wasn't as though she could do anything about it if he didn't answer the phone. She could try to see him in her mind—she usually could—but with the three cats there and everybody appearing and disappearing, Reg felt off-balance and wasn't sure she wanted to expend the psychic energy. Who knew if Harrison might change his mind and suddenly reappear, and she would have to try to talk him out of freeing Samyr Destine herself, without any help from Francesca or Corvin?

Reg watched the cats grooming each other and looking completely comfortable, as if they were a little family. But she caught Horace watching her, his head turning to examine her when the others were not paying any attention.

* * *

The phone rang. Reg looked at the face of the phone, but it wasn't a number she knew. It was a long number, international maybe, and Reg didn't want to end up talking to some salesperson from India or Pakistan about her phone plan.

As it rang, though, Reg realized that it could be someone else. Maybe someone whose phone didn't work outside his network. Reg swiped the call to answer. She could always hang up if it were someone she didn't want to talk to.

"Hello?"

"Regina." Corvin's voice came out in a huff, irritated, like she had taken too long to answer.

"Hi. Where are you? I tried to call you."

"My phone won't work."

"Did he send you to Siberia?"

"Not Siberia, no. A lot hotter here than it is there."

"Where?"

"Egypt."

"Oh. He sent you back to Horace's home?"

Corvin was silent for a moment. "I don't know. I don't speak the language fluently and I didn't stop to find out if someone with a black cat lived close by. I was just trying to call you or figure out a way to get back."

"Maybe you could talk to Horace's owner and find out... if something happened. Was Horace really unhappy there, or did Harrison just show up without any warning and take him away? Do they know... what Horace is and what Harrison is?"

"I'm trying to arrange passage back," Corvin growled.

And he wasn't interested in doing any investigating for her. Fair enough; Reg probably wouldn't have wanted to do anything for him either. But it wasn't her fault that he had ended up there.

"Okay. Fine. I'll see you when you get here."

"Regina."

"What?"

"I could... use some help."

"Oh, you called me for help, did you?" Reg couldn't help the sarcastic tone that entered her voice. "You have an interesting way of asking for it."

"I'm sorry. As you can imagine, it was a bit disorienting to suddenly find myself in another country, where I do not speak the language well or know the customs or how to find my way through the bureaucratic red tape to find my way home again."

"You speak Egyptian?"

"I know some Middle Kingdom. It... doesn't translate well to communicating with the people here. It would probably be better if I didn't know any at all."

"Just talk to them in English, then. Tell them you're American and someone kidnapped you."

Corvin considered this for a moment. "I'm not sure I want to get mixed up with the police here. It isn't exactly like at home. I don't want to end up behind bars in some hot, filthy cell while they try to decide whether I'm the victim or a criminal trying to pull some kind of con on them."

His voice went up just a little at the end of the sentence, as if he were asking Reg a question. She was the con man. Maybe she could give him some pointers on how to make people trust him.

"Why don't you just charm them?"

"That doesn't work so well on police and politicians. They are remarkably distrustful. Especially in a country like this."

Reg chuckled. "Aw, poor Corvin."

"Reg, do you think I would laugh at you if you were in this situation?"

"If I was in that situation... I wouldn't be talking to police and bureaucrats."

"Who would you talk to?"

"Some fly-by-night airplane pilot who could get me over a few borders into a friendlier country. And then... I don't know... I'd think of something."

"I'm here without a passport or any papers saying how I got into the country. It sort of throws a wrench into the works."

"There are always people willing to break laws for enough money," Reg offered.

"I didn't exactly bring cash."

"You must have credit cards. You can take money out."

"Regina." Corvin's voice was low, plaintive. Even across the ocean from her, it gave her goosebumps.

"There should be plenty of women over there you can charm into doing whatever you want. Call someone at your club. Don't they have connections?"

"Reg, I was hoping that you could help me. I know you can *call.*"

Reg had been able to use her psychic gifts to call Calliopia when she and Ruan had been far away, bringing her back through space to Black Sands to see her sister Karol Blackmoor. Corvin didn't know that Reg had done a call far more recently than that, when she had needed Ruan to help her with the cursed gemstones.

"You think I'm going to call you back into my house? There's no way I'm going to do that."

"It doesn't have to be into your house, although that would be the most discreet."

"It takes a lot of energy. If I do that, then how am I going to deal with clients? Or figure out what to do with these cats and Harrison?"

"Is he still there?"

"No. You know him. He appears, has a little chat, he disappears. But it isn't like we have solved the problem. He made you disappear and he made Francesca disappear. I got him to leave Horace here, but I've got no idea what to do next."

"He made Francesca disappear? Is she in Egypt too?" Corvin's voice rose hopefully.

"No. He sent her back to her house. I don't know why he sent her home and you to Egypt. Maybe because he's been to her house before."

"Well, nice for her. I guess I need to start inviting immortals over for dinner so when they disagree with me, they can at least send me to my room instead of halfway around the world."

"You haven't exactly been friendly with them before this. I wouldn't accept an invitation if I were one of them."

"Well, considering they can provide their own food, it isn't like they'd have to eat anything I had prepared." Corvin sounded a little more relaxed. Now that he'd asked for Reg's help, maybe he figured it was a forgone conclusion that she would help him.

"Where would I call you to?" Reg asked.

"Somewhere private. People tend to take a dim view of people just appearing out of nowhere. Despite the way Harrison and his friends seem to think that they can just appear and disappear anywhere and anytime they like."

"Well… they don't have to stay here and deal with people, so I guess it doesn't matter to them."

"Sarah's house?" Corvin suggested. "How about mine?"

Reg suspected that Sarah would take an equally dim view of Corvin appearing in her house. He had helped her in the past, and they were on reasonably good terms considering Corvin's "condition," but Reg suspected she would not want him in the house.

She had been to Corvin's house to drop him off once before,

when he had been ensorcelled by Norma Jean and hadn't been able to drive himself, so Reg had an approximate idea where it was, though she would need the exact address to get her to the right place.

But meeting with Corvin alone at his house was probably not a good idea either. Especially if Reg were tired from calling him all the way across the ocean. Would she be able to resist his charms?

How could she call him somewhere that was both private enough to hide what they were doing and public enough that he would not be able to take advantage of her?

The last time Reg had been to the police station, she had seen a sign in the parking lot for a safe exchange area. When someone was buying an item from an online vendor and wanted to meet them somewhere safe to make the exchange, they could make use of the safe exchange area. It was not directly supervised, but was out in public and was on camera in case someone did get ripped off. Crooks didn't like to meet there because they knew they would get their pictures taken.

If she called Corvin there, it might cause some consternation for anyone reviewing the video feed because he would seem to appear out of nowhere. But it could easily be brushed off as an electronic glitch. Videos were often jumpy. Sometimes surveillance cameras didn't even take an actual video feed, but shot a frame every few seconds. Enough to catch anything that went down, but taking up far less storage space than a video shot at 30 frames per second.

If there were any issues, Corvin could ask Detective Marta Jessup to smooth them over. The two of them were friends, or Corvin was a consultant for Jessup, or some similarly murky arrangement. Enough that Jessup would probably do what Corvin asked of her.

"How about the police station?" Reg suggested.

"The police station?"

Reg explained about the safe exchange area.

"What if someone else is already there?" Corvin demanded. "Or you're wrong and it is under direct surveillance?"

"Then whoever is watching will have to explain to the authorities what exactly they saw and, if they don't want to be laughed off the police force, they can't exactly say that a man appeared out of thin air. They will have to leave off the fact that they didn't see you approach."

Corvin grunted.

"And if someone else is there, I'll just wait until they're gone. No one will stay around for long. You don't exactly stop for a long visit with the stranger you're buying a DVD player from."

CHAPTER TWENTY-EIGHT

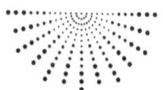

*R*eg drove by the police station once. She told herself that she was just checking to make sure that no one was hanging around who shouldn't be and that the safe exchange area was as she had remembered it.

But she knew on another level that she was driving by because she was afraid. She didn't like to be at the police station. She had never called Corvin before and wasn't one hundred percent sure she would be able to. She didn't want to end up in any trouble or having to call on Jessup to smooth things over.

But she couldn't call Corvin to her house or his; it was just too big of a risk. And she couldn't think of another place that provided the same benefits as the safe exchange area.

She drove by a second time. Corvin would be getting very impatient for her to get there and call him. But she wanted to make sure that she was safe. There was no one else using the safe zone. There was a prominent surveillance camera, but no cops sitting around watching from cars or park benches or smoking a cigarette outside the building. It seemed like the perfect setup.

With a sigh, Reg eventually pulled into one of the parking spaces designated for users of the safe exchange area. She got out of her car and walked over to the open space. There were no eyes on her. She was sure she would be able to tell whether someone was lurking nearby watching. She was a little anxious of what a cop who was watching the video feed might think of her hanging around there on her own. Most people probably sat in their cars until the second party showed up.

But not everyone. Some of them must get up and smoke, or pace, or do something else to get some exercise or fend off the anxiety of waiting. Reg leaned against the wall of the police station. She took a few deep breaths and closed her eyes. She'd had Starlight there to help her with calls before. She hadn't thought about that. Could she do it without his help? She hadn't even thought to bring him with her. Cats tended not to take to car travel well, but she had taken him in the car a few times and he was pretty good about it.

She envisioned Corvin in her mind and reached out to him. They had a strong psychic connection, so she didn't anticipate having any difficulties with seeing him.

It took a few minutes of breathing and focusing before she started to see him. Dressed just as he had been when Harrison had made him appear in Reg's cottage. Standing on a quiet street looking around. It wasn't how she had pictured Egypt, all sand dunes and tents or a busy, colorful bazaar. It looked like the dusty streets of any other city she had been in. He could have been in Texas.

She could feel Corvin locking on to their psychic connection, strengthening it from his end. He was a powerful warlock, even if he couldn't access all the Witch Doctor's powers that he had absorbed. Maybe it wouldn't take so much energy out of Reg if he were helping from his end. As if he were pushing the heavy wagon that she was pulling.

Reg tried to keep her thoughts focused and relaxed. Corvin was impatient, angry, and irritated. He didn't like to wait, that one. He would not have done well on the street pulling a long con. Sometimes it took days to set something up. Hours of surveillance and setting up details.

"Just call," Corvin muttered aloud.

Reg took one more deep breath and let it out slowly. "Corvin, come."

She experienced a kaleidoscope of images, emotions, and the sensation of falling through empty space, and then Corvin was there, landing heavily beside her in a heap.

Reg steadied herself against the wall, trying to reorient herself in space after feeling like she had been flipped over. She sighed and bent down to offer Corvin her hand.

"Are you okay?"

Corvin didn't take her hand, but moved gingerly until he could sit up and look at her. Then he blinked and shook his head at her.

"Well… I've never done that before. It's a lot smoother when Harrison does it."

Reg had experienced travel with Harrison. It was definitely smoother, though it did leave her with a sense of disorientation and nausea.

"Sorry. I haven't had much experience. And I didn't bring Starlight to help."

Corvin pushed himself up to his feet. He too leaned against the wall for a moment to get his equilibrium back.

"That would have been one more thing for anyone looking at the video to explain. Why did this crazy lady bring her cat to the safe exchange area?"

"Yeah. I supposed we could pretend to swap him, but…"

"People do come to places like this to pick up kids who are visiting the other parent. I suppose… there's no reason you couldn't do the same with a cat that you share custody of."

"Yeah. But we don't."

Corvin looked mildly puzzled by this comment. "No, of course not. I'm not suggesting that we actually do it."

"Right." Reg was still feeling a little bit disoriented. "So you're good to get home from here? You can call an Uber or something."

"You could drop me somewhere."

"I think I've already done plenty."

"You're just going to leave me here? At the police station?"

"It isn't like I'm turning you in. You can go wherever you want. I just don't want to drive you."

"I thought the deal was that you would get me home."

"And I thought it was that you wanted to avoid all the red tape of trying to get out of Egypt and back to Florida without any papers."

Corvin made a growling noise in his throat, his lips pressed together in a straight, angry line. "After all this travel through space, you think I want to get an Uber? Your car is right there, Reg. I'm too tired to deal with strangers and having to wait for someone to show up."

He leaned against the wall as if he really were tired. Reg analyzed his face and body language and probed at his consciousness. He had pretended to be too tired to do anything to hurt her before. But Reg had been warned not to be fooled. He did seem to really be tired from his movements from one continent to another and trying to figure out travel arrangements while in Egypt, so maybe it would be safe…

She had taken him home once before, and he hadn't done anything.

Corvin waited, gazing into Reg's eyes, trying to will her into doing what he asked.

Reg sighed and looked around, looking straight at the video camera for a minute. "If you try anything, you've been caught on camera. I have proof that I came here to help you, and that you got into my car."

Corvin shrugged. "What do you think I'm going to do, Regina?" He leaned a little closer to her. "I'm grateful to you. Haven't you heard the saying about not biting the hand that feeds you?"

"Yeah, but I've never seen you follow it."

Corvin scowled. "Just drive me to my house. I'm not going to do anything to hurt you. I just want to get back home."

Reg rolled her eyes. She gestured toward her car and then walked over to the driver's side. "Fine. But you're on video. You try anything, and…"

"Why would I do anything to harm you when I'm trying to get reinstated by the coven?"

"I don't know. Because you're hungry?"

Corvin stopped at the passenger's side, looking across the roof of the car at her before either of them got in. His eyes glittered. Of course he was hungry. He was always hungry. Even when he had consumed the powers of the Witch Doctor and his artifacts, he had told Reg that he still had room for dessert. Her powers.

Reg slid into the car and put her key into the ignition. She pulled her door shut and didn't wait for Corvin to get settled and put on his seatbelt before pulling out. She remembered the general area of his house and pointed the nose of the car toward it. The sooner she could get there, the sooner she would be rid of Corvin and the danger that he would turn on her.

He made disapproving noises over her pulling out so quickly, and jabbed the tongue of his seatbelt against the buckle a few times before managing to get it inserted properly. Reg heard it click into place.

CHAPTER TWENTY-NINE

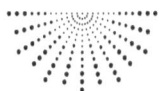

"*W*hy do you think Harrison is doing this?" Reg asked Corvin abruptly, voicing the thought that had been running through her mind since Harrison had disappeared. "He knows that releasing the Witch Doctor would be dangerous and put a lot of people at risk, so why would he consider doing it?"

"I don't know what his motivations are. He has never struck me as being particularly close to the Witch Doctor."

"No, I don't think they are. They're both immortals, but I don't think they spend any time together or are friendly. In all the old myths, the gods are usually competing with each other and jealous and everything. I would think that he would be happy that Destine was bound to the kattakyns."

"Maybe he just enjoys causing chaos. Have you ever heard of the law of entropy?"

Reg glanced away from her driving to give him a look of disbelief. "What? What kind of law is that?"

"It's physics."

"And you think I know physics because…?"

"I just asked," Corvin said in irritation. "The law of entropy says that everything is becoming gradually more chaotic. Everything in nature tends to degrade over time. To break down instead of spontaneously becoming more organized."

"Okay."

"We can organize things. Plant a garden, build a house or a machine, impose our order on the things around us. But as soon as we step out of the picture, it starts to degrade again."

"Yeah."

"Maybe... Harrison just likes chaos. Maybe when things are going well and seem to be well-organized, he feels the need to upset the applecart. Impose some chaos."

It matched Reg's own theory that Harrison got bored easily and liked to stir things up. Imagine being able to do whatever she wanted to. How long would it take before it all got old? She nodded. "I think you're right."

Corvin raised an eyebrow, maybe surprised to hear her agree with him. Maybe he had thought that she would defend her Uncle Harrison and say that none of this was his fault.

"So do you think he's actually thinking about freeing all the kattakyns? Or is he being impulsive? Trying to get a reaction out of us?"

"You know him better than I do. What do you think?"

"I've known him longer... but I don't know whether I know him any better. I mean, I was only a kid before. I've seen him a few times now as an adult, but... I don't know if I understand him any better now than I did then."

"What was he like when you were a kid?"

"I don't know. Fun. We played games. A lot of hide and seek, which I guess was to teach me how to hide from the Witch Doctor. I would call him sometimes when I was scared." Reg shrugged. "He'd make me feel better."

"How?"

"Well... giving me food, stuff I wasn't allowed to have or that the family couldn't afford. Playing little games. Telling me stories."

"What kind of stories?"

"I don't know. Silly stuff." Reg thought about it. "Maybe some of it was stories from mythology. It's hard to tell, because I guess they've changed over the generations, but I remember him telling me about his friends and the trouble they got into. It was nice to hear about adults getting in trouble. I always got in trouble, even if I was trying to be good. So it made me feel better to hear about these powerful grownups who still got into trouble."

Corvin nodded slowly. "You remember any of those old stories?"

"No... I don't really know. It was so long ago, and there were so many different people in different homes. It all blurs together. I don't remember any particular story. Just that somebody always got in trouble." Reg laughed. "And seeing Harrison now, through the eyes of an adult, I can understand that. He's just so..." Reg tried to think of a word or a phrase that would describe Harrison.

"Like an ADHD kid someone just gave a million bucks to?"

Reg laughed hard at that, trying to stop so that she could focus on her driving and not end up in an accident. "Yeah, just like that," she agreed breathlessly.

Corvin nodded his agreement.

When Reg pulled the car in front of Corvin's house, she turned to him, suddenly feeling serious.

"If he releases all of the kattakyns and the Witch Doctor reforms..."

"Yes?"

"That's really bad. If Destine keeps raising zombies and getting more power, like before... it could be the end of the world. He could destroy everything. He said he wanted to. That we were all like bugs he wanted to squash."

Corvin stared out the windshield, not looking at his house, but at something off in the distance. "There are many ancient texts that refer to an Armageddon. A last battle of humans against insurmountable odds. Sometimes against each other, but sometimes against a dragon or some other monster."

"So you think it could be the end of the world?"

"Not the end of the world..." Corvin hesitated. He put his hand on the door handle and considered for a few more seconds before popping the handle and pushing open the door. "But maybe the beginning of the end."

CHAPTER THIRTY

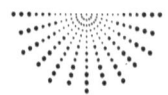

*S*leeping with three cats in the house was not nearly as easy as sleeping with just one cat in the house. Starlight was pretty quiet. He sometimes disturbed her sleep running and jumping onto the bed as if he were running away from something or chasing a mouse across her face. But usually, he just played by himself at night or watched out the window.

Having three cats in the house was a whole different story. Nico had been bad. When Reg had been taking care of Nico temporarily, with Starlight still there, things had been pretty tough. He seemed determined to break anything in the house that was fragile. Reg tried to put things away or out of reach, and he still managed to get at them. Starlight had been irritable with a kitten around demanding all Reg's attention and trying to engage Starlight in play or a fight.

Starlight and Nicole were fine when they had a play date. Reg enjoyed having Nicole over and she never caused any trouble. In fact, she would keep Starlight occupied and out from underfoot so that Reg could get things done without him always there watching her and silently passing judgment over what an inept human she was.

But she'd never had Nicole overnight. With Starlight, Nicole, and Horace all put together, looking for some fun to have while Reg was sleeping… There was not much sleep to be had.

"What's gotten into you?" Reg asked the big kitten as he sat on her nightstand looking down at her. "You were always so calm before!" That was one reason they had sent him to the old warlock in Egypt. They'd matched him with the kattakyn that was the quietest and most sedate, thinking that he would match the old warlock's needs the best.

Horace looked at Reg, a barely visible thread of green iris around his wide black pupils. She had owned a cat long enough to know what that meant. He would attack her at the first chance of weakness. All she had to do was to turn her back on him, drum her fingers on the counters, or flip her braids the wrong way, and he would be on top of her.

"You behave yourself. I'm not a bird. I'm bigger than you."

Horace just continued to watch her with those big black eyes. Across the bedroom, Starlight and Nicole started wrestling. Starlight ran away yowling loudly, and Nicole took off after him. She could hear both of them crashing around the cottage, knocking things over.

"You guys had better not break anything! And if either of you draws blood…!" Reg looked back at Horace again. "And that goes for you too. Especially if it's my blood. Why don't you go see what the others are doing? Supervise for me."

Horace didn't move. Reg reached over and shoved him off the nightstand. He meowed and headed for the door, turning to look at her to show her how disappointed he was in her behavior.

"Tell me about it," Reg muttered. "I'm not too happy with yours either."

* * *

When Francesca came back the next day, Reg was still in her bathrobe, sipping a cup of coffee which she hoped would wake her up enough that she would be able to do something constructive for the day. As it was, all she felt like doing was going back to bed. Where, of course, she wouldn't sleep anyway.

Although, the cats had finally settled down and gone to sleep after she had gotten up. Not all together, like when the kattakyns were new and had all slept in a heap, but all in their different spots around the cottage. So that Reg couldn't really find anywhere to sit down and relax without bothering at least one cat.

"Come in," Reg called out when Francesca knocked on the door. Reg had left it unlocked and she didn't have the energy to walk from the kitchen counter where she was leaning not-so-comfortably to answer the door.

Francesca tried the doorknob and peeked in to make sure she had heard properly before entering. "Regina...?"

"Yes, come in. Let yourself in."

Francesca obeyed. She looked at Reg for a moment, then looked around the cottage. She didn't make any comment about the various items scattered around the floor. Pillows, dishes, ornaments, candles, Reg's crystal ball, and various other knickknacks. On the couch, Horace was snoozing peacefully.

"Was everything all right?" Francesca asked.

"Not exactly. I don't think the three of them should stay together any longer than necessary."

"Well, I am here to pick up Nicole, so you won't have them all. I thought... did they not get along?"

Reg rolled her eyes. She took another long drink of her coffee. "Oh, they got along all right. But they were acting like the circus was in town and they were part of it. They were so loud. They were all over the place." She shook her head. "You wouldn't believe that three cats could be so loud. I was sure that Sarah would be over here any minute asking what all the ruckus was about."

"They were just playing?"

"I don't know whether I would say just playing. They were fighting, but they didn't draw blood, so I guess that counts as playing. And they were knocking things over. And Horace was looking for an opportunity to attack me."

"Horace?" Francesca looked at the snoozing cat with disbelief.

"Yes. Don't believe that innocent look. He was just as rambunctious as the others. I thought that he was the sleepy one. They don't change personalities when they get older, do they?"

Francesca scratched her head, looking at him. "Well… normal cats don't. They get quieter and more sedate as they get older, but they don't go through big personality changes. And they don't get wilder as they get older."

"Is it something to do with the Witch Doctor, then? Or did Harrison put a spell on him to make sure that he caused me as much trouble as possible?"

"I will examine him." Francesca moved into the room, gliding across the floor as if she were on wheels. Reg didn't know how Francesca could always look so polished and glamorous. Reg felt like she'd been dragged behind a train. A speeding train.

She probably looked like it too.

Francesca sat down on the couch, taking care not to disturb the cat sleeping there. For a few minutes, she just sat looking at him. Reg didn't know what she could be looking at. Horace just continued to sleep. He was a pure black cat and looked just like any other pure black cat. What could Francesca tell just by looking at him? Reg expected her to pick him up and to examine him as a doctor would, listening to his heart and stomach, prodding and palpating.

After a few minutes of silence, Reg realized that Francesca was singing. A barely audible hum to start with. Reg thought that she was hearing things. But it got louder and louder until Reg could pick up the wandering melody. It wasn't any song that she knew. Nothing popular or on the radio.

It had to be a spell. She was a charmer and, when she had bound the kattakyns, she had done so by singing them a song and weaving her hands around them in a complicated way. And now she sang again, the notes rising and falling, questioning, exploring. Horace moved, curling into a tighter ball and turning so that he was belly-up.

As much as Reg would have wanted to rub his furry belly if she were closer to him, there was no way. She'd lived with Starlight long enough to know that even when a cat showed you its belly and looked as cute as a button, it was just waiting for the chance to rip your hand off.

Francesca continued the song for a long time. Then she stood up, silent, and walked around the room. She walked around the cottage without looking at Reg or saying anything to her. As if she were there completely alone. And Reg let her. It wasn't like there was anything Reg could do to help; she had no idea what Francesca was even doing.

Eventually, Francesca returned to the kitchen and stood close to Reg.

"You want some coffee?" Reg offered.

Francesca nodded. When Reg made no move to get it for her, Francesca moved to the coffee pot and poured one for herself.

"Thank you."

"So, did you find anything out?"

Francesca frowned, a tiny M appearing in the wrinkle between her eyebrows. "It is very strange."

"What is? That he was behaving so differently last night?"

"No. I do not think that was the strange part."

"What, then?"

"The part of the Witch Doctor that was bound to Horace... is no longer there."

Reg nodded. "Okay."

"I bound it there very tightly."

"But Harrison unbound it."

"Yes. Apparently." Francesca sipped her coffee.

"Then what is it that you find so strange?"

"If they are unbound... then where is that piece of Samyr Destine?"

"Uh... I don't know. Where do pieces of immortals go?" It was far too philosophical a question for Reg to answer.

"Even though it is no longer bound to Horace, I would still expect it to be with him. They are not bound anymore, but that is where the immortal sent the piece of himself, and I would expect it to stay there. Unless..."

"Unless what?"

"Unless... someone took it. Someone did something with it."

"Harrison, you mean."

"Yes... Harrison is the likeliest suspect. Who else would recognize it as a piece of the Witch Doctor? And what would they do with it. But Harrison…"

"What could he do with it? Does that mean that he is trying to get Destine to form again? Or is he taking the power for himself, like Corvin would…?"

Francesca looked at Reg sharply. "Oh!"

CHAPTER THIRTY-ONE

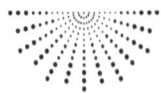

*R*eg nearly dropped her mug at the exclamation. She looked around to see what had startled Francesca, then looked back at her. "What?"

"Corvin was here. I had forgotten that."

"Yeah, he was here for a few minutes. But Harrison made him disappear, like you."

"Or he caused himself to disappear."

"That's not one of his gifts."

"Do you know what all of his gifts are? What he might have picked up recently in one of his liaisons? You don't know."

Reg had been ready to argue the point, but she reconsidered. It was true that she didn't know much about Corvin's gifts, other than his ability to steal others' powers. But the ability to steal others' powers meant that he could use the powers that he stole. His abilities were always shifting and morphing with each feeding. He had talked to Reg about her psychic powers and the voices when he had taken her powers. But he had never talked about what he had taken from anyone else. Or from the magical objects he was similarly able to absorb powers from.

"I know that Harrison sent him to Egypt."

"How do you know this?"

"Because I saw him there. I called him back."

"And you know that Harrison sent him there? He did not send himself?"

"Of course. If he could transport himself over there, why would he need me to transport him back?"

"Indeed."

"He was talking about how he couldn't get out of the country, couldn't get a plane ticket without a passport and other documentation. And he couldn't, could he? The laws don't make exceptions for people magically transported to other countries."

"You still do not know whether he sent himself there or whether Harrison did. Other people have the power to transport themselves somewhere, like you called Corvin. I did not know you could do a call."

Reg shifted uncomfortably. Not only could she do a call, but she could transport herself and others somewhere else. She had traveled with Ruan and Calliopia to return some of the gems to their source. Even Corvin didn't know that was what she had done to solve the problem of the cursed gems.

"If he sent himself over there, he could send himself back," Reg insisted.

"Not if he used up all his strength on the journey there."

"Well… I suppose."

"It takes a great deal of energy."

"I guess it would. But he could just take a nap until he felt better."

"Perhaps. Perhaps not."

"You think that Corvin went to Egypt on his own? Why?"

"He already absorbed much of Samyr Destine's life force. That is why Samyr sent himself into the kattakyns."

"Yeah."

"Corvin would be able to consume the portion of Samyr that was bound to Horace."

Reg's heart pounded. "How could he do that? Would he have to hold him? Or pet him?"

"I do not think so. I have not seen him in action as many times as you, but when we were at the warehouse, he was absorbing power from the artifacts without touching them directly. And he was able to begin to absorb power from Samyr before they were in physical contact with each other."

It was true. Reg breathed out hard. Was it true? Had Corvin disappeared not because Harrison had grown tired of him, but because he had taken the piece of the Witch Doctor which had been bound to Horace? Did he have to go somewhere else to assimilate it? Home or to Egypt?

"He wouldn't have to go to Egypt, would he? I mean, Horace was here, not there."

"Maybe he was hoping to find something in the old warlock's papers. Or maybe just misdirection. Maybe he never was in Egypt. Would you know?"

"Well... I don't know. He wasn't here; he was somewhere very different. Dry and dusty, not green and humid like Florida."

"But it could have been somewhere much closer. Did you see anything Egyptian?"

"No, just a street. It could have been any city, I guess."

Francesca nodded. She paced back and forth, thinking about everything. "You do not need to know where someone is to call them to you?"

"No. I never really know where they are. I think of them in my mind, picture them, and then I can see them and call them. I can see things around them, but I couldn't tell you what country they were in unless they were standing next to a road sign or a landmark I knew. Why would he want to mislead me?"

"So you would not guess that he had gone voluntarily? He had seen Harrison send me back. So he knew that if he disappeared, you would assume that it was Harrison too. You wouldn't guess that he had gone voluntarily and taken something with him."

"And if he didn't take that piece of the Witch Doctor, it would still be here. Attached to Horace."

"If someone didn't take it."

"But it might have been Harrison."

"Of course. It could be. But Harrison does not need more power. He is already an immortal. He has more power than he needs."

"You thought he was going to free all the kattakyns. So that the Witch Doctor could re-form."

"Yes."

"So maybe that is what he has done. Maybe he took that piece, and he's collecting all the other pieces, and then he will put them together."

Francesca nodded. "That is possible, yes."

"So it isn't necessarily Corvin. That's all I'm saying."

But then, she wasn't sure she liked the alternative either. She didn't want to think that her godfather was going to reassemble the Witch Doctor, someone who had wanted to destroy her.

"I will take Nicole home," Francesca said. "But I think we should start calling the owners of the other kattakyns. We should find out how many others Harrison has gone to see. And whether… any of them have changed."

"You think the change in Horace's behavior is because the piece of the Witch Doctor is gone?"

"When we first were trying to match them to the right owners, we thought that they had each inherited a different part of Samyr's personality. They weren't all the same; some had very different traits than others."

"Right."

"So the part of Samyr that went into them was what gave them that particular personality trait. And when it is gone…" Francesca looked around the room at all the things that the cats had knocked over that Reg hadn't yet bothered to pick up.

"Horace was quiet and sedate. You think that was part of the Witch Doctor's personality? He sure didn't strike me as calm."

"We do not always see what is inside. We only see the dominant personality traits. There could be many others that the person keeps hidden."

"I suppose so." Reg knew that there were parts of herself that she didn't share with others. And parts of her that could only come out when she was alone and didn't have the stresses and distractions of other people around her. She wasn't exactly the same person when she was by herself that she was when others were around. "So Horace had the quiet, calm part of the Witch Doctor. And now... he doesn't anymore. And that's why he has started behaving differently."

Francesca nodded. "That is my best guess. It isn't like there are a lot of cases of this happening that we can examine. I do not know of anyone who has put parts of his spirit into a kattakyn before. I know that the draugar can only be animated by the spell caster, but he does not send his spirit away from himself when he does."

Reg thought back to that day in the warehouse, when she had seen the Witch Doctor's body disappear in a bright starburst. She had felt his dark aura in the kattakyns before Francesca bound them.

"They have rules," Francesca said slowly, "but I do not understand them. And I do not know whether they are the natural rules of physics or imposed rules of their order that can be broken. They do seem to be bound by one physical manifestation... usually. But if they can step through time, then there could be many of them in one time and place, could there not? And if they were faced with destruction, could they not just go back to a different time? And as we saw, Samyr was able to leave his physical form to go into the kattakyns. Was that against their rules? Or natural laws?"

Reg's head hurt when she tried to understand it. Her brain told her that there had to be specific natural laws that the immortals were bound by. Just because a human had a difficult time understanding what the rules of that order were, that didn't mean that they didn't have the same natural laws of physics that humans did. They were just able to manipulate atoms or energy in a way that humans couldn't or didn't yet know how to.

They knew from what had happened that an immortal could be bound. Either in his body, as Weston had been when he had locked himself away, or dissolving his body and inhabiting another, or others, as the Witch Doctor had. They knew that the Witch Doctor would remain bound for as long as Francesca's spell lasted.

Francesca had said it would be at least a thousand years. She hadn't anticipated Harrison unraveling it before then.

CHAPTER THIRTY-TWO

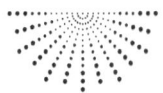

"*W*hat are you going to do about Horace?" Reg asked.

Francesca raised her brows. "What can I do about him?"

"I mean... where is he going to go? Are you going to keep him or return him to Egypt?"

"I am not going to do anything with him. We have eight other kattakyns to worry about. I need to focus my attentions on them."

"But you're going to take him with you. Him and Nicole."

Francesca shook her head. "You will need to look after him. I cannot at this time."

"But he was one of your kattakyns. You took care of them all before."

"When he was bound to Samyr, that was my responsibility. Now... it is not. And I have more important things to worry about."

"So you think you're just going to leave him here with me?"

"I'm sorry, Reg, but I have very important things to do. Can you not do this one small part?"

Reg opened her mouth, trying to marshal an argument. Of course she couldn't keep Horace. She already had another cat. All Francesca needed to do was to look around and see how much destruction the cats had wreaked in just one night. If she had to keep Horace for the longer term, who knew what problems he might cause? And Sarah, her landlord, would have something to say about it. She hadn't been too happy about Reg bringing Starlight home from the animal shelter and had made it clear that Reg was not to have any other animals.

"I… I can't."

"Then you need to find someone who can take care of him. Would you please do this thing? I cannot. If you cannot keep him here, then you must find somewhere else."

Reg looked for a way to make it Francesca's responsibility, but the fact that Francesca had looked after him before was all she could come up with. And she didn't have any way to research what they could do about Harrison releasing the kattakyns, and Francesca apparently could. Reg was in possession of the cat, which pretty much made it hers. Possession being nine-tenths of the law and all that.

On one hand, she wished that she hadn't gotten Harrison to leave Horace there but, on the other, Francesca wouldn't have been able to find anything out if Harrison hadn't left Horace behind. At least with Francesca taking Nicole, Reg would be down one cat.

Reg sighed and shook her head, but didn't argue. She couldn't change what had happened or convince Francesca to change her mind, so she would have to deal with it.

* * *

Horace continued to sleep, which was a relief. Except that it meant he would probably be up causing havoc all night again. Reg was determined to enjoy the peace while she had it so, when the phone rang, she was sitting on the couch with Horace beside her and Starlight snoozing in her lap, a cup of tea cooling on the coffee table, binge-watching a new sitcom series.

Reg looked down at the phone screen, hoping that it would be Francesca rather than Corvin, but it wasn't either one of them. It was not Gwythr's number, but it had the same area code and prefix, so Reg figured it was a call from one of the other dwarfs in the colony. She swiped the phone to answer the call.

"Hello?"

"Reg Rawlins, it is Brimir, son of Fraeg."

"Hi. Did you and Gwythr sort out whether you wanted to buy some of these stones?"

"I am the son of King Fraeg. I do not need to deal with the smithies."

"Okay. Does that mean that you're interested in them or not?"

Brimir grunted, probably displeased with the fact that she wasn't subservient to him. But Reg wasn't kowtowing to anyone, princeling or not. "We are willing to negotiate."

"Great. Do you have a starting offer?"

"I will send you an email."

Reg shrugged. He could have done that in the first place. He didn't need to call her just to say that he was sending an email.

"Great. I'll look at that. When we settle on a number, is there a courier service that you use? Or how do you want me to get them to you?"

"You would not bring them here?"

"I'm not going all that way on my own, no. Do you have someone you trust? I don't know anyone here that well."

"I will talk to the court. We will arrange for someone."

"Good. Okay. I'll get back to you."

"Do you have other stones? We are often looking."

Reg was cautious. "I have some others, but I am not ready to deal with them yet. I'm just starting with this lot."

"It would be good to know what else you might have. So that we know who to ask in the future. It could be quite profitable for you."

"Uh… yeah, let me think about that." Reg wasn't sure that telling anyone what else she had was a good idea. What if the courier who came to get the gems decided that he could get a little more for his time? Or if the dwarfs decided that they were entitled to all the gems, even though they hadn't made a deal for them? Pixies believed that all gemstones were theirs because they came from the earth. Dwarfs might have the same attitude. She didn't know.

"This could be a very beneficial relationship," Brimir encouraged.

"I'll definitely look into it."

"Hmmph. Reg Rawlins is very tight-lipped."

"I don't think you would tell me about all of the gems you have in your castle or in your colony either, would you?"

"Of course not. And what need would humans have to know such things?"

"What need do you have to know what gems I have that I'm not ready to sell yet?"

"You are not going to use them. It is best if they go to the kingdom. We know how to deal with such things."

"Doesn't matter. If I'm not ready to sell I don't need to tell you what I have."

"You are a heartless negotiator." Brimir's voice held a grudging note of respect.

"Thank you."

"I have further to ask of you."

"Okay, sure."

"It is about the devil that visited you."

"The... devil?"

"You warned that he might come here, to steal the warrior cat away."

"Oh. Him. I didn't say he was a devil."

"What else is a powerful practitioner who wishes to take our cat from us?" Brimir challenged.

"Well... okay. I don't know." Reg didn't want to tell them more about Harrison than she had to. If he hadn't shown up at the dwarf mountain, she didn't want to reveal that he was an immortal or that he had a relationship with her. "Has anyone come?"

"No. You still think that he will?"

Reg nodded, although he couldn't see her. "Yes. He was here yesterday... with another of Nico's litter mates. I don't know what his intentions are. And I don't know whether the dwarfs can do anything to stop him. I don't want any of your people getting hurt."

"We are ready to fight. The dwarf kingdom is strong!"

"I know. You are very tough opponents," Reg agreed, building his ego. She didn't want him to think that she was looking down on them, thinking they were helpless just because they were shorter than human beings. Reg knew very well that you could never judge a person's spirit or toughness by their body size and shape. People were too quick to make that assumption, and Reg knew better.

And she had seen the dwarfs' armor and weaponry, and some of the drills and training they did. They were very capable fighters.

But against Harrison?

Swords and shields would not be effective against him. Dwarf weapons were imbued with magic, of course, but she didn't know what or if they would have any effect against someone as powerful as Harrison.

"I just want you to be careful," Reg reiterated. "He is a formidable opponent and I don't want him to hurt anyone. And if he just wants to *visit* with Nico…"

Brimir laughed. "He does not just want to visit with the cat."

"Well… probably not, but you can't say you know that for sure."

"Has he merely visited the other cats?"

Reg thought about Horace. She didn't know the details of his visits with any of the other cats, but she knew that he had done something to Horace. Taken the piece of the Witch Doctor's soul, or unbound him, and removed him from the home that they decided was best for him. He hadn't just gone to Egypt to say hello.

"No."

"We will not allow him to take or harm our warrior cat."

"I'm just saying… be wise. Don't rush into anything impulsively. If you can negotiate with him… words are better than bloodshed. Maybe you can get somewhere with him, even if no one else could."

"We will not waste long on words."

Reg sighed. Hopefully, Harrison would know not go to the dwarf mountain until they had a better idea of how to stop him from freeing the Witch Doctor. Maybe Francesca could find something that would help them.

"We'll talk later, then. Email me your offer."

"Fare thee well," Brimir said brusquely, and hung up.

CHAPTER THIRTY-THREE

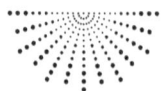

*R*eg checked her email and reviewed the detailed offer that Brimir had sent her, with a detailed itemization of each of the stones and their value for the dwarfs and how they would be used. It was on the low side, but she had expected that. The dwarfs were used to negotiating. You didn't go to a used car lot expecting to pay sticker price, and you didn't sell to dwarfs expecting to pay the first price that was bandied about.

She wanted to think about it for a while and see what she felt like after letting it simmer. She had only negotiated with the dwarfs once before and had to get a feel for it.

Reg did want to look at her other gems and see what else she had that they might be interested in. Future considerations were a big part of negotiations. It wasn't just a single deal they were working out. As Brimir had said, it was a relationship.

She pulled out each of the bags of gems, looking them over and remembering what she had sensed about each. She was not as good at reading the gems as a pixie or dwarf might be, but she could sense something about them. Their power, their affinity, where they had come from. The gems were grouped together by where they had come from, so that she would be able to return them to their rightful owners in their countries of origin. It seemed to be the only sure way that they could be cleansed from the curses on them. There were other ways that might work. She had been able to cleanse a few of them with fire or by other methods.

She was thinking of Egypt, of Horace being brought back from Egypt and Corvin being sent there by Harrison. Or saying that he had been sent there by Harrison. Her eyes kept returning to a bag containing a variety of precious and semiprecious stones, some of them lapis lazuli or turquoise. The blues were used in a lot of Egyptian statuary or decorations. The color of royalty for the Egyptians. Reg picked up the bag and examined the various stones through the plastic. She had forgotten that there were a few rings and other bits of jewelry among the unset stones. Two of them were in the bag of stones from Egypt. Something else she could sell to the dwarfs? They liked jewelry. They already had channels they could sell them through. Etsy. Amazon storefronts.

Reg opened the zip top and fished out the two rings. They were beautiful, the colors so pure. The lapis lazuli was the same shade of blue as one of Starlight's eyes.

They felt heavy in her hand. The weight was a good sign. They were not just thin slices of stone, but good, weighty pieces. She could feel the power that imbued them. It had taken her some practice, but she could sense both the power and the curses very easily now. She closed her eyes and communed with the stones.

Maybe she could go to Egypt to inquire after the warlock who had owned Horace. Maybe he could tell Reg something about what had happened. Why Harrison had gone there and why he had taken Horace away. Harrison said that Horace liked it better at Reg's cottage. If that was true, why hadn't he liked it in Egypt? Reg and Francesca had thought that they had matched the kattakyns and their owners quite well. Reg had studied the pictures on each of the profiles Francesca had written up, trying to read everything she could from their faces. They had discussed each of the assignments and had not rushed into it.

Horace had been one of the first kattakyns that they had placed. Had they failed to assign him to the right new owner? If so, had they made the same mistake for the others? Or had they only failed with

Horace because he was the first and they didn't really know what they were doing?

The phone rang. Reg slipped the rings onto her fingers and picked up the phone. Corvin. Reg swiped to answer.

"Corvin."

"Regina." He sounded relaxed, more like his usual self. She didn't like it when he was irritated. She'd grown to expect him to be calm no matter what the circumstances, so it was disconcerting when he was not.

"Hi. Did you have a good night?"

"Slept like the dead. How about you?"

"No, not really. I'm not sure if I slept at all."

"Oh?" His voice was warm. "Something on your mind?"

"Yeah, three wild cats. It was chaos around here."

"Ah. Good reason not to have any cats! They always contribute to chaos."

Reg wasn't sure whether he was making a joke or referring to some other physics theory she wasn't aware of. She made a neutral sound in response. "So… were you really in Egypt?"

"Was I really in Egypt?" Corvin was silent for a moment. "Why would you ask me that?"

He didn't deny it, Reg noted. His question was thrown up in defense against her question, leaving it unanswered.

"I want to know whether Harrison really sent you there, or whether you just said that. Or whether you sent yourself somewhere else."

"Sent myself somewhere else? Where is this all coming from? You know where I was. You called me back from Egypt."

"But I can't tell where you were. I can find you in my mind, but it isn't as if you have a geolocator chip built into your head. I don't see you on a map with borders neatly marked out."

Corvin gave a short laugh. "Well, trust me, I was in Egypt. Did someone tell you I wasn't in Egypt? Harrison?"

"No." Reg did not feel a twinge of guilt at lying to him about Francesca's theory. "I just wanted to know. I can't see, so… I mean, you could have been anywhere. Anywhere hot and dusty, anyway. Could have been Texas, for all I know."

"Why would I be in Texas?"

"I don't know. You could have been."

"I… wasn't."

"What was it like in Egypt?"

"What it's always like in Egypt. Hot and dusty."

"Did you see anything interesting there?"

"Like… what?"

He was certainly being cautious about his answers. Reg would have expected him to have been more glib with his answers. Especially if he'd been up to something. When people knew they might get in trouble, they started rehearsing excuses. Explaining their behavior and coming up with cover stories. She'd seen it many times. She'd done it almost as many times. He seemed not to know what she was fishing for and was trying to avoid any potential traps. Throwing her questions back at her, avoiding committing himself to any particular story.

"I don't know. Did you see the Sphinx? The pyramids? King Tut's tomb?"

"No… I was not there sightseeing. I was just in the city for a few hours. It was noisy and smelly and hot. Crowded. Dealing with people who I did not want to deal with. Everyone trying to make a buck and rip me off if they could. Do you know what it would have cost me to get out of the country if you hadn't called me? How many people I would have had to bribe and pay off to get safely out without someone reporting me to the police? Prisons in Egypt are not nearly as nice as the ones in the United States."

"Did you talk to anyone?" She anticipated his next question. "Anyone interesting, I mean?"

"The people I talked to were very unhelpful. And… no one you would know. I don't know where these questions are going, Regina? Why don't you just ask me what you really want to know? Or explain what you're worried about. I'm a bit lost."

"Did you meet Horace's owner?"

"Who is Horace?"

"The cat. The one that Harrison brought back from Egypt."

"Oh. Him. How would I know? I wasn't looking for any cat owner. There wasn't anyone stapling up 'missing' signs or crying in the street."

"Well, if Harrison sent you back, then he would have sent you to where he had been, wouldn't he? To Horace's house?"

"I don't know. Maybe he went somewhere else after picking Horace up. Maybe he has a favorite restaurant in Egypt. You can't expect him to be logical."

"He sent you back to a restaurant?" That didn't sound right. Yes, Harrison enjoyed eating human food. But Reg was pretty sure that the warlock who owned Horace did not work in a restaurant.

Unless he had lied. Reg supposed that people inserted lies into all kinds of applications. Resumes for job opportunities, dating profiles, why not an application to become a pet parent? He said that he was the leader of a coven, but that didn't mean he really was. Had Francesca actually done any kind of background checks on the candidates? She supposed Davyn still had a day job, even though he was the leader of Corvin's coven.

"No, I didn't say he sent me back to a restaurant," Corvin said in exasperation. "I just said, you have no idea what Harrison had been doing before he appeared at your house and you have no idea what he might have been thinking of when he made me disappear. Who knows why he does any of the things that he does?"

"So where did he send you? He just dropped you in the middle of a street or on a sidewalk somewhere in the middle of Egypt."

"Pretty much, yes."

Pretty much. More waffling. Being imprecise so that he could take back the words later and say that he hadn't lied or misled her. She had just made wrong assumptions.

"You weren't in someone's house or place of business?"

"Well... initially, I suppose."

"And you didn't talk to the warlock who lived there?"

"What makes you think that a warlock did live there? Or that I would know him or approach him?"

"Why do you keep answering with questions? Why won't you just give me a straight answer?"

"You seem to think that I did something wrong. That I made myself disappear in order to get into some kind of mischief. Nothing could be farther from the truth."

"Then why don't you want to answer me truthfully?"

"I don't know what you're looking for."

"For the answers to my questions!"

But she wasn't going to get it from him. Whatever he had done while he was in Egypt seemed to fall into the category of "top secret."

"Maybe we can get together," Corvin suggested. "We could have a long and frank discussion about everything."

"You're not going to be any more honest to my face than over the phone."

She could see the slow curl of his mouth in her mind. Infuriating and attractive at the same time. Sometimes she hated how easily she was drawn to him.

CHAPTER THIRTY-FOUR

A plan was starting to form in Reg's mind. She could do several things at once. She could take the Egyptian stones with her to see whether she could pass them on to whoever was supposed to have them. Maybe it would even be Horace's owner. That would be very serendipitous. Sometimes things did come together like that. She would find out from Horace's owner exactly what had happened. Both when Horace had been unbound and when Corvin had been sent to Egypt. If he really had been. And if he'd been sent to the same place as Horace had come from. There was no guarantee, but Reg would feel better if she knew whether she could trust that Corvin was telling the truth about being to Egypt. She was sure he was, but Francesca had planted doubts in her mind and it was not helpful that Corvin wasn't answering her questions properly.

"Regina?" Corvin's voice reached Reg. Nudging her out of her thoughts.

"Oh. Sorry. I got distracted."

"I was asking about dinner."

"Oh. No, I think I'm going to be busy."

"You have clients tonight?"

"Um… I have to check; I'm not sure. I suppose I'll have to cancel them. Unless it doesn't take very long to talk to him and get things sorted out."

"Talk to who? Sort out what things? You're on a whole different plane than I am."

"I'm going to go to Egypt. Where you were."

There was a startled silence from Corvin. It seemed like a long time before he was able to find his voice.

"Why are you going to Egypt?"

"I have some things to do there."

"Just… a few errands to run? Have you ever even been out of the country before?"

"Yes." Reg smiled, thinking about her previous trip. Corvin knew nothing about it. He thought he was so superior because of his experience. But he didn't even know what she had experienced. "I have."

"Where?"

"That's none of your business."

"I think you're going to find that it's a lot harder getting to Egypt than you thought. There are a lot of arrangements to be made. You can't just go there on a whim like you might drive to Grandma's."

"It would be a lot harder to drive to Grandma's, since as far as I know, my grandmothers are both dead. Besides, it isn't like I'm *driving* to Egypt."

"Do you even have a passport? You'll need papers."

"Well, if I was going through the border, I suppose."

"And how do you expect to get there without going through a border?"

"The same way as I got you out."

"The same way…" Another silence as Corvin sorted this out. "You can't *call* yourself."

"No. But I know how to jump. I've done it before."

"When?"

"I don't need to explain myself to you."

"Well, no, of course not, but… how? Why haven't I heard of this before? How long have you had that ability?"

He was probably thinking of when he had held her powers.

169

Wondering if he had been able to jump at that point and just didn't know it.

"I've only done it a couple of times," Reg admitted. "But I know how. So I thought... I would go to Egypt and talk to Horace's owner."

"By yourself?"

"Sure."

"You don't know anything about this warlock or his abilities."

Reg thought back to the profiles that Francesca had prepared on each of the candidates for kattakyn ownership. Reg hadn't done anything more than skim over it. She had studied the man's picture and Francesca had told her a few details in summary.

"I know some things about him. I know he's well-respected in his community and that he's the leader of his coven. Which is more than I can say for you."

That might be a bit of a low blow, but Reg didn't know where he got off acting so superior to her. Sure he had lived longer than she had and had grown up in a magical home, so he knew all the ins and outs of the community that Reg did not, but those were just practical matters that would be remedied with time. They didn't make him superior to her.

Maybe she shouldn't mention Horace's owner being the leader of his coven when Corvin couldn't even talk to anyone from his. But that was his problem, not hers, the punishment for his choice to break the rules of the community.

"I think you need to know a little bit more than that about him before you go over there. Don't be in such a hurry," Corvin warned.

"You were over there for a few hours and you were just fine. What do you think is going to happen to me?"

"A lot of things could happen. For one thing, it is not as safe for a woman to be there unaccompanied by a man."

"Really? You're going to play the gender card?"

"It's an important cultural factor to consider. And I at least know a little of the language. You haven't learned to speak in tongues without me knowing about it, have you?"

"Francesca talked to him on the phone and emailed with him in English."

"I still think that you would have better luck if I went with you. An old Egyptian warlock will have a lot of prejudices about women. He may refuse to talk to you at all."

"We are the ones who sent him Horace. So he'll talk to me."

"Reg. Let me go along with you. I really don't think it's safe for you to go alone."

Reg was actually reassured by the idea of his going with her. She was prepared to go on her own, but it would be easier if Corvin went with her. He could watch her back. Help her with any cultural or language issues.

But she wasn't going to tell him that. His ego was big enough without her pumping it up any more.

"Well… I suppose I could take you along if you really want to go. Are you sure you want to go back there so soon? I mean, you were just there and you didn't seem too keen on staying."

"And I'm not going to stay this time either. Just long enough for you to take care of your business. If I go with you, I know I won't be stuck without a way to get back." He paused. "Assuming you don't get yourself into some kind of trouble."

"If I get into trouble, I can still jump back."

"It depends on what kind of trouble you get into. What if you find that this warlock is more powerful than you think and he wants something from you?"

"Oh." Reg hadn't considered that. She had assumed that the warlock would be a kindly old man. "Well, yeah, I guess. But I don't think he will do anything to hurt me, do you? I mean… he's not like you, right? He doesn't have your 'condition'?"

"Very few do, but I don't know him. I assume that he does not, but I could be wrong. He might have been able to keep it a secret. Or he might have other powers that you don't know of. You don't know what kind of a person he is."

"Francesca did a background check on him. We wouldn't have given him Horace if there had been something wrong with him."

Corvin was silent.

Reg sighed. "How do you want to do this, then? You want to meet me somewhere?"

"Your safe exchange zone again? Why do we need to do something like that if you can jump? Just come here, or call me there, and we can go. You can save all kinds of money on transportation costs and commute time now that you have this ability," he teased.

"Yeah, except it takes energy. I can't just jump everywhere, or I'll be exhausted."

"Do you want to come here or should I come to you?"

"I guess… I'll come to you. I still don't want you in my house."

"There's no need to treat me like a pet who hasn't been housebroken," Corvin muttered.

"I wouldn't have to if you *were* housebroken."

He didn't have anything to say about that. "I'll see you soon, then?" he asked in a clipped tone.

"Yeah. I'll be there in a bit."

CHAPTER THIRTY-FIVE

*R*eg felt a little strange getting ready to go. She didn't have to pack her bags, since she would be back in an hour or two, not staying overnight. But she didn't feel like she should travel halfway around the world without some kind of preparation and packing. She carefully tucked away the bag of gems. No need for Corvin to see them before she was ready to reveal them. Maybe Horace's owner would be the right person to give them to and maybe he wouldn't. Hopefully, though, he would be able to give her some indication of where she should take them.

She decided to pack some granola bars and snacks, just in case she was there longer than expected and didn't have anything to eat. She didn't know what the hospitality rules were in Egypt, how much the food cost, or whether she would like it. And she didn't exactly have Egyptian drachmas or whatever they used for money.

Starlight followed her back and forth as she made her preparations. She thought at first that it was just because she kept going into the kitchen, and of course when she went into the kitchen Starlight thought that she was going to get him something to eat. Or that she would if he reminded her of his needs. But it occurred to her after a few minutes that he wasn't begging for food, and that the feeling she was getting from him wasn't concern for his own belly, but a worry about her and what she was doing.

"What is it?" Reg asked, stopping and crouching down to talk to him. "Everything is fine."

He stared at her with his one blue eye and one green, his gaze intense.

Reg raised her brows and shook her head, exaggerating her body language. "What?"

He bumped his head against her leg, rubbed his cheeks against her a couple of times, and then stood on his hind legs, putting his front paws on her leg.

"What? You can't come with me."

He bumped his head against her again and gave a low *mrrow*.

"You want to come with me? To Egypt?"

She got warm feelings of approval from him. Reg started to tell him again that he didn't want to go to Egypt, that he wouldn't like it there and he couldn't travel back and forth with her. But he had lived in Egypt before, had been a powerful being there, worshiped and venerated.

Maybe he just wanted to go back to visit his home country. To see how much had changed in the time since he had lived there, centuries ago.

"I doubt whether it's the same anymore."

He meowed again, more insistently. Reg looked down at him, thinking it through. She had taken him with her on a couple of other trips, and it had always turned out okay. There had been times when she hadn't taken him with her and had regretted it later, wishing that she had the extra psychic strength that he provided her with. He always helped to focus and strengthen her own abilities.

"I don't know. Are you sure?"

He meowed again.

"Corvin will be there," Reg warned.

He made a snorting, snuffling sound Reg took for contempt. But he kept looking at her, confirming that he wanted to go even if Corvin was going to be there.

"Well... okay. I guess. But you'll stay with me, right? You can't go running off anywhere. I won't know how to find you. And I'm not going to be staying for very long."

Starlight waited.

"Okay," Reg said again. "Do you want to go in your carrier? Or should I just take you…?"

He walked over to the door.

Even though he had agreed not to run off, Reg wasn't about to open the door and let him go where he pleased. He had run away once before and, even though that had been a long time ago and it had turned out that he was seeking out an herb that would help to heal her, she was still worried that he could run off and get lost.

She picked up her shoulder bag, then picked up Starlight and fumbled through her bag to find her keys. She locked the cottage door behind her, despite the fact that it was already protected by wards and anyone who could get by the wards could undoubtedly also get past a locked door. She had to do what she could to protect the gems, which she still had not put into a safe deposit box as Sarah had told her to do more than once.

Reg released Starlight in the car and he settled onto the passenger seat and started washing. He did not act startled or worried when she started to drive and, in a few minutes, stood up on his hind legs to be able to see out the front windshield and side window. He watched the scenery go by and did not yowl and complain.

"That's a good boy," Reg murmured in approval.

Starlight turned his head to look at her, then back to the window.

* * *

Reg had not expected to be at Corvin's house again so soon when she had dropped him off after his return from Egypt. She pulled up to the curb outside his house and wondered whether she was supposed to go in, or whether he would come out to the car. She supposed that he would not want to take the chance of their vanishing before the eyes of anyone who happened to be walking down the street, so she ought to go inside.

She was reluctant to cross his threshold. Who knew what kind of traps he could have set for her? She knew that letting him into her house granted him certain privileges and abilities. But she didn't know what risk she might be putting herself at by willingly walking into his lair.

Maybe it was a good thing she had Starlight with her. He could help to guard her against Corvin and warn her if she were walking into danger.

Reg slid the straps of her purse back over her shoulder, picked up Starlight from the other seat, and opened the door to slide out, awkwardly shuffling and climbing out of the car without the use of her arms, her shoulder bag bumping and catching on everything on the way out. Reg powered the locks and hip-checked the car door shut.

Corvin must have been watching for her or had sensed her approach. He was standing at the open door when she got up the sidewalk to his house. He looked at the cat in her arms with distaste.

"You didn't tell me you were taking that cat with you."

"I didn't tell you that I wasn't."

He shook his head. "And what about the other one? Did Francesca take him?"

"No... he's alone at my place still. He's sleeping, and hopefully won't get in any trouble while we're gone." She looked at Starlight. "Hopefully, we won't be gone too long, so he won't destroy anything while we're gone."

"I thought he was the quiet one."

Reg was surprised he had paid any attention to the fact. "Yes... he was."

She didn't tell him more than that and, while he looked like he wanted to know more, she pushed ahead.

"Are you going to invite me in so we can get on our way?"

Corvin stepped back and motioned for her to enter. "Please."

Reg stepped into the house. She paused for an instant, reaching out with all her senses. There was no one else in the house, of course. She didn't sense any traps or danger, but she hadn't always been the best judge of that. At least this time she was taking the time to check. That had to at least increase her odds of not being caught in whatever

Corvin might have planned in the short time since she had hung up her call with him.

She looked around curiously. Although she had remotely viewed Corvin in his home several times, she had never actually been there, and she had wondered how accurate her visions had been. It was an older home, but not ancient. The furnishings were a mixture of classic and more modern styles. Muted colors, as she would have expected. She didn't see any TV or computer, but thought that he must have one somewhere, maybe in his study or library. He would need some kind of computer for all the research he did. And he must communicate with other professors or scholars by email.

"Nothing too shocking, I hope," Corvin said, smiling at her.

"No. About what I had pictured."

"Maybe you'll feel more comfortable coming in now and then. There's no reason we can't see each other in a private setting."

There were several reasons that visiting with Corvin in a private setting was not a good idea. Reg shook her head and didn't answer him. She spun in a circle in the living room, looking around, Starlight still in her arms.

"Well... I guess we should go, huh?"

Corvin nodded. "I suppose you want to get your business over with quickly."

Reg drew in her breath a few times, trying to visualize the place they were jumping to. She had seen it when she had visualized Corvin in order to call him home. It shouldn't be too hard for her to reverse the process and jump both of them back. She looked at Corvin sideways.

"Do you mind if we hold hands to make it easier to stay together? I don't want to leave you behind."

"Of course. I love to hold your hand any time."

He touched her arm, ran his finger lightly down the back of it, then closed his hand around hers. Reg was braced for the electrical charge that flowed through the two of them whenever they made skin-to-skin contact, but she still jumped and had to steel herself not to pull away.

She tried to think of her destination instead of their contact with each other. She used her channel into Corvin's mind to strengthen the picture of Egypt and to drink in the other senses. The sounds, the smells, the feel of the air on her skin. Everything was different.

CHAPTER THIRTY-SIX

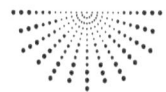

*W*ith barely a whisper, they were there. Reg had never called or jumped with such ease. One second, they were in Florida and she was imagining Egypt, and the next second they were there, the changed landscape flooding her senses. She opened her eyes and looked at Corvin. He looked back at her, eyes wide.

"That was... incredible. I've never traveled so smoothly."

Reg nodded. She let out her breath. "I'm getting better. But I think part of it was you."

"How?"

"Because you've been here before, so I could see and feel it through you."

"I always told you we make a great team."

Reg wasn't sure she'd ever heard him say that. The only time he talked about their doing something together, he was trying to get something from her. Trying to talk her into something that was against her better judgment. She pulled her hand out of his grasp.

"So..." Reg looked around. The streets were quiet. She could see, though, that it was not Texas. There were signs on buildings and litter on the street with letters written in a curly script that was completely unfamiliar to her. "When you came here, is this exactly where you landed?"

"No." Corvin shook his head. "This is where I was when you called me. But I had done quite a bit in the hours in between."

"Can you remember enough about where you landed to take me back there?"

"I think I can manage that."

Reg glanced at him. She wasn't sure whether that was sarcasm because she had asked him to do something that was simple, or whether it was more difficult for him and he was really sincere about thinking he could do it.

Either way, he was going to try. As long as he took her there, she didn't care.

"Why the place where I landed? I thought you had some specific tasks to do here? Why not go there, instead of relying on something that might be a wild goose chase?"

"It isn't a wild goose chase," Reg told him firmly, hoping she was right. Was he trying to distract her? Trying to keep her from finding something out?

Corvin looked at Starlight, still cuddled close in Reg's arms. "A wild cat chase, maybe?"

Starlight put his ears back and hissed at Corvin. He laughed.

"Starlight wanted to come along," Reg said. "I'm not exactly sure why. I think he wanted to protect me. Like you."

"From me, you mean."

"I don't know. But he didn't want me coming here without him. So…"

"The ancient Egyptians venerated cats and worshiped a cat god. Maybe he's hoping someone will worship him."

Reg didn't fill Corvin in on the details she knew of Starlight's past. As far as he knew, Starlight was just what he appeared to be. "Maybe," she agreed neutrally.

Corvin looked around, then began to lead her. "This way. Stay close. Egypt isn't well-known for the respect they pay to female tourists."

Reg didn't argue. Even though she had said that she was not

afraid to go to Egypt alone, she was glad to have someone at her side. Especially someone with powerful magic and a knowledge of the culture and history of the place. Even if he didn't know the language well, at least he knew it better than she did. She knew exactly nothing about the Egyptian language, ancient or modern.

Corvin seemed confident in the direction he took. Hopefully it would not be difficult for him to find his landing place of the previous day. They would scout around, talk to Horace's owner, and Reg would find out what she could about what had happened with Harrison. And maybe find something out about where to take the gems. If she were lucky, maybe Horace's owner would even be able to do something with them himself. Some kind of ceremony or ritual he knew that would cleanse the gems so that they could be given back to the Egyptian people, with a portion going back to Reg in appreciation.

That was the way it had worked with the previous mission. Though she hoped that this time it wouldn't mean also going up against some powerful magical warlord.

They walked by a lot of businesses, with Corvin occasionally pointing one out to say that he had made inquiries there about money or a passport or other papers. Being dumped there so unexpectedly, without even any American cash in his wallet, it had been difficult or impossible for him to make any headway.

They covered quite a distance. Reg's arms were getting sore from carrying Starlight. Of course he could walk by himself, but she was afraid that he might take off if she put him down. Cats were not well-known for heeling. There were not many people out on the street, and those that they did see looked at Reg and Corvin with curious expressions. Clearly, Americans holding cats did not walk through their neighborhood very often.

Corvin pointed down a narrow lane. "Okay. We're close. Just down here."

Reg was nervous preceding him into the enclosed area. It felt too much like a trap. Only one way in and out, and it could be blocked by one man.

"You go first."

He looked at her, waving her ahead of him impatiently.

Reg shook her head.

"What do you think I'm going to do?" Corvin demanded. "This is where you wanted to go."

Why would Harrison put him into that close, dark alley? Reg looked around, wondering whether Harrison was close by. Was he watching her? Waiting for her to show up there? Or was he completely oblivious, off doing something else. Maybe seeing Nico or one of the other kittens.

"Reg," Corvin encouraged, impatient.

"You go first."

He shook his head and stepped in ahead of her. Which of course meant that he blocked her from seeing anything as they moved forward. Maybe not such a good idea. But she still had a clear exit behind her, which she wouldn't have if she'd gone first.

The alley was dark and the piles of trash stank. Not exactly somewhere Reg would have chosen to go on her own. But she'd been in enough dark alleys and questionable circumstances previously in her life. She'd survived. And she would survive this time too.

They reached the terminus of the alley, the two buildings forming walls on three sides of them. Corvin turned and knocked on a wooden door set into the brick building. He rapped it hard with his knuckles. His blows boomed inside the house as if amplified.

Reg stood rigidly as the sound died away. It seemed ominous. She wondered if she should turn around and go the other way. Who said she had to come back to this place to find out why Harrison had sent Corvin there? It had just been the whim of a changeable, distractible god who didn't know what he wanted from one moment to the next. It meant nothing.

Corvin turned partway toward Reg, opening his mouth to speak. To make a joke about the situation or to ask her a question.

There was a sound on the other side of the door. Scratching. Bolts sliding. Chains jangling. An echoing click, and the door swung out of its frame slightly.

CHAPTER THIRTY-SEVEN

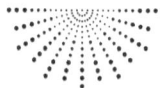

"Who is it?" a hoarse voice inquired.

"It's me," Corvin replied "I was here yesterday."

The door opened a fraction farther. "You? I thought you left. You didn't go home?"

"I did, but I'm back, and I brought a friend." Corvin shifted to the side slightly so that the old warlock could see Reg as well. "She has some questions for you."

The man didn't open the door. Reg could not see him very well in the dimness of the evening, and there did not appear to be a light on inside the residence.

"Are you Horace's owner?" Reg asked. "I'm looking for the person who owned him."

"Horace? What do you know about Horace?"

"Are you?"

After another moment of consideration, he opened the door far enough to admit them. Corvin entered the house first, followed by Reg.

It wasn't a hovel, but it wasn't a modern place like Reg or Corvin lived in either. The building felt ancient. There was a woven mat inside the door with a couple of pairs of shoes beside it. The man pointed to them. It took Corvin and Reg a moment to get the idea and take off their shoes, and then they entered his home.

"Is that because this is a sacred place?" Reg asked in a hushed voice.

"It is to keep people from bringing the mud and sand from outside into the house."

"Oh."

Starlight twisted his head this way and that as Reg carried him through the house. She was glad that they were finally there, because she really wanted to put him down. Once she was seated in a dimly lit living room or sitting room, Reg rested Starlight in her lap and let go so he could decide whether to stay with her or to jump down and look around.

"Who is this?" the warlock inquired, looking at Starlight. He didn't get close or hold his hand out for Starlight to sniff. He didn't rush in and pet him as if he were a stuffed animal without any feelings of decorum or personal space.

"I'm sorry, I forget your name," Reg said. "This is Starlight, and I'm Reg."

While she waited for the warlock to answer, Reg studied him. She vaguely remembered seeing his picture in the profile Francesca had prepared. He was an older man. He looked older than Corvin, though she was learning that a person's appearance didn't necessarily reveal their true age. Some witches and warlocks seemed to know secrets that made them age far more slowly than others. Sarah had a special emerald that kept her young and healthy. Reg didn't know what Corvin did, but he claimed to be decades older than he looked, so she assumed he used some kind of potion or spell to keep him looking that way. The old man might be the age that he looked, in his sixties or seventies, or he might be ancient. His skin was dark, his face round. He had a sparse black beard, the rest of his hair gray and white. He was on the heavy side, but didn't look fat, just comfortable and settled. Someone who spent a lot of time sitting, but was still active. Maybe going for long walks in the evening as the day started to cool.

"I am Kareem," the warlock said finally, bending at the waist to give Reg a slight bow. He looked at Corvin.

"Corvin Hunter," Corvin said with a nod. He had apparently not introduced himself when he had seen the man the previous day.

"When you came yesterday, did you land inside or outside?" Reg asked curiously.

Had he surprised the warlock by making a sudden appearance inside his house? Or had Corvin knocked on his door to ask for help after being dumped outside by Harrison?

"And why are you here?" Kareem said, ignoring Reg's question and talking over her. He addressed Corvin. He was the man, after all. A warlock in the States would probably have assumed that Corvin was in charge too. Reg had found them to be remarkably sexist. "What brings you back to my home again?"

"Reg wanted to speak with you," Corvin said, nodding in her direction. "She asked me to accompany her."

Kareem looked in Reg's direction, but didn't seem to think much of her. He continued to address Corvin, eyes intent on him.

"You could not get back to the US and here again in a day."

"I did. But not on a plane."

"You said you had to catch a plane. That you needed help. You lied?"

"No," Corvin assured him. "I was looking for a plane in order to get out of the country, but that's not what I ended up doing. It turned out… there was no way I could get on a flight without papers or a significant amount of money, and I had not been prepared with either before I was sent here."

"Of course you cannot fly without papers or money. You should have known that."

"I didn't come here by choice. I was brought against my will."

"You are a warlock. I can feel that your powers are great. Why would you let someone do that?" His eyes flicked to Reg again. "It was her?"

"No. She brought me back today. With my permission, of course. Yesterday was… somebody with greater power than I."

The man scratched at his scrubby beard. "What are your questions?" he asked, finally looking at Reg and meeting her gaze.

"Are you Horace's owner?"

"Yes. I didn't call him that, but... yes. Do you know what happened to him?"

"I was hoping that you could explain it to me. I know where he is, but I don't know what happened before. What happened here before he was brought back to America?"

"You say he is in America?"

"Yes. He's at my house right now. He's safe, you don't need to worry about him."

"Of course I am very concerned. Everything that happened here was very confusing."

Reg nodded. She found pretty much everything Harrison did to be confusing. "Can you tell me what happened? Did Harrison just show up here and demand to see Horace?"

"He did not so much demand..." Kareem trailed off, thinking about it. "He was suddenly here. Without coming through the door or setting off my wards or any kind of warning. He was not here, and then he was. Like..." he looked at Starlight. "Like one of them."

Reg was going to say, "Like a cat?" But then she thought maybe he meant "like an immortal" and she didn't want to reveal anything about Starlight's previous life and history to him, so she kept her mouth shut. There were far more important things to focus on.

"What did he say?"

"He was here, petting Hassam. Horace."

"Yes?"

"He called the cat another name. Not Horace."

"Destine?"

"Yes. Yes, I think that was it. Destine. Why did he call him that? I thought that Hassam was owned by that other woman before me. That Haitian woman."

"Francesca."

"Yes. She was his owner before, was she not? She was the owner of the mother?"

"She owns Nicole. Yes." Reg looked at Corvin, asking him in her mind whether she should give Kareem the history, to explain to him about the Witch Doctor being joined to each of the kattakyns and their efforts to keep the kattakyns away from each other permanently. Or as permanently as magic and physics would allow.

Corvin gave a slight shake of his head. *Don't tell him.*

Reg shifted uncomfortably. She looked down at Starlight and petted him. He shook off her touch and jumped to the floor. Kareem said nothing. For a few minutes, they all just watched Starlight exploring the room.

"The man who came, he didn't say how he knew Horace?" Reg asked. "That is, Hassam?"

"He did not say he owned him," Kareem admitted. "I thought that must be why he was here and how he knew the cat. But... maybe I was mistaken. Or maybe he just knew Hassam casually, and the Francesca woman owned him."

Reg nodded. "Did he say why he was here? Did he do anything? Or did he just take Horace away?"

"He petted him, talked to him..." Kareem shook his head. He put his hands out, palms up, in a pleading gesture. "I do not know. I could not understand it."

Reg knew how Harrison behaved around Starlight and assumed he had been the same way with Horace. As if Starlight were an old friend, or an old enemy. An old acquaintance, anyway, one that he was apparently eager to talk to and engage with. Harrison always seemed too intimate with Starlight, too familiar with him. As if there were no social or species barrier between them.

"Yes. I know what you mean. Did he say anything in particular? Did he say that he wanted to take Horace away? Or to do something with him?"

"He just... petted him. Then took him. The two of them disappeared." Kareem shook his head. "That is all. He picked him up and talked to him, and then he took him away."

CHAPTER THIRTY-EIGHT

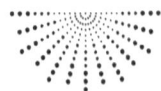

*R*eg sighed. She followed Starlight with her eyes while trying to figure out what else she could ask Kareem. He didn't seem to know anything at all. She had been hoping that he would be able to provide a little background and insight at least. But that didn't seem to be the case.

She looked over at Corvin, who didn't have any suggestions or questions of his own.

Reg was getting a prickly feeling from Starlight. He didn't like it there. Was it because something had happened to Horace there? Because Harrison had been there and taken Horace away? But Starlight liked Harrison. They were friends. He wouldn't have minded that.

But he didn't like Corvin, so maybe part of it was Corvin's presence there. And he didn't know the other warlock.

Reg looked at Starlight and waited until he turned and looked her in the eye. The sense of unease grew. Not just a wariness, but a sense that something was very wrong.

She supposed she had done what they had gone there for. To talk to Kareem and see if he knew anything. Unfortunately, he didn't. But Reg didn't want to turn around and go home again so quickly.

She still had the gems. Maybe Kareem could help her with those.

Reg reached into the pocket of her skirt and touched the bag of gems. She looked at Starlight's blue and green eyes, remembering the lapis lazuli and turquoise among the other precious stones.

"Can I ask you something else?" Reg asked. "Changing the subject. Do you know… about gemstones in Egypt? Where they come from? Who mines them?"

Kareem blinked at her, slow and thoughtful, like a cat. "Who mines the gemstones in Egypt? What does this have to do with Hassam?"

"Nothing. Like I said, it is a change of topic. Just something that I thought I would look into while I was here."

Corvin's eyes were sharp, his attention fully on her. He hadn't sensed her intention before that. Hadn't realized that she had gone to Egypt for something other than just asking Kareem about Horace and Harrison.

"There are mines here," Kareem said slowly. "I do not know much about them. They are mostly run by large corporations. Very few are privately-owned anymore. The mining for precious stones is done by big companies."

"And where do the workers live? Are they in the city? Or do they have a camp or a village somewhere else?"

He stroked the patchy whiskers on his chin. "I do not know… they do not circulate in my circles. Why do you ask this? What do you want with miners?"

"I have… something that belongs to them. Something that I wanted to return to the rightful owners."

Corvin's consciousness was pressing against hers. She tried to push him out of her head. He wanted to know what she was talking about, what she had, what she intended to do. None of it was any of his business, and she was regretting that she had brought him with her. She hadn't thought about how he was going to behave if he found out that she had precious gemstones with her. That she hadn't gotten rid of them all on her previous mission. Corvin was just as greedy as anyone else. Though more for the power of the stones than their monetary value. Maybe he would be interested in their history as well. He liked all that history stuff.

Reg turned her head to glare at Corvin. It had always been difficult to keep him out of her mind. And now he was even more insis-
tent. He gave a slight shake of his head. Because, of course, he didn't
want to be kicked out. He wanted more information. Much more
than she intended to give him.

"I am not the right person to talk to," Kareem told her, shaking
his head. "Perhaps... I can find those who can help you. But it will
take time."

The stones were warm in Reg's hand in the pocket of her skirt.
They were eager to be returned to their rightful owners. Reg had
brought them all the way to Egypt and she hated to go back to the
US without dealing with them. The stones would not be happy if she
just turned around and took them back home.

"You're sure you don't know anyone who could help me today?"

"Tonight?" Kareem shook his head. "Everyone is closing up their
businesses and going home. That hour is past. Even if I had someone
for you to go to, I wouldn't be able to get you any help until the
morning."

"Okay. Well. If you can't, you can't, of course. I guess... maybe
I'll leave you my information, and then when you find something
out, you can call or email me?"

He shrugged.

Reg dug into her purse, moving things around to look for her
business cards. She'd had some nice ones printed when she had first
come into possession of the gems. Not the cheap paper ones printed
on a personal inkjet printer, but properly engraved cards on thick,
glossy ivory stock. They looked and felt very sophisticated.

She found the card wallet and pulled one out. She passed it over
to Kareem. It wasn't until she reached out to him with the card that
she saw the rings on her fingers. She didn't even remember putting on
the rings as she had looked through her stones and selected the ones
to bring with her to Egypt. The rings should have been in the bag in
her pocket, with the rest of the stones. She hadn't intended to put
them on.

Kareem took the card from her, but he wasn't looking at it. He
was staring down at the rings. Reg pulled back her hand and tried to

fold her fingers into a position that looked natural and that hid the rings from sight. Of course, it was too late. Kareem had already seen them.

"Where did you get those?"

"They are not mine," Reg said quickly. "I'm just holding on to them."

"No, they aren't yours," Kareem agreed, his dark eyes getting darker and more suspicious. "Where did you get them?"

Reg didn't tell him. "I am trying to find the rightful owners."

"This is not something for someone like you to do. One would need to trace the histories of those rings. Where they came from. The genealogies of the true owners. Treasures like this, taken from tombs. Wars have been fought over them. They have traveled the world as men have fought over them."

Reg nodded. "I know all that. But I can find out. I can find out where they came from and who should get them." She glanced at Corvin and then away again. "I've done it before."

"Not stones as ancient and acclaimed as these."

Reg looked down at them self-consciously. "What is the difference? It is still the same thing. They were taken out of this country and traded between people who had no right over them. I want to make that right. Bringing it back to this country is what I need to do to cleanse them."

"Simply bringing them here does not wash the blood from them! And there are thousands who could claim to be the rightful heirs to these treasures. You will never find the one person who should hold them. It needs to be carefully researched and negotiated."

Reg had hoped that it would be easier. When she had jumped with Ruan, the stones had led her directly to the mines that they had come from. It had been easy to determine that the miners should be the ones who got the stones to try to care for their families, rather than the warlords, soldiers, and politicians who would have fought over them. But she had jumped to the location she had seen Corvin in, rather than letting the Egyptian stones guide her, so she had not arrived at the right place to find the rightful heirs of the gems and jewelry.

"I will have to look into it further," Reg said. "I'm not making a decision today. Maybe when you get back to me with the name of someone who knows about mines in Egypt…"

"You cannot be allowed to take those stones back out of the country. You must leave them here. I will safeguard them until you return with more information."

Like she would let him hold the stones.

Starlight's wariness and distrust of the warlock was starting to affect Reg. It was not a safe place to leave the gems. She wouldn't have been likely to anyway, not unless she'd had some reason to believe that Kareem knew about gems and was an appropriate guardian.

Even then.

Reg looked at Corvin, warning him mentally that they would be leaving soon, and it might be in a rush rather than a carefully prepared-for jump. She made kissy sounds to call Starlight back to her and put her hand close to the floor, rubbing her fingers together to encourage him.

Starlight looked at her hand, looked her in the eyes, and then walked directly over to her. He understood why she wanted to leave that place and he agreed. That made it easier. She wouldn't have wanted to be chasing around after Starlight trying to catch him while avoiding any attempts by Kareem to keep them there. Or to keep the rings there.

Reg had the rings turned around facing her palm so that they were out of sight. She folded her fingers over into a fist and crossed her thumb over. It didn't exactly do her any good, since Kareem had already seen them, but she hoped that if he weren't looking at them, his emotions would cool. He could remember what he had seen, but if he weren't looking right at them, hopefully those feelings would be transitory and he wouldn't be drawn to the power of the stones.

Corvin stood up. "We should probably be leaving, Regina."

"Yeah. It's getting late. We'll want to get home and have some supper. I have clients coming tonight." She was babbling, pretending that it had just been an ordinary visit and that they had other things to do. She could feel Kareem's anger and outrage building. She didn't want to still be there if he blew his top and decided to act.

"You must leave the rings here," Kareem insisted again, his tone sharp. "I will keep them safe until you are able to find the correct owners."

"No. I'm not leaving them here."

Maybe it would have been wiser to keep her mouth closed instead of broadcasting her defiance. Or pretended that she would give them to him, to allow her time to get ready for the jump and not botch everything up.

But Reg had always been a little bit oppositional. She hated people telling her what to do. Even if someone told her to do something that she wanted to do, a sure way to get her not to do it was to tell her she had to. Her instinct was to push back, to refuse to do anything just because someone told her to.

Reg picked up Starlight and stood beside Corvin. She was trying to quiet her mind, to picture home and to feel it with all her senses. It was not an ideal situation. She should be calm and relaxed in order to get to that meditative place where jumping across the ocean was just as easy as breathing in and out.

Corvin put his hand on her arm. Reg breathed raggedly in, unable to close her eyes because she had to keep looking at Kareem to make sure that he couldn't reach her before she managed to jump. She couldn't take her eyes from him and focus on something else, no matter how hard she was berating herself for it. Her body's instinct for self-preservation and her knowledge of what she had to do to escape were at odds with each other.

Corvin said her name from somewhere far away and encouraged her that it would be a good time to jump. Reg breathed in and out again as Kareem came toward her threateningly.

CHAPTER THIRTY-NINE

*K*areem was an old man, but he advanced on her quickly, pushing himself up from his chair and reaching toward her. Reg threw up a psychic shield around herself to prevent him from reaching her. It surrounded the three of them—Reg, Starlight, and Corvin. The warlock got closer, as close as he could to the shield. His face was an angry scowl, tight and hard and cold.

"You are a thief! You know that which you hold is not yours! You have no right to possess them or to use their power. I command you to turn them over to me. You cannot continue to hold them. You cannot take them out of the country. This is where they belong, and you know that. Give them to me!"

Reg shook her head. She kept the shield strong around her. She had fought people much more powerful than Kareem before. He was an old warlock, not someone who was used to fighting. He wasn't an immortal or another siren. He wasn't the most powerful wizard in the world. He couldn't do anything to her while she was within the shield.

But unfortunately, neither could Reg. She couldn't switch from holding the shield in place to jumping them back home. She could only do one or the other. Corvin would not be able to perform any magic outside the shield either, to hit Kareem with a spell that would disable him so that Reg could take them out of there. She hadn't thought; she had just reacted, and now Reg wasn't sure how to get out of the situation. She couldn't do anything without dropping the shield, and she couldn't drop the shield.

She swore under her breath, and then more loudly. There had to be a way out of it. Maybe Kareem would get tired and decide it wasn't worth attacking her over. Maybe he would have a heart attack and keel over. Or a stroke. Or an anvil would fall out of the sky, through the roof of the building, onto his head and knock him out. Anything would do, she didn't really care what it was.

"Reg, maybe you could—"

"I can't do anything," Reg snapped. "If I do something other than hold the shield, then the shield will go down."

"We could walk out. If you keep the shield around us."

"Where? He's just going to follow us."

"Let's at least get out of his house."

That resonated with Reg. Get out of Kareem's house. He had more power there. He might have ways of breaking through her magic. They were guests in his house, and there were a whole bunch of rules about magic surrounding guests and what they could and couldn't do. And Reg had no idea what all the rules were and how they would pertain to her.

"Yes," she agreed curtly. "Let's do that."

Corvin tugged her backward gently. Reg let herself be pulled along, letting him guide her, while she kept her eyes glued to Kareem to make sure that he couldn't do anything without her knowing about it. She didn't know what he could do while she had the shield in place. If he were very powerful, he might still be able to break through somehow and harm them.

She heard the door open behind her, and something banged into the backs of her heels. Reg stumbled over something placed behind her. How could Corvin be so inept in guiding her?

"Your shoes," Corvin said. "Put them on."

Reg glanced down. That was what she had tripped over. He'd been trying to guide her over to them to put them back on. She couldn't see whether he had put his back on, but assumed that he had. Reg slid her feet into her shoes, carefully watching Kareem the whole time. He continued to yell at her to stop, calling her a thief and worse.

When Corvin guided her over the threshold, Reg felt a sense of relief, and a lightening around her shoulders, as if a weight had been removed. There had been some kind of magic in the house that she had been fighting against.

"You will not leave!" Kareem howled, incensed. "You will not!"

"Can you leave now?" Corvin asked.

Reg shook her head. "Not while I'm keeping him back."

"Let me do that part. I'll hold him back, you jump us."

Reg nodded.

She intended to do exactly what he had said, but she could not drop her shield. Just as she had been unable to close her eyes and not watch for danger, she couldn't drop her shield and open herself up for attack. It was like not flinching when someone punched her in the face, not sneezing when the urge hit her. A physical impossibility.

"It's okay, Reg. I'm ready."

"I can't."

Tears of frustration broke free from Reg's eyes and started to trail down her face. Starlight made a meowing, growling sound in her arms. She knew that he wanted her to release him, that he was ready to take on the crazy old warlock himself, but Reg couldn't let him go and put himself at risk.

"We go together," she murmured to him.

The rings on her hand were getting warm, she was holding them so tightly in her fist. Was she willing to do all this for a couple of rings and a small baggie of gems? She could just give up and leave them with Kareem. He would be the one who would bear the curse on the gems. Maybe he would die some horrible death, like those who had opened the tombs of kings in the past.

There was a brilliant flash of light. Reg threw her arm up in front of her eyes to shield them, still holding Starlight in her other arm. The gems of the rings turned burning hot when they met with the white light that was too bright to look at.

"Now," a quiet voice said in her head.

CHAPTER FORTY

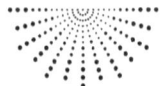

*T*hen there was silence. Reg still had her arm in front of her eyes and her lids squeezed tightly shut. Her whole body tense.

"Regina," Corvin's husky voice reached her ears. "It's okay. We're back."

Reg didn't believe it. She stood there in the darkness behind her lids for a time, listening to every tiny sound. She wanted to believe Corvin, but she didn't dare. She stood there, holding tightly to her shield, until Starlight squirmed to be put down.

She finally opened her eyes. She was in the space between her kitchen and living room, near the front door. It was her cottage. There were still objects scattered around the floor where the cats had knocked them down during the night. She hadn't yet bothered to pick them up.

"What happened?"

She turned to look at Corvin, who was still positioned behind her, as he had been as he led her backward out of the house. He jerked his chin toward the kitchen. Reg turned the other way to look into the kitchen and saw Harrison standing there. He absently stroked Horace's midnight black fur as the cat wandered around the top of the kitchen island sniffing at Reg's appointment book and being the king of the castle.

"Uncle Harrison? What are you doing here?"

Harrison raised his brows. He didn't seem as pleasant and amused as usual. "What were you doing in the land of the ancients?"

"Egypt?"

He just looked at her, waiting for the answer. Reg tried to come up with a logical explanation that wouldn't make it sound like she suspected him of doing anything wrong.

"I was just… I wanted to talk to Horace's owner," Reg nodded to the cat. "See if I could find out why he was unhappy there. If we need to find a new home for him, then I should make sure it is somewhere he'll like better, right?"

"I told you he did not like it there. He likes it here."

"Yes, you told me that. But he's not going to stay here. I already have a cat."

"People can have two cats."

"Yes, I know. But I have enough to do with just one. That's enough responsibility for me. We need to find someone else who will take him."

Harrison twirled the ends of his long, thin mustache.

"You should have stayed here with him."

"I was doing what I thought was best. You didn't say I had to stay here with him."

Harrison rolled his eyes. "Reg Rawlins does not stay when she is told to stay."

"Well… no, that's true." He was probably right. If he had told her to stay in the house to look after Horace and not to go anywhere else, especially back to Egypt, that was probably exactly where she would have gone.

Harrison nodded his agreement. "Now I must make sure you stay," he told her. "And do not go back there."

"I am not going to go back."

He stood there looking at her. Reg felt the rings, warm on her fingers, and looked down at them. She wouldn't go back to Egypt? She had to go back to take care of the gems and the rings. But she wouldn't go back to Kareem's house. She would go where the gems took her. To the mines or the people who should rightfully possess them. That was different.

"I'm not going back to see Kareem. I won't see him again."

"You do not know what you meddle with."

"I'm not meddling! Okay... maybe I *was* meddling, but I'm sorry. I didn't mean to cause any trouble, just to find out what was going on. What happened with Horace? You could explain it to me. Then I wouldn't have any reason to go back there."

Harrison shook his head. "He wants to live here."

"What happened to Destine? The piece of him that was bound to Horace?"

Harrison petted Horace. He held Horace's head to scratch his ears and kissed him on the top of the head. He didn't tell Reg what had happened to the part of the Witch Doctor that had been bound to the kattakyn.

"You will take care of him? Do not take him back to the warlock."

Reg didn't say anything. She wouldn't take Horace back to Kareem, but she would not promise to take care of him, either.

Harrison gave Horace one final ear scratch, then vanished. Reg looked around to make sure that he was really gone.

"Immortals," she said to Corvin in a light voice, as if it were something funny instead of something that frustrated the heck out of her. "Can't live with 'em..."

"He transported us from Egypt?"

Reg nodded. "It wasn't me. Like I said, I couldn't do that while I was trying to maintain the shield."

"You should have jumped before that. Before there was a danger."

"I didn't know."

"You shouldn't have gone there in the first place. I told you it wasn't a good idea."

"I needed to see if I could find something out from Kareem. Harrison clearly isn't putting all his cards on the table."

"No," Corvin agreed, looking over at Horace and the space Harrison had occupied. "But I think there would have been wiser approaches."

Reg shrugged. "I don't know where else I could have gone. Harrison and Kareem are the only ones who know what happened."

Corvin looked at the cat. "And Horace."

Reg considered that. "I guess so. But what is he going to tell me?"

"I don't know. You're the one who can communicate with these creatures."

"Well… not exactly. I mean, I can on a certain level, and I can see their auras or feel what they are feeling. But it isn't like with people… with words."

"Words are a very limited means of communication."

It was true. Reg could read far more from someone's face and actions and by their feelings and their unconscious psychic communication. But words were still preferable for some things. She knew when Starlight was hungry or tired or wanted to play games, but she wasn't so good at figuring out what he was thinking about or what his opinion was on different subjects.

"I don't know. Maybe there is something I can learn from him," she admitted. "But I'm feeling kind of out of sorts now. I don't think it's a good time for me to try to read him."

Corvin nodded. "It's been an interesting day."

Reg looked around. She was, once again, alone in the house with Corvin. She needed to get him on his way before he started getting ideas.

They had jumped from Corvin's house, so she needed to either drive him home, jump him home, or make him order an Uber or find another way to get home.

Corvin's eyes glittered, and she thought he sensed that she was trying to get rid of him. His gazed dropped to the rings on her fingers. "So are you going to tell me about those?"

Reg shrugged. "You already know about those. They're some of the gems that I'm trying to deal with."

Corvin gazed at her, considering the information. "You didn't tell me there were any set pieces. I thought it was all just loose gems. The gems that you showed me."

"There were a few more that I didn't show you."

"Any more jewelry?"

"I don't think I need to give you all the details."

"Of course they are your treasure, but it is curious... that you would show me some of them and leave these two pieces out. Two powerful rings like that. I would think they would be the first pieces that you would want to cleanse, to either use them for yourself or find a buyer."

"I figured it would be easier to liquidate the loose gems. Quieter. Not draw as much attention to myself."

"Well, that is true. You certainly attracted some attention today, wearing those when we went on our little trip." His eyes slitted halfway shut, like a cat sitting in the sun. "What was your reason for wearing them to Egypt? You wanted to see what the reaction to them was?"

"No. I forgot I had them. I was looking at them... and I just put them on my finger when I had to answer the phone. Then later when I put the rest away, I forgot they were there. Until I handed Kareem that business card, they completely slipped my mind."

Reg gazed down at the beautiful rings. Turned the right way around and no longer held in the middle of her fist, they were not as warm as they had been. But they did seem to have a glow and an aura that they hadn't before. They had seemed mild before. Pretty, certainly valuable, but not something that spoke to her. Now, they were completely different. The two rings demanded her attention, pulsed with a magic that made her want to examine them and find out their names and their purpose. These were not rings that someone had picked up at a Middle Eastern bazaar.

"I didn't know they were so powerful."

"Maybe they were dormant before. I didn't sense them before you showed them to Kareem. But now..." Corvin stared at the rings, apparently able to sense their power the same as Reg did. "Now it is unmistakable."

Reg rubbed her thumb over the face of each ring. "You think I activated them by taking them with me to Egypt? Ruan said before that some of the gems were at rest, but that they could become activated later, and I should deal with them before that happened. So that I wouldn't suffer the ill effects of the curses."

"I think that ship has sailed," Corvin confirmed.

Reg sighed. It wasn't easy trying to deal with the gems. She had thought that she would have all the time she needed. The gems had been dormant for a long time, maybe years or decades or even centuries. As long as they stayed asleep, she would be okay. Now her timeline was apparently sped up by quite a bit.

"Well… that's a problem for another day. I should get you home and get ready for my evening appointments."

"I thought that your comment to Kareem about having appointments this evening was a lie. You left clients scheduled for tonight when you didn't know what would happen in Egypt?"

Of course she hadn't. She didn't know whether she would have to stay overnight to deal with the gems, as she had before, so she had rescheduled her appointments for that day. But it was time to get Corvin home.

"Do you mind if I try jumping you there?" she asked, then held up her hand. "No jokes about that, please, I don't know how else to say it."

Corvin smirked. "If you are not too tired, then of course, feel free to take me home. I'd love to have company."

"I'm not staying." Reg didn't want to hold hands with Corvin, so she touched him on the shoulder and thought about his house. She focused on the sights and sounds and smells, the whole feel of the place. She opened her eyes, and they were still standing in her cottage.

CHAPTER FORTY-ONE

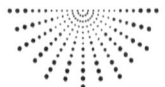

*C*orvin looked at Reg. "Anytime."

Reg frowned. "I thought… I was trying. Why didn't it work?"

He shook his head. "Maybe jumping twice in one day is all you can manage? You did expend a lot of power today."

"No…" Reg considered the way that her body and brain felt. She was a little tired, but not so much that she couldn't still perform.

Except that she couldn't.

"It must be something else," she murmured.

Corvin considered. "I could try boosting your power. You might be tireder than you think."

Without waiting for her to agree or object, he raised his hands and held them close to her without touching. Reg could feel the heat coming from him, filling her body with strength and vitality. She tried again, closing her eyes and picturing Corvin's house.

When she opened her eyes, she was still in her own house.

"Maybe it's because it is unfamiliar," Corvin suggested. "You've only been inside once. Maybe that isn't enough."

"I can jump places I've never been before," Reg pointed out. "I should be able to go back to your house without a problem."

She kept her eyes open, staring into Corvin's face and seeing and smelling and sensing everything about him. If she couldn't jump to his house by picturing the house, she should certainly be able to get there by filling her senses with Corvin. She'd been able to jump based on the almost indistinguishable smell of the stones when she had jumped with Ruan.

She still seemed stuck to the kitchen of the cottage.

"Try holding hands. Skin-to-skin contact," Corvin suggested.

Reg grimaced, but she took his hand anyway. It was strong and warm and her hand seemed to fit into it exactly, as if their hands had been made for each other. Reg resisted flinching at the electricity that buzzed between them and tried not to be taken in by his charms. The heady smell of roses rolled off of him, as he was clearly affected by her touch just as much as she was by him. Or else he was trying very hard to seduce her. Which, of course, wouldn't be surprising.

Skin-to-skin contact was proving to be more distracting than focusing. Reg pulled back from him.

"That's not working."

Corvin looked down at her hand as she let go. "The rings."

"The rings? But I was wearing them before and they didn't stop me."

"But now they have been activated. And removed from Egypt, which Kareem told you not to do. Maybe they are blocking you from taking them any farther."

Reg slowly took the rings off and pushed them down into the bottom of one of the pockets of her skirt, ensuring that they wouldn't fall out the minute she sat down. She put her hand on Corvin's arm once more and tried again.

Still, nothing.

How could it be nothing? There should at least be some sign. Some feeling. Even just a twinge. But there was nothing. Reg couldn't seem to move at all.

She shifted her feet experimentally, just to reassure herself that she wasn't pasted to the floor. She could still get from one place to another the old-fashioned way. Maybe Corvin would have to grab an Uber.

"I'm going to… put the rings away. Maybe if they're in the other room, in the jewelry box…"

Corvin nodded. She could feel his eyes on her all the way to the bedroom, hot on her neck, giving her goosebumps. She hurried into the bedroom and shut the door to keep his eyes off of her. She got out the chest of jewels and transferred the rings and the baggie of gems she had taken to Egypt back to the small wooden box. She took advantage of the time alone to slow her breathing.

The only problem was that she was distracted by what had happened in Egypt. Her powers were still all intact. It was just a matter of focus.

Starlight scratched at the door. He wasn't used to her shutting him out of the bedroom, except in the morning when she was still sleeping and he thought it was time to order breakfast. The rest of the time, all the doors in the cottage were always open.

Reg opened the door. Starlight sat looking up at her. He meowed loudly.

"Do you want to help me?" Reg asked.

Starlight was always a big help when she needed to concentrate on something or to extend her abilities. Corvin had given her more strength, but he was still a distraction himself. With Starlight to help her to focus, the jump to Corvin's house would be no problem at all.

"Thanks," Reg told Starlight. She picked him up and walked back over to Corvin. "Okay." She forced a cheerful smile. "I can do this now."

Corvin nodded.

Reg put her hand on his arm again and focused her being on Corvin's house. She remembered all the details she could of his furnishings, the smell of the place, Corvin's presence there. It was that easy.

Reg opened her eyes. She still hadn't moved.

* * *

She and Corvin looked at each other for a long time.

If it wasn't fatigue keeping Reg there, and it wasn't the rings of power or her distraction...

"Harrison said that he would have to keep you here," Corvin offered.

Reg swore. Yes, he had. She hadn't picked up on it, thinking that he was just telling her that she needed to stay put. That she needed to listen to him. She hadn't thought about his actually forcing her to stay there by preventing her from using her gifts to jump herself somewhere else. For all he knew, she could go straight back to Egypt again. And he'd decided he didn't want her investigating what he had done to Horace.

"Harrison!"

She looked around, but he didn't appear. Reg walked back to the bedroom to look for him, and checked the bathroom and the spare room, sure that he must be there somewhere. He came when she called. He had to be there somewhere.

But he wasn't. He didn't answer her call.

"This is crazy." Reg strode to the front door and opened it. She stood there, looking out at the pathway and the vegetation around her door.

"Not out there?" Corvin asked.

"I wasn't looking to see if he was out here. I was opening it to see whether I could..." Reg trailed off. It was a lovely day outside. Birds chirping, the sun low in the sky but the temperature still pleasant.

"What is it?" Corvin asked, his voice low, as he came up behind Reg.

Reg turned to look at him. "I can't leave."

"I know."

"No, I mean... even walking away. I can't leave the house."

"You can't physically step out of the house?"

"No."

He eyed her, expecting her to demonstrate. Reg didn't move.

"Is it like a force field?" Corvin asked.

"No, not like there's a barrier there. Just... I can't leave. I can't step out."

Corvin gave her a little push from behind. Reg stumbled forward, just an inch or two, not over the threshold. She turned to face him, blazing hot fury erupting.

"Don't *ever* do that!"

Corvin stepped back in surprise, putting his hands up defensively. "Regina, I was just seeing if—"

"You lay your hands on me or push me again and you're going to regret it!"

Corvin's cloak was suddenly engulfed in flames. Corvin yelped and struggled to quickly pull it off. He threw it on the floor and stomped out the fire.

Reg could have kept it burning. She could have made the fire larger and larger until it completely obliterated Corvin. She didn't have to put up with his bullying her or physically laying hands on her. But she let him stomp out the small fire and breathed slowly, trying her best not to reignite it.

Corvin glared at Reg, but she could see his surprise through the outrage. Reg hadn't lit him on fire since he had appeared before the tribunal. That had been before Davyn had taken her on and taught her how to manage her fire. She hadn't even believed back then that she was the one lighting the fires, though she had found the timing to be very propitious and his reactions quite satisfying.

"Don't ever do that again," Reg repeated, in a calmer voice.

"I hear you."

"You'd better."

They circled each other like dancers, watching each other and synchronizing their movements.

"So you can't leave," Corvin observed.

"No."

"He didn't say that *I* had to stay here."

Even so, Corvin made no movement for the door.

"Go then," Reg said.

"If I leave, I might not be able to return, and if you need my help..."

"I don't need your help." And she would make sure that he couldn't return. Harrison shouldn't have brought him into Reg's cottage to begin with. She had wards against intruders, and against

Corvin in particular. There was a reason for that. Harrison should have respected those boundaries. If he felt he had to transport them from Egypt, he could have returned them both to Corvin's house. Or to the garden. Or somewhere else he had seen the two of them together. He shouldn't have brought Corvin into her sanctuary.

Corvin still looked uncertain about leaving.

"Go ahead," Reg encouraged.

Corvin stepped past her and over the threshold of the door. He looked back at her as if to see whether she would follow him or if he had gone far enough.

"Should I go for help?"

"Who would you get? Who is going to be able to break Harrison's spell?"

"We don't know if we don't try."

Reg shrugged. "I don't know. I assume he'll come back, and I can talk him into releasing me…"

"If he's not coming when you call him…"

"He'll get bored sooner or later, won't he? He doesn't usually stay gone for long if I need him."

"What if he is going after the other kattakyns?"

Reg's heart sank. That was what they had been trying to stop. She had half-forgotten why they had gone to Egypt in the first place due to the attack by Kareem. Or maybe Harrison had made her forget as well as sealing her into her house.

Reg thought about all the fairy tales where princesses were locked away in towers or dungeons. Those fun, romantic stories. When she had played as a child, she'd always been the knight coming to save the woman from her prison. She'd never wanted to be the princess.

"We need to stop him. But how are we going to do that if he won't even answer when I call him?"

"What does Francesca think?"

"She was going to call the other kattakyn owners. See if he had been around."

"Have you called her to see how that went?"

"No." Reg patted her pockets for her phone. "I guess I should do that."

Corvin tried to walk back into the cottage and was unable to step through the doorway. He looked at Reg. "Invite me in."

"I thought you were going to go home."

"Not yet. I'll stick around and help you to sort this out."

Reg found her phone and tapped to find Francesca's number. "I don't need you to stay here. You can go home and you can call if there is anything to tell me."

"Invite me in and we can at least see what Francesca has to say."

Reg tapped her phone, ignoring the request. Corvin was left standing on the doorstep while she placed the call.

"Reg, where have you been?" Francesca answered the phone immediately. "I have been calling you!"

"Sorry, I was away for a while."

"You need to keep your phone on! This is important work."

"I know. I just… had to go do some checking myself. And I guess I was out of cell range." Reg changed the topic before Francesca could continue on this line. "I wanted to know whether you were able to find anything out. From the other owners of the kattakyns."

"I did not reach the dwarfs, but otherwise… he has been to see *all* of them."

Reg tried to process this. "Harrison has been to see all the kattakyn owners?" she said aloud, relaying the information to Corvin. He looked grim.

"Yes," Francesca agreed.

"Has he… done anything? Taken them away or…"

"The only one he took away was Horace."

"And are they all still bound?" Reg worried at the problem even before Francesca answered. "That is the main thing, isn't it? If he just went to visit them, that's one thing, but if he loosed the parts of the Witch Doctor, if he is trying to restore Destine…"

"The other owners did not say there were any changes to the personalities of the other kattakyns or to their abilities. They are all witches and warlocks who should have noticed the difference, if there was a change."

"You don't sound sure."

Francesca sighed. "I am worried," she agreed. "It is very bad, the immortal going to see all of them. He knows where they all are. If he wants to restore Destine…"

"We need to stop him."

"You must talk to him. You said that you would."

"Well… I have talked to him, but… things didn't go very well."

"You must try again. Until you are able to convince him."

"You are the charmer, maybe you should try to talk to him."

Francesca considered this. "He does not know me like he knows you. He is your protector. It is not the same with someone like me, who he does not care about."

Reg sometimes wondered whether Harrison really did care about her, or whether he just liked to play that role on occasion. Until now, he had never done anything to harm her, but if he had changed his methods and was now going to lock her up to prevent her from doing anything to derail his plans, then she had to reconsider.

"But you could charm him. I don't have that ability."

"We would have to find a way for me to see him. And the last time… he just sent me home."

"I've called to him, but he hasn't come. I don't know where he is." Reg looked at Corvin. "Maybe with the dwarfs. Maybe I should call them to see… find out what's going on out there."

"I didn't know how to get them," Francesca said. "You are the contact with the dwarfs."

"Okay… I guess I'll call them. And maybe…" Reg shook her head. "I don't know *what* I'm going to do about Harrison."

CHAPTER FORTY-TWO

*R*eg hung up the call with Francesca, the knot in her stomach growing tighter and heavier.

"What am I going to do? He's really doing this, isn't he? He's going to resurrect the Witch Doctor!" She tried to keep the feeling of panic from overwhelming her. "How could he? I told him it was dangerous. I told him he couldn't do that."

"You can't expect an immortal to listen to you and believe that you know better than he does."

Reg breathed out heavily and shook her head. She raised her phone and opened the contacts.

Brimir or Gwythr?

Brimir might be higher in the kingdom's hierarchy, able to make decisions over anything his father gave him authority over. But it was Gwythr who had taken Nico in and was in charge of him. He seemed to be the one who was helping to prepare the dwarfs for war against Harrison. He probably had the on-the-ground knowledge of what was going on in the mountain.

Reg tried to relax the clenched muscles in her shoulders and stomach. She tapped Gwythr's name.

"Put it on speaker," Corvin suggested.

Reg hit the button before Gwythr answered.

"Reg Rawlins," Gwythr's voice boomed from the speaker. Reg turned the volume down.

"Gwythr. Hi. I wondered… how things are going there. I hadn't heard from you, so I assume that… no one came to see Nico."

"I should probably have contacted you earlier," Gwythr said, his voice grave.

Reg groaned. "Oh, no. What happened?"

"One of the ancient ones."

She gulped. "Harrison?"

"I do not know how he is known to humans. To the dwarfs, he is known as Far."

"Has he done anything? Did he try to take Nico?"

"He has seen Nico, but he has not taken him away. We would not allow this."

Reg wasn't sure how they would stop him if they tried. Not when Harrison could transport himself, Nico, or anyone in the dwarf mountain at any time. They could go to battle against him, and maybe their mages and sorcerers would be able to do something to shield Nico from him, but Reg wasn't confident about it. She and Corvin had fought an immortal. That was why they were so averse to Harrison allowing the Witch Doctor to re-form.

"What did he do? Did he… did anything change? Nico is very special."

"We know he is special," Gwythr agreed. "He is a warrior cat."

"And Harrison—Far—he didn't… change anything about Nico? Take that fire away from him?"

Gwythr's voice was very serious. "No, Reg Rawlins. He has not harmed the cat."

Reg blew her breath out. Horace was the only one, then. If she and Francesca were to believe what all the kattakyn owners told them, then Horace was the only one that Harrison had unbound. Why? And why had he brought him back to Reg?

"So everything is okay?" Reg asked. "Truly? You have not had to fight?"

"We are ready if he comes back. We will not let down our guard."

"He's not there right now?"

"No. Not now. Earlier today. But then he said he had to go see you."

Was that when he had rescued Reg from Kareem? "Okay. Thanks. I appreciate it."

"And Reg Rawlins is well? She has not had any trouble with Far?"

"Well..." Reg didn't feel like telling Gwythr that she had effectively been grounded. Harrison would be back. He would release her, and they would forget all about what had happened. "We have had some problems with him. One of Nico's litter mates... It appears that Far took something from him."

"His fire?" Gwythr demanded, returning to their earlier conversation.

"Well, it wasn't exactly fire in Horace's case, but yes. He took away part of him that... made him who he was. And we don't understand why."

"He is not there now?"

"Harrison? I mean, Far? No. He's not here now. But he could come back. I've been trying to get him to come back. I really need to talk to him."

And for him to release her from her house so that she could go other places if she needed to. Even though Reg didn't have anywhere to go at that moment, she couldn't help feeling trapped. Staying in her house when she wanted to was far different from staying in her house because she had to. Because some being had decided to keep her there against her will.

Reg made excuses to Gwythr and terminated the call.

"Can I come in, Reg?" Corvin asked.

Reg shook her head. "No. Um... you should go home, I guess. We need to figure things out, but I don't think there's any point in you staying here."

Besides the fact that she couldn't trust him if she let him back in, of course. Which Corvin knew full well was the reason she didn't invite him back in and let him past the wards.

"Reg, we can work together much better if you let me in."

"No."

Reg closed her eyes, frustrated. Sooner or later, he was going to have to figure out that she would not give in and he would leave in a snit. And that was fine with her.

When she opened her eyes, she was seeing sparklers. She put her hand on the door frame to steady herself, worried that she was going to pass out. The flashes of light did not clear, but multiplied. Until they started to gather, coalescing to become a recognizable figure.

"Orri."

CHAPTER FORTY-THREE

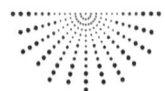

*C*orvin's eyes were wide, fixed on Orri as he materialized out of thin air. And fireflies.

"Your elf," he murmured.

"Yeah." Reg nodded. Although she was tired of Orri's appearances and bumbling around, she was a little proud that the elf had chosen her and that she had seen something so rare not just once, but multiple times. "My harbinger. *Orri.*"

Orri turned and saw Reg. "Reg Rawlins. I am here to give you—"

"A warning. I know."

He shook his head. "No. To give you assistance."

"Assistance." Reg blinked, surprised. "Assistance with what?"

"You are trapped? You are unable to get free from here?"

"Yes. How did you know?"

Orri nodded. He stroked his beard, and fireflies flew out from it. "I can help you."

"How?" Corvin demanded. "She cannot leave this house. She has already tried to leave, both by teleportation and by walking out."

Orri looked at Corvin. He gave a brief bow, and turned back to Reg. He indicated Corvin with his eyes and murmured so low that Reg could barely hear him.

"...fair of face..." Reg heard.

"I know." She told him. "I've already been warned."

Orri gave a nod. He reached a hand toward her. "Do you wish it?"

"Wish... what?"

"Do you go with me?"

"Yes, please, if you can get me out of here."

"Which direction do you wish to go?"

Reg was a little worried about his use of the word "wish." She had a certain aversion to the word, and he kept using it.

"What direction? Just... outside, I guess. I can get my car and go where I want, or I can jump. Whatever, as long as I'm not stuck inside."

"There are only two directions to go," Orri explained patiently. "Forward and back."

Forward and back? How could there only be two directions? Orri wasn't a train engine. Forward would take her through the doorway, so she supposed that was the direction she wanted to go. She nodded toward it.

"Forward."

Orri nodded. He put his hand on her arm. It didn't give her a buzz like when Corvin touched her, but it did feel very comforting. The elves had helped to heal Starlight when he had been sick, and maybe it was just her remembrance of that event that made her feel warm and comforted to have him touching her. Or maybe it was because of magic and healing in his touch. It soothed away the knotted muscles and nauseated stomach, so that she could feel calm and focused. Like a new person.

She saw the lights start to glow around Orri and around her. They seemed to be flying away from her, as if both she and Orri were dissolving into fireflies. Like a lit sparkler. She saw Corvin watching, eyes wide. And then he was gone.

For a long time, Reg felt as though she was suspended in space. In a nowhere place, where time did not pass, where she did not exist and neither did anything else. She couldn't sit and wait there, because there was nowhere to sit and nothing to wait for. Eventually, she started feeling her body. She could again see the fireflies and other brightly lit bugs swarming around her and Orri. They gathered in until they were all gone, and it was just her and Orri standing in the garden outside Reg's cabin.

Corvin coughed and cleared his throat. Reg looked around Orri and saw him.

"It worked!" she told him the obvious. "Why could you get me out of there when I couldn't jump myself out?" she asked Orri.

His raised his brows. "Because you were attempting to move through space."

"You moved us through space."

Orri shook his head. "I moved you through time and space." He looked back at the cottage, with the door standing open. "Janus did not prevent you from moving through time."

"Well, the joke's on him, I guess. Francesca says it's JAY-nus, by the way. Not Janice."

Orri shrugged. "Human pronunciation."

"Well, maybe I would have figured it out faster if you used human pronunciations. Or maybe if you didn't talk like a fortune cookie at all and just gave warnings straight out in normal human language. You could do that, couldn't you?"

"The rules are very exact."

"And you have to talk that way? You're not allowed to just give me a warning in plain language?"

"Your people and mine do not speak the same way," Orri told her slowly, obviously picking his words with great care. "Human language is very... blunt."

"Yeah. And that's the way we like it." Reg moved to the side so that she could see both Corvin and Orri. "So... I'm out. What should I do? Jump to the dwarf mountain?"

"Harrison isn't there. Your friend said that he had already left," Corvin pointed out.

"But he could go back. He didn't come back here. He didn't go to Francesca's. I don't think he would go back to Egypt; he already brought Horace back. It would help if he had actually told us what he was doing! Maybe we could help him, if it isn't something that wouldn't enable the Witch Doctor to re-form. I'd at least be able to predict where he might be."

"Do you know where he is?" Reg asked Orri. "Janus?"

"He has been here," Orri said. "And will be here soon. He will come back here."

Reg swore. She wanted to know what he was doing, but she didn't want him returning and finding her free again. What was the point in Orri releasing her if she was just going to be locked up again?

"We need to get out of here then."

There was a noise from the other side of the fence, the front yard of the big house. Reg thought at first that it was a caterwaul, it sounded so weird and otherworldly. Not like the noise that anything human would make. All three of them turned toward the noise, curious.

"What the heck is that?" Reg asked.

"Your other friend," Orri said, giving her a bow. "The other of the ancients."

"The other... who? Weston?"

"I do not know the human names."

Reg walked the path to the front gate. The back yard was protected from intruders by wards Sarah had set. There were beings who could get past it, obviously, Orri and Harrison, to name two. She wasn't sure why Weston could not get through it and Harrison could. Weston had been able to appear to her in the cabin before. But maybe he had approached the wrong way. Maybe he had to appear to her inside the cottage, not to approach it from outside. Or maybe he was prevented because of whatever Harrison had done to keep her there. Some kind of sealing power.

But the figure she saw outside the front gate was not Weston. Nor was it Harrison.

It was Kareem.

CHAPTER FORTY-FOUR

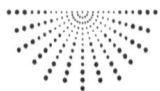

"*W*hat are you doing here?" Reg demanded. "How did you know…?"

"You invited me to contact you," Kareem reminded her. "If I knew anything about Hassam and your friend."

"Yes…"

"You gave me your card."

But Reg's address was not on her card. Her address was not published anywhere. She did give it out to clients when they made contact and wanted to set up a seance or reading, but she kept it off public records.

"How did you find me here?" Reg demanded again. "You didn't get my address from my card. And you didn't fly here on an airplane."

Orri had referred to him as another ancient. Was Kareem one of the immortals? If he was, then why hadn't Harrison explained that part to Reg?

"So… is that why Harrison took Horace away?" she asked aloud, following the series of thoughts. "Because he knew you were an immortal and you could take the part of the Witch Doctor from Horace?"

"You are a fool," Kareem sneered. "You still have no idea what it is going on. Even after activating the rings, you have no clue."

"I… haven't had much time," Reg explained. It was a lame excuse even in her ears. She was creative. She could come up with a lot better than that.

Corvin was thinking more quickly on his feet. He hadn't had to expend energy in maintaining a psychic shield and jumping halfway around the world and back. Of course he figured it out before Reg.

"Harrison went to see all the kattakyns, but the only one he took was yours. The only one that had been unbound."

Kareem rolled his eyes. He was an ugly man. An ugly man with an ugly attitude. Reg could tell him why it was he didn't have any friends. "You think I would not recognize the essence of an immortal when it was right in front of me? Rubbing against me every day?"

Reg pressed her fingertips to her temples. "*You* were the one who released the piece of the Witch Doctor from Horace? Why would you do that?"

"Why would I ignore that kind of power? I have lived many lifetimes longer than you, and this was my chance to increase my power. And now I know there are others. I only need to find them."

His eyes glittered and Reg followed his sight line to Starlight, who had apparently come out of the house when the door was left open. She tried to step between the two of them.

"Starlight does not have any of the pieces of the Witch Doctor. He's just a regular cat."

"A regular cat," Kareem scoffed. "There is no such thing as a regular cat. And *he* certainly is not one. Do you think I don't have vision?"

Sarah had shown Reg how to see the light around powerful objects, and Reg had been startled by the brightness around Starlight. She shouldn't have been, of course; more than one person had told her that he was powerful. But it was hard to understand sometimes that her cat was something other than a fuzzy little foot warmer who demanded fish.

She knew some of Starlight's history now. Maybe Kareem was hoping to take his power too.

"He is not one of the kattakyns," she told Kareem firmly. "The kattakyns are all pure black—"

Corvin nudged Reg. She scowled at him, turning to rebuke him for bothering her when she was trying to take control of the situation. He met her eyes, his consciousness burrowing into her brain, communicating with her as clearly as he could.

You are saying too much.

Reg opened her mouth to argue that she hadn't told Kareem anything he didn't already know. But maybe she was wrong. Maybe he was only guessing about the other kattakyns. Or maybe he knew that the Witch Doctor had gone out into several objects, but didn't know that they were all kattakyns. Maybe he didn't even know they were kattakyns, and had thought that they were just regular cats.

Except he said there was no such thing as a regular cat.

Instead of keeping her mouth shut, Reg had told him that there were others and had given him a basic description.

How do we get him out of here? Reg asked Corvin in her mind.

He shrugged with one shoulder.

Reg turned her attention back to Kareem. The wards that were set against intruders would not last forever. Especially if Kareem was stronger than Sarah. And if he were as old as he said he was and had acquired part of the Witch Doctor's power from Horace, then she needed to act while she was still able instead of waiting until he could break through the barriers and take them down one at a time.

"Why don't you go back to Egypt?" Reg told him. "There isn't anything for you here. I only have Starlight and Horace, and you already took Horace's power. So you might as well just go back to where you came from."

"You think yourself powerful. But you do not have the strength to fight me. Even in Egypt, still wearing the rings, you were barely able to hold me off. Now you have removed the rings..." He shook his head. "Why would you take them off instead of wielding their power?"

Reg looked sideways at Corvin. It was at his suggestion that she had taken them off. Now they were put away in the cottage. It didn't exactly make sense for her to run back into the house, dig under her bed for the chest, open it, and recover the rings from the plastic bag that held all the jewels from Egypt. It would take too much time and she would look foolish in front of Kareem. She needed to look as though she knew what she was doing, that she had a reason for everything she did, not that she was ignorant of the fact that she should have kept the rings on.

"I don't need the power of the rings," she told him confidently. "Not in my own country. I will save them for the day that I require them. There is no point in wasting their power." She lifted her chin so that she was looking down her nose at Kareem. Not saying *no point in wasting their power on you,* even though that was what she intended to convey.

"You witch!" Kareem yelled. He kicked the fence and he held up his hands in front of the open gate, working on the wards that kept him from entering there. "You unschooled, incompetent witch! You don't have what it takes to fight someone like me! Not even with the rings!"

Reg could feel the power of his magic against the wards. She and Sarah had worked on them together, since the yard was their joint domain and Reg needed to be trained in the most basic of crafts. It felt as if someone were pushing her in the chest, forcing her back.

Reg hated being bullied. Hated the feeling of being overpowered. She had been in that position too many times as she grew up. Surrounded by people with greater physical strength, more authority, more experience, and more violence inside them. She'd been pushed around and abused enough times as a child and had sworn that it would never happen to her as an adult.

And here she was, taking it. Waiting for Kareem to break down her wards and invade her space. She wouldn't be able to stop him from hurting her, from trying to take Starlight's power. She would stand there, helpless, while he took everything that mattered to her.

"No," she said firmly. Her face was as tight and frozen as a mask. "You cannot enter here. You cannot do any harm here."

CHAPTER FORTY-FIVE

"*H*ow do you think you're going to stop me?" Kareem challenged. "What do you think you're going to do, *little girl?*"

Reg's anger flared. She was having trouble focusing her thoughts and keeping herself under control. That was how the Witch Doctor had addressed her. He remembered her from when she was small and she could do nothing to stop him from torturing and killing her mother.

And now he remembered her and the others challenging him in the warehouse, taking the immortal and his draugar minions on with their tiny force.

Little girl.

Reg hated to be called a little girl.

She wasn't that four-year-old child anymore. She had learned of her power and had been training and developing it. She had helped to defeat the Witch Doctor once already. She had also challenged Weston openly, and she and Corvin and her younger self had overcome him and forced him to leave Norma Jean and her child alone. She had overcome others who thought that she was a weak child or woman.

Being underestimated was one of her gifts. Like a mother bird pretending to be injured to lead a predator away, and then flying up in his face and leaving him far behind. She could use it to her advantage. *Appearing* to be weak wasn't the same as *being* weak.

Reg closed her eyes. They were swimming with tears, but not tears of distress or fear. Tears of anger. There was so much rage bubbling up inside her over the injustices she had suffered as a child and now faced again that she could not contain it. It had to get out somehow.

Kareem laughed.

"You are a child. Picking up rings of power as if they were baubles. Playing dress-up in vestments that are too powerful for you to even understand. You will fall here."

Reg opened her eyes. He had transformed. She was aware that it was only a trick of her mind, that he hadn't actually physically transformed, but she could see the Witch Doctor in front of her now, mocking and challenging, ignoring the fact that she had helped to overcome him once before. She could see the immortal's face superimposed over Kareem's features. Her mouth twisted into a grimace of pain and fury both at once.

"Stop! I am not weak. I'm stronger than you ever were, in all the centuries you have lived." She spat the words out, her inner convictions taking over. Her brain was still trying to sort and correlate all her scattered thoughts and impressions. "You cannot enter. You cannot find any more of the kattakyns. You have overestimated your own powers and have expended more than you should have."

She fought back against him, pushing back against the force on her chest. The fire inside her was raging to get out. Unable to contain it any longer, Reg released it. The Egyptian's cloak was in flames. He angrily shook his head and tried to pat out the fire.

"You think I'm afraid of a little party trick?" he demanded. "You don't have anything on me!"

"I do!" Reg argued, her voice strained as she tried to keep herself under control. "You are the one who doesn't know what he is dealing with."

"You think I can't fight a little girl?" Kareem's eyes went over the others. "And her little kitty cat? You think that this fallen warlock and bumbling harbinger can help you? They can't do anything. And neither can you."

"You've already lost. We've already beaten you once before. In fact," Reg looked at Orri, "we've already beaten you today, haven't we?"

Orri put on his dark glasses as if he would be able to see Kareem better with them on. He looked at his wrist, where he didn't wear a wristwatch, but a wide brass bracelet sparkled in the sun, nearly dazzling Reg.

"Yes," Orri agreed. "The child will prevail."

"No, she won't!" Kareem screamed. "You are *nothing* to me! My power is beyond anything you have ever encountered!"

"Isn't it the same thing I have encountered before?" Reg argued, "just one-ninth of the power?"

"No!" Kareem insisted "You cannot do anything to me! You have no idea of my power!"

Reg faced him, determined. He couldn't extinguish the flaming cloak, and eventually tore it away from himself and threw it down.

"Watch out," Corvin intoned. "She'll have your jacket next."

"Tricks," Kareem insisted. "You think that a few sparklers are going to scare me?"

"Sparklers?" Reg looked at the cloak on the ground, nearly consumed, and made it flare up, forcing the warlock to step back despite himself. Reg wanted to burn everything around him, but it was Sarah's yard, and she would not be very happy if Reg burned her trees, bushes, and fence to the ground just to prove a point.

She stepped toward the open gate. Corvin put his hand on her arm to stop her. "Regina..."

"You really think this guy can stop me? He can't even get past the wards."

Reg stepped through the barrier that prevented Kareem from entering the yard, feeling herself pass through it as if it were water or thickened air. She hadn't felt the full brunt of Kareem's attack until then. And Corvin was right, she should have exercised more caution. She wasn't prepared to face the full force of Kareem's power.

His magic seemed dark and sticky. Like something she didn't

want to touch. The tacky floor in a public restroom. She would have to battle Kareem face on, but wanted to turn away from him in distaste.

Reg didn't put up a shield this time. She was tired of using shields, of passively trying to avoid or fend off attacks. People needed to know that she was dangerous in her own right. That she was strong and confident and would not be cowed by witches or warlocks who thought they were something special. Or even wizards or pieces of immortals.

She put up both hands and pushed Kareem back. He didn't like it. He resisted and stepped forward to gain the upper hand.

"No," Reg insisted. "You are not welcome here. You're not bugging me or my cat or any of my friends. You can go back to where you came from."

She wasn't sure whether she was telling Kareem to go back to Egypt, or the Witch Doctor to go back into hiding or to attach himself once more to Horace. But she didn't want him there.

"I don't take orders from little girls."

"You should!"

Reg held him, preventing him from moving. He couldn't attack her. He couldn't retreat or transport himself. All he could do was stand there, his eyes wide and angry, trying to overcome her by effort of will.

Gradually, he started to push forward, gaining ground on Reg a fraction of an inch at a time. He smiled. A tight, frozen smile filled with effort.

Reg could feel Corvin behind her. His hand was no longer on her arm, but she could feel his presence there and could feel his power. She turned her head slightly. Not far enough to look at him, just to acknowledge his presence. She felt for him in her mind.

Give me some power.

CHAPTER FORTY-SIX

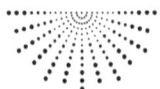

*S*he would not ask most people for such a favor, though she had skimmed from others' power before, but Corvin was different. He had helped her on several occasions, both by feeding her power when she was too weak and still needed to perform, and when she couldn't control the power she had and needed a relief valve before she ended up blowing everyone up.

He had chastised her before for not asking before accessing his power, so this time she did, though she fully intended to take it even if he did not agree. She knew that the two of them together could defeat Kareem, even with part of the Witch Doctor to help him. Corvin had drunk most of the Witch Doctor's power and it was only the dregs that had been able to go into the kattakyns.

She could feel warmth radiating from behind her and an immediate boost in her strength. She pushed back against Kareem, and like in a tug-of-war where one side suddenly overbalanced and was dragged through the mud, she forced him back several rapid steps without any apparent resistance.

"No!" Kareem howled. "You cannot!"

He drew back and to the side. Reg thought he was trying to figure out another avenue of attack, some attack that she was not expecting, but she was ready for him. He was not as strong as he thought he was.

She had thought that someone from Egypt would have been trained in many ancient arts that she had no idea about. He would have kinds of magic that she knew nothing of. He might put her into a trance or put a mummy's curse on her. Something she had never seen before.

But instead of attacking her, he went suddenly after someone behind her. Reg was too slow to turn around. Her first thought was that he had gone after Starlight. He had talked, after all, of her cat and how he was not strong enough to defend them. Reg had seen Starlight fight before, in several different forms, and she knew that he was a formidable foe. But still vulnerable to certain attacks. She didn't want him to end up sick or cursed again, as he had been at Yule.

At death's door.

She hadn't known from one day to another whether she would find him still alive when she next went to the vet's office. Reg's heart squeezed a little just thinking of it. So she turned as quickly as she could, prepared to protect Starlight against magical attack.

Orri stood there, his eyes wide, hands held up to protect himself. But it was too late, the warlock had clearly already struck. There was no blood or gore, nothing gruesome, but Orri's round, dark eyes showed his shock. His pale skin was paper white, as if all the blood had been sucked from him.

"Orri?"

He didn't respond to her, but slowly started to crumple on the spot. Reg hurried to him, trying to keep her eyes on Kareem at the same time. He would attack again given half a chance, Reg was sure.

"Leave the elf," Corvin advised. "You've got Kareem on the run. You have to finish him before he has a chance to retreat and gain in strength."

"Will you help him?" Reg obediently turned back toward Kareem, leaving Orri where he fell.

"I will aid *you*."

"No—Orri—" Reg wanted to turn back toward him, but she didn't have the time. Corvin was right, of course; she had to take care of Kareem before he had a chance to recover. There was nothing she could do for Orri until Kareem was out of the way. But she still felt like a traitor for turning her back on him when he had returned to her, over and over again, to try to warn her against danger.

"Give me back..." Reg didn't even know what to ask for. The piece of the Witch Doctor? Was it a soul? Powers? Essence? Was it something that could be trafficked between two people? Francesca had bound it to the kattakyn and Kareem had loosed it. Did that mean that it was now part of him? Could it be removed like a piece of clothing? Excised like a tumor? "It is not yours," she told him. "If you want to get out of here safely, you have to return that which is not yours."

"I give you nothing. I give no quarter. You cannot defeat me. You are weak and there are too many others I can hurt."

Reg's heart pounded hard. That was the one thing he could do. He could keep harming people that she cared about. Or even people she didn't care about. She would keep trying to fight him, but if he wouldn't face her and kept attacking others...

She closed in on him, her racing heart powering movements that were too quick for her body and had to be supernatural. She grabbed him and yanked him around, then clamped both hands over his arms to hold him still and prevent him from causing any more harm.

"No. You cannot," she insisted.

He squirmed not just in her hands but also inside her mind. He was not going to go easily.

"You are evil," Reg snapped, staring into his eyes. "You attack the weak and defenseless."

"Defenseless? You're not defenseless."

"I wasn't talking about myself."

Reg felt scattered, trying to keep her senses on everything at the same time. On Kareem and the Witch Doctor. On Corvin behind her, supplying her with strength, whispering prompts in her brain. She was aware of Orri, on the ground behind her somewhere, injured by whatever Kareem had done to him. Was he mortally wounded? Reg couldn't forgive herself if the elf died because of her, because he had kept coming back to warn her and she hadn't heeded him.

There was a movement in the trees beside her. Reg's mind snapped to Starlight. He was out there with her too. He also needed to be protected. And Horace? Where was he? If Starlight had left the cottage, then Horace could too. He might have followed Starlight or have gone off in his own direction. He might try to go to Kareem, his owner, not understanding that the man hadn't wanted anything to do with the cat, but had stolen something from him. Something that had given him power, and now he had none.

Reg glanced to the side to see if it was one of the cats. Instead of one of her four-legged friends, it was a child.

Where had a child come from in her yard? Reg tried to process the new information, while holding on to Kareem and trying to keep him pinned down both physically and psychically. Another glance to the side. The child was dressed in brown and green. He had slightly pointed ears and was creeping toward Orri. An elf child. Had Orri brought the child with him, or had one followed where he wasn't supposed to? Either way, there was yet another life in the balance. How could Reg protect all of them at once?

Finish him off, Corvin told her, directing her attention back to Kareem. *It is within our power.*

Reg didn't know what that meant. She felt there was enough on her conscience already with the death of the wizard in the graveyard. And then there was Vivian's disappearance when a sinkhole had opened up in the middle of the street. Reg knew that wouldn't have happened if she hadn't tried to help Vivian. And Jacky Lane.

She didn't feel bad about the Witch Doctor. Maybe if they had been able to do something other than bind him when they had bested him at the warehouse, none of the rest would have happened. But they hadn't been able to finish him off then, and that meant that he came back, and could keep coming back, in the shape of the kattakyns. And if they managed to band together? Or Harrison released each of them?

Reg renewed her attack, holding tightly to Kareem, squeezing his arms and drawing power from him. If she couldn't overpower him easily, then maybe she could de-power him, pulling strength from him until he couldn't fight her any longer. Until he had no strength to fight back or to hold on to the piece of the Witch Doctor.

Kareem tried to strike out at the elf child, laughing in Reg's face, knowing that she would protect him. That she cared more for the welfare of a child she had never seen before and who was of a completely different species than she did for herself.

"No!" Reg insisted. "You can't!"

He tried harder to break free of her and attack the child, and Reg fought harder to pull his strength from him.

Kareem's knees buckled. Corvin moved in. He raised his hands and tried to get in close to Kareem, pushing past Reg. Reg remembered his taking the essence of the dying wizard. And previously, of his sucking the massive power surge from the Witch Doctor, doing the best he could to destroy the entity completely. Reg put her arm out.

"No. He's weakened. Leave him alone."

"You can't stop there," Corvin insisted. "It's not safe. He needs to be neutralized."

Reg turned, looking for the elf child, who was still creeping towards his father's body, ignoring everything that was going on around him. Normally, the elves didn't travel in their bodily form, and Reg wasn't sure what had made him materialize when he was still so far away from his parent. Maybe it was inexperience. Or he might have been hiding there all along, left alone by Orri to blend in with his surroundings like a baby rabbit or deer.

"Corvin…"

Corvin looked in the direction that Reg was looking, but shook his head. "What?"

"The elf. We need to protect the little one."

Corvin blinked at her. "I only see one elf."

"But the little one…"

"No. I only see Orri. And when we have taken care of Kareem, we can make sure he's okay."

"But—"

Reg looked back at Orri and the young elf. Where was Harrison when she needed him? Why had he left her alone, grounded like a disobedient child, leaving her to handle everything all by herself? He should have been there to help fight the Egyptian warlock. Even if there were rules about the immortals not being able to hurt each other, she didn't need him to cause any harm to the Witch Doctor, only to help with Kareem.

"Reg."

Reg looked in the direction of the voice. Now he showed up? Now, right when they were in the middle of a heated battle?

CHAPTER FORTY-SEVEN

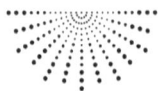

"*U*ncle Harrison!"

"What are you doing?" Harrison looked at Reg, then turned and looked at the guest cottage, where she was supposed to be locked in. He made a huffing sound and shook his head.

"I am trying to fight."

"This is not your battle."

"Well, Kareem made it my battle. What am I supposed to do, walk away?"

"Stay in the house." Harrison looked back at the house again. "Why are you no longer in the house?"

"I got out. So that I could do what I had to. We needed to overcome Kareem, the warlock who owned Horace. Because he—"

"He holds what was bound," Harrison acknowledged testily. "Why are you out here?"

Reg looked at Corvin, kneeling over Kareem, still sucking the life force out of him.

"You have to stop him. He's going to go too far!"

"When are you going to train this warlock?" Harrison said it as if Corvin were a puppy who should be trained but had just pooped in the house.

Reg snorted. "I'm not sure this one can be trained."

Harrison flicked his hand and Corvin went tumbling away from Kareem. "Hey!" he growled, baring his teeth at Harrison, more than just irritated at being stopped. He looked like a wild animal; a wolf-man stopped mid-feed. There was no blood, but that was the image that sprang to Reg's mind. An animal, fangs dripping with blood, snapping at the hand that got too close to his food.

Reg left Harrison to deal with Corvin and hurried over to Orri and the elf child. The child drew back immediately, frightened by the woman moving toward him. They were not used to being seen. They normally kept out of sight and, from what Corvin had said, even he hadn't been able to see the elf child as Reg did.

"It's okay," Reg murmured. "I'm not going to hurt you. I just want to see how Orri is." She hovered over Orri's long, slender body, holding her hands out over him, pushing the heat of her fire into him. She wasn't a great healer, but she knew the basics, and she hoped that all Orri needed was a little strength to get back on his feet again. Kareem hadn't had any chance to think of a strategy, so she had to assume that he had just struck out swiftly and reflexively, without really thinking about it. A quick blow and then retreating from Reg.

The smaller elf leaned forward, staring at Reg's hands and then looking up into her face, curious and questioning.

Reg couldn't feel anything wrong. The elf's heart and lungs were still operating, blood was still flowing through his veins, he was probably just stunned and low on energy. Reg fed more into him. She reached out to Corvin, supplementing her energy with his, so that she wouldn't collapse with the loss of her own strength. Corvin was an endless reservoir of strength, always getting more from somewhere.

After a few minutes, she could tell that Orri's face was getting pinker, regaining some of its ruddy coloring.

"See?" She smiled at the younger elf. "He will be okay."

The little one crept forward to his father's side and took his hand. He looked at Reg, waiting for her to pronounce his father healed. Reg rested her hand directly on Orri's chest for a moment, then went over to Corvin and Harrison who were having a heated discussion.

"Where is it?" Harrison demanded of Corvin.

"What?" Reg asked.

"The unbound essence. Where? It must be retrieved."

"No idea," Corvin said, raising his brows. "I'm sorry, things have been kind of crazy here."

"He had it."

Corvin folded his arms across his chest. "You left Reg alone and undefended. I helped her."

Harrison waved this away as if none of it mattered. "What happened to Destine?"

Corvin looked at Reg, shrugging. "Do you know? There was so much going on... I didn't feel any of the Witch Doctor passing through me. Maybe you? Or just into the universe..." Corvin made a gesture indicating the air around him, fingers graceful.

Reg looked back at Harrison with concern. "What does that mean? You didn't find him? That piece that was bound to Horace?"

Harrison nodded his agreement. "It is gone."

Reg looked over at Kareem, lying on the ground, still moving slightly. Not dead, as she had feared. Harrison had been able to stop Corvin before he had consumed all the man's life force. No more lives on Reg's conscience.

"Maybe he still has it?"

"No."

Reg shrugged widely. "Then it must be like Corvin said. It just... went out into the world."

Harrison looked at Reg, his mouth a straight, angry slash across his face. "Why did you not stay? How got you out?"

Reg ducked her head. "Well... the elf. He is a time traveler."

Harrison turned to look at Orri on the ground, beginning to waken. "A time traveler?"

"Yeah. So he kind of... moved me in time to where I wasn't in the house anymore."

"Where?" Harrison repeated

"When," Reg amended. "And then... for his troubles, Kareem attacked him too, to try to distract me."

"They should return to their time."

"They?" Corvin repeated.

"There is a young one too," Reg informed him. "His son, maybe."

"There are more of them," Harrison said.

Reg began to see other twinkles and movements around Orri and the child elf. The trees were alive with lights and the faint tinkling of bells. She hadn't noticed before. Reg looked around, but the others did not become visible to her. She returned to Orri's side.

"Wake up," she murmured, shaking Orri's shoulder gently. "Time to get up now."

Orri's eyelids fluttered and he opened his eyes, looking around him in confusion. He lifted his head, struggling to get up.

"It's okay," Reg said. "Just take a minute. Everyone is safe now."

"Jon? Where is Jon?"

Reg leaned back so that he could see the young elf beside him. "Is this your son?"

Orri relaxed, resting his head back down again. "Jon. You are safe."

"He's fine," Reg assured him. "You're the only one who took any damage."

"You protected him."

"Well… I did my best. I'm sorry that you got hurt, though."

"That does not matter." Orri closed his eyes for a moment and squeezed Jon's hand. "As long as my son is okay."

Reg smiled. They looked a lot alike; she could see Orri's features in Jon's face. "He's a very handsome boy."

Orri looked at him. "You should not have appeared," he chastised. "Elves must remain hidden to stay safe."

"You did not remain hidden," Jon pointed out.

"I had a debt."

"A debt?" Reg repeated. "To who?"

"To Reg Rawlins. Because you kept my son safe."

Reg tried to wrap her mind around this one. "You came to warn me, and to help me, because you knew I was going to help protect Jon?"

Orri nodded.

"But he wouldn't have been in danger if it wasn't for me. And for you appearing to me."

Orri smiled. He scratched his beard, fireflies twinkling in its strands. "Yes. It is hard for humans to understand," he admitted.

"Uh… yeah. It is. So does that mean this is the last time I'll see you? You won't be coming back anymore?"

"No more." Orri pushed himself up into a sitting position. He rubbed his temples, looking around. "It is a beautiful garden."

"Yes, it is," Reg agreed. "Forst has made it very beautiful and inviting."

"You must continue to protect it."

Reg hadn't thought about how the wards and protections they had placed might help other species who lived in the yard and garden as well. She and Sarah had only been thinking of themselves and their own safety.

"Yes. Of course. I'll make sure that we protect it."

CHAPTER FORTY-EIGHT

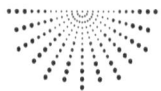

*H*arrison and Corvin approached, looking curiously at the elf. Reg could tell that there was still tension between Harrison and Corvin. But they had never really liked each other.

"So this is your elf," Corvin observed. "Your harbinger."

Reg nodded. It was sort of sad to think that Orri would never come back, that she was seeing him for the last time. But on the other hand, he had been driving her crazy with his appearances and she was glad she wouldn't have to listen to any more warnings.

"Fair face," Orri said, looking at Corvin. "And Janus."

"Why do you call him Janus?" Reg asked.

Orri raised his brows. "He is a human god. So you would understand."

Reg didn't tell him how difficult it had been for them to work the riddle out. "And you said that Kareem was an ancient. But he's just a warlock."

"He carried a piece of the Witch Doctor with him," Corvin reminded Reg, "So there was an immortal. Part of an immortal."

"I was mistaken." Orri shrugged. "The human world is... difficult."

Reg shook her head and ran her fingers through her braids as if straightening them could order her thoughts too. "You can see things in the future? You know what's going to happen?"

Orri didn't answer.

"So… now what is going to happen? Can you see where the piece of the Witch Doctor went and whether any more of the kattakyns will be loosed?"

She could feel Corvin in her mind again, cautioning her against saying more than she should to him, as she had done with Kareem. Reg looked over at the spot where Kareem lay to make sure that he was not conscious and listening to them. But he was gone. There was no sign of him.

If Orri could already see the future, then it didn't matter if she told him; he already knew what would happen. At least, if the world ended because Harrison or other witches or warlocks released the other kattakyns, Orri would know it. Because it would impact on his future.

"It is not our place to tell humans what will happen," Orri said apologetically.

"But that's exactly what you've been doing. What are you talking about, you can't tell us what is going to happen?"

"There are certain times when we are chosen to share what we know." Orri stroked his son's hair affectionately. "But normally… that is not something we may do."

"You could tell me what's going to happen with the Witch Doctor. You were already warning me about him, remember? About the cat with nine lives? Remind me again why I have to beware of the cat with nine lives."

"It is not done," Orri repeated. He put his sunglasses on. "Now, we must go."

As they watched, the lights started to sparkle around Orri and his son and, in a few seconds, they were gone. Corvin shook his head. "It's fascinating."

"It's confusing," Reg griped.

"Many things in the magical world are."

"I like things to be… simple and straightforward."

Corvin grinned. "You are in the wrong profession."

Reg looked over to where Kareem had lain after they had overcome him. "Where did he go?"

Harrison flicked his fingers toward the spot. "I sent him away."

"Where?"

He raised his brows at her. "He is no longer here. The question is," Harrison looked suspiciously at Corvin. "Where is the missing piece? Where is what Horace had?"

Corvin shook his head. "I told you. I don't know. Maybe he put it into some other creature before he attacked us. Maybe it was dispersed."

"You would know if Corvin had it, wouldn't you?" Reg prompted Harrison.

"Not if it was hidden well."

Reg couldn't help looking suspiciously at Corvin as well. But what reason would he have had to take a piece of the Witch Doctor away? This was the second time they had fought. He didn't have any reason to wish for the return of the Witch Doctor. None of them wanted that.

Well, maybe Harrison wanted it. And he could be deceptive if he wanted to be. He might just accuse Corvin when he himself knew the answer.

"Well," Reg sighed. "I'm beat. You're going home?" This was aimed at Corvin.

He looked disgruntled. "I suppose." His eyes slid over to Harrison. "And what about him?"

"He'll go home too," Reg said. "After we talk."

CHAPTER FORTY-NINE

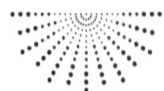

*C*orvin was past the gate and would not be able to return. Reg swept Starlight up in her arms, even though he yowled in protest at this handling. Reg and Harrison walked back into the guest cottage, each lost in thought.

Horace was waiting for them inside. He sat near the doorway, watching them with inscrutable eyes. Reg reached out to him with her mind, but was unable to read him. He didn't want to connect with her like Starlight usually did. He remained distant, not telling her what he was thinking and feeling.

"Know anyone who wants a cat?" Reg asked Harrison lightly.

"The cat does not want me."

"I'll have to find him something sooner or later. So... how did you know what had happened in Egypt? How did you know that Kareem had found out about the Witch Doctor's form being bound to the kattakyns?"

"The immortal can see many things. Things that humans cannot."

"I don't doubt it. Did you know because you went to visit him? Is that how you knew? Or did you go to visit him after you found out he had been loosed?"

"We can sense our own. If they are not hidden."

"And then you went to visit all of the others? To make sure that they had not been unbound too?"

Harrison tapped the tips of his fingers together. "If his power is unleashed, we must know."

"Because of his destructiveness? How evil he is?"

"His power needs to be balanced. Humans worry only about loss of human life. Immortals know… there is more at stake than human lives."

He was silent after that portentous revelation. Reg took a deep breath and tried to calm the pounding of her heart.

"So, what's for dinner?" Harrison asked brightly and opened the fridge door.

Reg was about to tell him that she had cleaned out the fridge— twice now—so there wasn't really anything in there he would be interested in. But she saw that it had been well stocked.

By Sarah? Harrison himself?

"I don't know. What's in there?"

They would have a feast. And they would worry about the Witch Doctor's power being unleashed on an unsuspecting world again some other time.

Did you enjoy this book? Reviews and recommendations are vital to making a book successful.

Please leave a review at your favorite book store or review site and share it with your friends.

Don't miss the following bonus material:
Sign up for mailing list to get a free ebook
Read a sneak preview chapter
Other books by P.D. Workman
Learn more about the author

Sign up for my mailing list at pdworkman.com and get
Gluten-Free Murder for free!

PREVIEW OF UNDISCOVERED TOMB

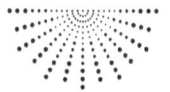

CHAPTER 1

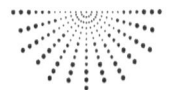

*R*eg rubbed her eyes and yawned, not particularly ready to face her day and Sarah's disapproval. The gray-haired, older woman was usually pleasant and easy to get along with. Reg's landlord, she rented out the guest cottage in her back yard at a very reasonable rate, fully furnished in a rustic Florida style, and could frequently be found stocking Reg's fridge or writing new appointments into Reg's appointment book on the kitchen island, which Reg didn't pay her to do. She was helpful and grandmotherly and had helped Reg through some difficult situations.

But Sarah did not like cats, and that was a problem. She had an African gray parrot as her familiar and bird feeders in the beautiful gardens on the property, and cats were high on her list of pests to be eliminated.

Starlight, Reg's black and white tuxedo cat with a white marking on his forehead, had been lucky to escape Sarah's wrath. Reg had adopted him before she knew of Sarah's anathema, so Sarah had overlooked Reg not consulting her first. Sarah even fed Starlight when she popped over—which was frequently. Too much, if the truth were told.

But the recent addition of Horace was another story. Reg had not gotten permission to take in another cat and had known that Sarah was strict in her rule that Reg was not to have any more pets.

Especially cats.

Of course, Reg knew that the pure black cat was not actually the usual, run-of-the-mill domestic short hair that he appeared to be.

And she hadn't adopted him. Not intentionally, anyway.

"I can't help it that Harrison left him here," Reg told Sarah for the hundredth time. She gathered her box braids into both hands to pull them all back behind her shoulders, and let the red strands fall. "I told him not to. But he did. And it's going to take me a little time to find a new home for Horace."

"You can't keep him."

"I know that. And I'm not planning to, I told you that from the start. He's not going to stay here. But... I need to find a new home for him. And I can't just dump him on someone."

Sarah's sour look indicated that she didn't see why not. "That's what you said last week."

"I'm trying. It isn't like I can return him to his previous owner. That warlock was in Egypt, and I don't even know if he exists anymore."

It seemed like a strange thing to say about a person, and maybe it was, but Reg didn't know how else to put it. Uncle Harrison had made the warlock disappear, and whether he had used his powers as an immortal to teleport him back to his house in Egypt, or had annihilated him, Reg had no idea. And she didn't really want to know. Even if she asked Harrison, he would probably give her some nonsensical answer or ask her something about the nature of human existence and she would be no closer to the truth.

"Didn't he have heirs? Maybe the cat could go to his children."

"I hope he didn't have children." Reg gave a little shudder, thinking about the evil, power-hungry warlock. "And if he did, I wouldn't give Horace to them. He wasn't happy in Egypt."

"Egypt is a wonderful place for cats. They are worshipped there," Sarah pointed out.

"They *used to be* worshipped there. That was a long time ago.

Now... who knows how they treat them. Probably let them wander the streets and get eaten by dogs."

"There is a natural order of things," Sarah said with a nod, as if this were a sad truth that nothing could be done about.

"Just like cats eating birds?"

Sarah's face got red.

Not the right thing to say. Not when Reg wanted Sarah to calm down and relax about Horace being around for a few more days.

"Sorry." Reg rubbed her eyes again. "I just got up. I need my coffee. Then I'll be in a better mood. I shouldn't have said that."

"You know that I said no more cats. Even having that other one over to visit..." Sarah rolled her eyes over the concept of kitty play dates. But Starlight really did like having Nicole over. Horace's adoptive mother, Nicole was also black all over, and she and Starlight were very close.

"I know. But I didn't take in another pet. You wouldn't want me to just open the door and shoo him out, would you? Have him stalking around your garden?"

"Certainly not!" Sarah's voice got noticeably shriller. "But we do have animal shelters. You could take him to one of those."

"You want him to be put down? How is that fair? He hasn't done anything to hurt anyone. His owner turned out to be an evil warlock who should never have had a pet. Who knows what kind of abuse Horace had to put up with while he was there. You think he should just be turned out and put down for something that wasn't his fault?"

Reg's own experiences with being abused and frequently moved from home to home in foster care meant that this hit much closer to home for Reg than it did for Sarah. It wasn't Horace's fault that he had been treated that way. Harrison had rescued him from a bad situation and dumped him on Reg, believing that she would be the best person to take care of him. And in other circumstances, maybe he would have been right, but as Reg couldn't take on another pet under the current circumstances...

Reg pulled the coffee pot out from the coffee maker, even though it was still dripping a little and the drips sizzled on the hot plate and filled the room with the smell of burning coffee. She sloshed a good amount of coffee into a mug and quickly put the pot back in place.

"I'll give Francesca a call later today," she promised. "She was going to be looking for some other homes too. Okay?"

"Yes, fine," Sarah agreed grumpily. "Why doesn't she take this cat in until she can find a new home for it? She had all of the kittens before. She can easily manage two."

"I've tried to get her to take him, but she says there is too much else going on and she needs to concentrate on the others... she's worried about... things."

Reg didn't want to get into it too deeply. She too thought that Francesca should be able to take one more cat. Even if it were just short term. But Francesca's worries about Horace and his eight litter mates were serious and not something that could just be brushed off. And Reg would prefer that Francesca was the one taking on that responsibility. Reg didn't want anything else to do with the Witch Doctor and the other kattakyns.

"Just see that you deal with it soon," Sarah reiterated, looking at the black cat, who for the moment was curled up on the cushion of the wicker sofa, looking perfectly happy and at home.

"I will," Reg promised.

But she didn't know how she could find him a home any faster than she was already doing.

Sarah did a quick flip through the date book on the island, showing that she was moving on to other things and would not stop being involved in Reg's life.

"Let me know when you do."

CHAPTER 2

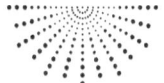

*R*eg decided to take a page out of Harrison's book and just show up at Francesca's with Horace. Maybe if Francesca actually had him in the house, and he showed how well he got along with Nicole (pronounced NEE-cole in Francesca's beautiful Haitian accent) she would let him stay there, at least until the two of them could find him another home. Then Reg didn't have to listen to Sarah's lectures three times a day and could focus on her psychic services business.

And they would find Horace another home. Eventually. Unless Francesca decided he could stay there permanently.

Francesca raised her brows when she saw Reg on her doorstep with Horace in the cat carrier. She swept long blond curls back over her ear, frowning.

"Why did you bring him here?" Francesca asked. She looked at her watch. "We did not have anything set up today."

"No, I know. But he wanted to see Nicole and has been moping around my place. So, I just took the chance that the timing would be okay. You don't need to do anything; he won't get in your way. He can just have a visit with Nicole..."

"You know I have other things to do."

"I know. You're a busy person," Reg agreed crisply. "Lots of responsibilities. I don't need to stop and visit. You can keep working on whatever…"

"I am not working on 'whatever'. I am working on preventing a disaster!"

Reg stepped toward the door and angled to get through it before Francesca decided to slam it in her face. As she expected, Francesca elected to be polite and stepped back, allowing Reg in. Reg put down the cat carrier, and as soon as Francesca closed the front door, Reg opened the carrier and let Horace out. He slunk out immediately and began smelling the floor around the carrier. He had lived there before and Reg was sure he would recognize the place and be happy to be there with his adopted mother again.

"Can you take a break from your work to have some tea?" Reg suggested.

Francesca sighed. She rubbed her forehead and nodded. "Come into the kitchen," she conceded.

Reg followed her in and sat at the kitchen table while Francesca turned the kettle on and got out cups. Bright sunlight was streaming in the kitchen windows, making the glass fronts of the cupboards sparkle.

"So, I take it things are not going as well as you would hope?" Reg hoped that sympathy would go a long way to greasing the wheels and convincing Francesca to take Horace for a few days.

"No. It is… difficult" Francesca puttered around waiting for the kettle to boil and thinking about what she wanted to say. When she sat down at the table, she was ready to talk. "This is the problem. First, we fought the Witch Doctor, who was raising draugar from the dead to do his will. Not just one or two of them, but an increasing army."

Reg nodded. "Nine zombie guys."

Francesca rolled her eyes and shook her head. But Reg's summary was correct, of course.

"We battle this immortal and together we are able to do what is not possible. With the help of Corvin and Damon, we are able to defeat him. Take most of his power away, until he flees, sending his essence into the nine draugar."

"Which have shifted form from huge zombie guys to cute little black cats."

"I use my charm to call them to me and bind them with a spell so that the being of the immortal cannot separate from the kattakyns and re-form as Samyr Destine."

"Which you figure should hold him bound for a thousand years."

"More or less," Francesca agreed. "But I did not count on any interference in the process. I thought that once we found homes for the kattakyns all around the world, we would be safe from them rediscovering each other and re-forming even when the binding spell wore off. So scattered, they would have a difficult time finding each other."

"But we sent Horace to Kareem."

Francesca sighed and nodded. She pulled a file out of a pile of papers beside her and opened it up. Reg saw the research profile she had done on Kareem before they sent Horace to him. Everything they needed to know about his background. Except for the fact that he had merely been waiting for opportunity to present itself so that he could make his grab for power. He was an older, well-respected warlock, the leader of his coven. He had recently lost his cat familiar and was looking for his replacement. They thought that he would do well with the sedate, often sleepy Horace.

But Francesca's profile had not suggested that the warlock might recognize the kattakyn for what he was, and even worse, recognize the portion of the Witch Doctor's power that had been bound to the kattakyn. And that he would have the knowledge and skill to unwind Francesca's charm and separate that piece of Samyr Destine from the creature for his own use.

"I cannot believe..." Francesca started. She stopped and shook her head sadly. "He seemed so *perfect* on paper. And I talked to him on the phone, corresponded with him in email. Everything seemed to be ideal."

"He's sneaky," Reg comforted. "He was being deliberately deceptive. How were you supposed to know that?"

"I should have sensed it. Things that he said, I should have known."

"You couldn't," Reg asserted. "Don't spend time beating yourself up. You have enough to do without that."

Francesca rubbed the bones around her eyes, looking tired. She nodded. "I know. You are right. So now... Kareem unbinds the kattakyn and takes that part of Samyr to himself. That is one thing. A powerful warlock with a portion of immortal powers that is not good."

Reg nodded her agreement.

"But after losing that piece... *now* what are we to do?"

Reg didn't actually need a refresher on the problem. She knew that Francesca was just trying to lay it all out logically, to look at it again and find a solution they might have missed.

"It depends on where the piece went," Reg offered.

"If you are sure that Kareem no longer had it..."

"Well... yeah. Harrison wouldn't have *disappeared* him if he still had it."

"Why not?"

"Because... he and Samyr are both immortals. Harrison always follows the rule that immortals are not allowed to harm one another."

"Or so he says."

"So he says," Reg agreed. But she didn't think that Harrison would do anything to harm one of his fellows. That was one thing about him that had remained constant. Even when she had asked him for his help, he had refused to do anything that might harm another of his kind. Or even one-ninth of his kind.

"He wouldn't have done anything to Kareem if he still held a piece of the Witch Doctor."

"Not even to return him to Egypt?"

"Well... I don't know. But he said that Kareem no longer had that piece. And I believe him."

"Then explain where it went." Francesca took a sip of her tea and then folded her arms across her chest. She'd already heard the story from Reg enough times, there were no new details to give to her. They just kept going over the same facts over and over.

"Harrison thinks that someone hid it."

"And he would not be able to sense it?" Francesca's tone was skeptical.

"He said that if it was hidden well enough, he would not be able to."

"He was able to find each of the kattakyns."

"But..." Reg struggled with magical concepts, not having been raised in a practicing home. "Were they *hidden?*"

Francesca considered. She chewed on her lip and had another sip of the tea. "I do not know how to hide something from an immortal. My skills are not in hiding."

"If Kareem could sense the piece attached to Horace, and he is just a human, just a warlock, then it couldn't have been hidden very well."

"No. Perhaps... just because I could not sense it after they were bound... that doesn't mean that *no one* could."

Reg nodded her agreement. They sat for a while, nursing their cups. Reg knew where the conversation was going next, but she really didn't want to go there. Talking about the past, about their battle with the Witch Doctor and finding the kattakyns homes; that was one thing.

Talking about what danger there might still be, a danger that was no longer a millennium away; that was something Reg didn't want to do.

"The options are very limited," Francesca said. She raised her index finger. "One, Harrison was lying, and he has the piece of Samyr."

"If he does, I'm sure it's just for safekeeping," Reg said immediately. "I explained to him how dangerous it would be for him to put the pieces of the Witch Doctor back together again. How it was dangerous to me and the whole human race."

Francesca didn't look impressed by this. Harrison was not well-known for an overwhelming concern for the human race. Reg had caught his fancy, at least the child Reg had been years before when he had tried to protect her from the Witch Doctor. Reg was no longer that little girl, and she feared he might be withdrawing from her, recognizing that she was no longer an innocent little child but had powers and gifts of her own. She wasn't helpless any longer.

But against the Witch Doctor if he were re-formed and came after her? Reg shuddered at the thought of what he might do to her.

"Possibility two," Francesca raised the next finger, "someone is hiding the piece of Samyr. Namely Corvin Hunter."

Reg nodded.

This was entirely possible. Corvin had been sucking the powers from Kareem, intent on his destruction. He might have taken the piece of the Witch Doctor during that process. And as a creature hungry for power and who already had absorbed much of the Witch Doctor's powers, he would be loath to give it up. He would hide it from Harrison and anyone else who was able to sense it. He did not have control of all the powers that he had absorbed from the artifacts and the Witch Doctor the day of their battle, but he might control enough of them to access memories and powers that would allow him to hide what he had stolen.

"Or," Reg held up three fingers, "it just dispersed out into the universe, like Corvin suggested."

Francesca shook her head. "That seems very unlikely. The more I research... the more certain I am that these final pieces of Samyr cannot be destroyed or dispersed. They must remain intact somewhere."

Reg thought of mythology stories she had heard in school. Very powerful beings were difficult to kill. Even if you cut them into little pieces, those pieces had to be scattered or burned to prevent them from resurrecting, re-forming, or reincarnating.

"It isn't like the pieces are his physical body," she countered. "His spirit or powers or whatever is left of him... it isn't like a body that has to stay the same size and shape."

"No," Francesca agreed thoughtfully. "They could be present in many different forms."

"I don't think that Corvin took that piece and hid it. I would know if he did that."

"How?"

"Because... he can't hide from me. We are connected."

"He cannot hide *anything* from you?"

"Well..." Reg wavered.

Of course he could.

Francesca read Reg's expression and nodded. "You do not even know all the powers he has absorbed. From Samyr and his artifacts and... anyone else he has drunk." She grimaced as she said it. The thought made Reg a little queasy as well. She had been one of Corvin Hunter's victims. He had charmed her and tricked her into agreeing to his proposition, which she did not realize meant taking her powers from her.

She had awakened empty and hollow, the silence as loud as a klaxon in her head. But he had returned her powers to save her from torture, and she had guarded them carefully—or *tried* to guard them carefully—ever since.

"It's either Harrison or Corvin," Francesca told her. Her lips pressed together in a line as Reg shook her head, not wanting to attribute the theft to either one of them. "If it isn't them, then the only other person who could have taken it was... you."

* * *

Undiscovered Tomb, Book #15 of the *Reg Rawlins, Psychic Investigator series* by P.D. Workman can be ordered at pdworkman.com

ABOUT THE AUTHOR

P.D. Workman is a USA Today Bestselling author, winner of several awards from Library Services for Youth in Custody and the InD'tale Magazine's Crowned Heart award, and has published over 90 mystery/suspense/thriller and young adult books, including stand alones and these series: Auntie Clem's Bakery cozy mysteries, Reg Rawlins Psychic Investigator paranormal mysteries, Zachary Goldman Mysteries (PI), Kenzie Kirsch Medical Thrillers, Parks Pat Mysteries (police procedural), and YA series: Tamara's Teardrops, Between the Cracks, and Breaking the Pattern.

Workman loves writing about the underdog, who the reader may love or hate. She has been praised for her realistic details, deep characterization, and sensitive handling of the serious social issues that appear in all of her stories, from light cozy mysteries through to darker, grittier young adult and mystery/suspense books.

> P. D. Workman, does not shy from probing the deep psychological scars of childhood trauma, mental illness, and addiction. Also characteristic of this author, these extremely sensitive issues are explored with extensive empathy, described with incredible clarity, and portrayed with profound insight.
>
> — —KIM, GOODREADS REVIEWER

Some of Workman's titles have been translated into Spanish, French, Portuguese, German, and Italian.

Workman began writing at an early age and is a prolific reader as well as writer. She is also passionate about teaching and learning, expresses her creativity through art and cooking, and loves exploring the Calgary parks and green spaces where the Parks Pat Mysteries are set. She was a legal assistant for many years and has done extensive charitable work.

Workman was born and raised in Alberta, Canada, and is married with one adult son.

* * *

Please visit P.D. Workman at pdworkman.com to see what else she is working on, to join her mailing list, and to link to her social networks.

* * *

If you enjoyed this book, please take the time to recommend it to other purchasers with a review or star rating and share it with your friends!

facebook.com/pdworkmanauthor

twitter.com/pdworkmanauthor

instagram.com/pdworkmanauthor

amazon.com/author/pdworkman

bookbub.com/authors/p-d-workman

goodreads.com/pdworkman

linkedin.com/in/pdworkman

pinterest.com/pdworkmanauthor

youtube.com/pdworkman

Find P.D. Workman's books at

PDWORKMAN.COM

Scan the QR code below